I0564689

Frances Elizabeth Murray

Memoir of LeBaron Botsford

Frances Elizabeth Murray

Memoir of LeBaron Botsford

ISBN/EAN: 9783337396251

Printed in Europe, USA, Canada, Australia, Japan

Cover: Foto ©Raphael Reischuk / pixelio.de

More available books at **www.hansebooks.com**

MEMOIR

OF

LeBaron Botsford, M.D.

BY HIS NIECE,

FRANCES ELIZABETH MURRAY.

———•———

" A doctor for near half a century,
He lived and laboured for the good of men,
Though called to watch the sick bed of the rich,
And earn the fee for care and 'tendance due,
He never shrank at all unseemly hours
From waiting on the poor man's couch of pain,
And seeking to alleviate the ills
That human nature is foredoomed to bear."

SAINT JOHN, N. B.
J. & A. McMILLAN, 98 PRINCE WM. STREET.
1892.

Entered according to Act of Parliament of Canada, in the year 1892, by

FRANCES ELIZABETH MURRAY,

At the Department of Agriculture, Ottawa.

TO

SIR SAMUEL LEONARD TILLEY, K.C.M.G., C.B.,

AND TO

DR. BOTSFORD'S OTHER FRIENDS AND FELLOW-CITIZENS IN ST. JOHN,

THIS MEMOIR OF HIS LIFE

IS RESPECTFULLY DEDICATED.

PREFACE.

In presenting this memoir of Dr. Botsford to the public, the writer's aim has been to narrate the moulding circumstances which surrounded Dr. Botsford's childhood and youth, vividly to depict him as he walked among us for so many years—a physician, friend, and citizen—and partially to reveal the hidden motor-power of Christian principle which impelled the various professional, social, and benevolent activities of his life.

The work is offered especially to St. John citizens, trusting they will appreciate and endorse the effort which has been made to produce it. It is the first record that has appeared in book form of the life of a St. John citizen. May we not hope that it will not be the last, but that in future such memorials may be given us from time to time, to serve as incentives and encouragements in the battle of life.

The writer wishes to thank those who have assisted in the work by furnishing letters and papers, especially Dr. Henry Hartt, of New York, and Mrs. Hartt, Rev. W. O. Raymond, Mr. J. W. Lawrence, and Senator Botsford.

Thanks are also due for the picture of the interior of Old Trinity Church, the plate for which was kindly lent by the Rector.

FRANCES ELIZABETH MURRAY.

St. John, May 22, 1892.

TABLE OF CONTENTS.

CHAPTER I.

> Our times are in His hand
> Who said "a Whole I planned."
> Youth shows but half;
> See all. Trust God,
>   Nor be afraid.
>   — *Browning.*

On a low, wooded hill, overlooking the head waters of the Bay of Fundy, stands the "old-fashioned country seat" built upwards of a hundred years ago by Dr. Botsford's grandfather, Amos Botsford — "Speaker Botsford," as he was popularly called. From the "antique portico," across which

> " Tall poplar trees their shadows throw,"

you see on the right, upland pastures, fragrant with sweet-scented grass (*anthox-anthum odoratum*); on the left the garden and orchard. Before you stretches the trim lawn, shaded by chestnut trees, bordered with flowers and sheltered from bleak winds by a high, well-clipt hawthorn hedge. Beyond the syringas and flowering shrubs at the foot of the lawn, the eye ranges over wide meadow-lands or marshes, dotted with trees. Then, as now, the cloud-shadows floated over the green expanse and the Bay beyond, over the little settlement to the north and the Wood-Point ledges to the south. Then, as now, the coast of Nova Scotia, with the Cobequid Mountains and the old Fortress Beau Séjour, closed the eastern horizon.

(9)

Then, as now, the great tides of the Bay of Fundy swept up sixty feet over the rich mud banks—then, as now, but all else has changed. The little settlement has grown into thriving Sackville, with its colleges, its Conservatory of Music, its churches, its pretty houses, and, of course, its station. The ledges of Wood-Point resound with the quarryman's pickaxe, and send their building blocks of freestone to New York, Chicago, Toronto, while close to the old, dismantled fortresses one of the great engineering enterprises of the day has been commenced, the Chignecto Marine Railway, on which ships are to be carried overland from the Bay of Fundy to the Gulf of St. Lawrence. Thus has this colonial outpost kept pace with the march of the age.

But this is only the framework of the picture. The old home itself cannot so easily be described. Comfort reigned within — a pretty dining-room, a large, handsome family drawing-room, a library (or office) well lined with books, wide halls, sunny bed-rooms and the "old clock on the stair." Behind the house was the large, low kitchen, with its old-fashioned fireplace, the "moss covered bucket" at the well, the ample barnyard and farm buildings, protected by a grove of spruce trees, the huge wood pile, the lowing cattle, the twittering swallows; these are some of the main features of the homestead.

Its hospitality was well known. The red Indian, wrapped in his blanket, slept at the kitchen fire. French labourers bivouacked at harvest time in the barn. Weary immigrants stopped for a mid-day meal at the kitchen table. Officers, both military and naval, came for a few days of snipe-shooting. Clergymen

WESTCOCK, THE IDEAL OF A COLONIAL HOME.

passing with their families to distant parishes rested there. Judges and lawyers on their circuits, bishops on their confirmation tours, governors and their suites, all were given a warm welcome by the old Speaker or his still more genial son, Judge Botsford. All carried away a pleasant impression of Westcock, the ideal of a colonial home.

The Botsfords were an old family from Leicestershire, England. They emigrated and settled in Newton, Connecticut, where they rose to eminence and wealth. Speaker Botsford was educated in Yale College. He graduated in 1763, and was tutor in Yale in 1768, but when the Revolutionary War broke out he felt that duty and honour called upon him to join the royal cause. He was then in the prime of life, and, when the fight was fought and the victory gained by his opponents, he took his wife, daughter and little son (nine years old), and sailed from New York for Annapolis, Nova Scotia, arriving there in October, 1782.

Amos Botsford may very fairly be considered as the *pioneer* of the extensive loyalist immigration which laid the foundation of the City of St. John and of the Province of New Brunswick. This will be more apparent from a consideration of the following documentary evidence :

[*Extract from the* " *Political Magazine,*" *Published in London,* A. D., 1783.]

" When the loyal refugees from the Northern Provinces were informed of the resolution of the House of Commons against offensive war with the rebels, they instantly saw there were no hopes left them of settling down again in their native country.

"Those of them, therefore, who had been forward in taking up arms and in fighting the battles of the mother country, began to look out for a place of refuge, and Nova Scotia being the nearest place to their old plantations, they determined on settling in that province.

"Accordingly, to the number of 500, they embarked for Annapolis Royal; they had arms and ammunition, and one year's provisions, and were put under the care and convoy of his Majesty's ship *Amphitrite*, of 24 guns, Captain Robert Briggs. This officer behaved to them with great attention, humanity and generosity, and saw them safely landed and settled in the barracks at Annapolis, which the Loyalists soon repaired. There was plenty of wild fowl in the country and at that time—which was last fall—a goose sold for two shillings and a turkey for two shillings and sixpence. The Captain was at £200 expense out of his own pocket in order to render the passage and arrival of the unfortunate Loyalists in some degree comfortable to them. Before Captain Briggs sailed from Annapolis, the grateful Loyalists waited on him with the following address:

" *To Robert Briggs, Esq., Commander of His Majesty's Ship* ' *Amphitrite*':

'The Loyal Refugees, who have emigrated from New York to settle in Nova Scotia, beg your acceptance of their warmest thanks for the kind and unremitted attention you have paid to their preservation and safe conduct at all times during their passage.

'Driven from their respective dwellings for their loyalty to our King, after enduring immense hardships, and seeking a settlement in a land unknown to us, our distresses were sensibly relieved during an uncomfortable passage by your humanity, ever attentive to our preservation.

'Be pleased to accept our most grateful acknowledgment, so justly due to you and the officers under your command, and be assured we shall remember your kindness with the most grateful sensibility. We are, with the warmest wishes for your health and happiness, and a prosperous voyage, with the greatest respect, your most obedient humble servants,

In behalf of the Refugees,

> Amos. Botsford,
> Th. Ward,
> Fred. Hauser,
> Sam. Cummings,
> Elijah Williams.

Annapolis Royal, the 20th October, 1782.'

"The Rev. Jacob Bailey, the S. P. G. missionary at Annapolis (himself a refugee from the Kennebec in Maine), speaking of the arrival of this party said: 'Every habitation is crowded and many are unable to procure any lodgings. Many of these distressed people left large possessions in the rebellious colonies, and their sufferings on account of their loyalty, and their present uncertain and destitute condition render them very affecting objects of compassion.' On October 27 Mr. Bailey preached 'a refugee sermon' from Psalm cvii. 2, 3."

Amos Botsford was selected as an agent for the Loyalists, and he proceeded to make an examination of the country on the shores of the Bay of Fundy and of the St. John River. The results of this examination were communicated in a letter of January, 1783, to the Loyalists in New York, and there cannot be the slightest doubt that the information thus conveyed determined the large emigration from New York to "Saint John's River" the following spring. The first fleet of over thirty vessels arrived May 11 and landed a week later. A second fleet of thirteen ships arrived

June 29, and a fleet of about the same size on October 4. These fleets carried about 6,000 people, and nearly 4,000 more arrived at intervals during the summer.

Amos Botsford had associated with him a civil engineer, Frederick Hauser, who probably accompanied him on the explorations made of the St. John River.

Amos Botsford drew lots 202 and 203, in Parr Town, situated on the south-east corner of Union and Prince William Streets, directly opposite the Odd Fellows' Hall.

The letter written by Amos Botsford is found in Beamish Murdoch's Hist. of Nova Scotia, Vol. III.*

Amos Botsford remained in Annapolis a year or two. He then moved northward to Fort Beau Séjour. He bought the hill called by the Indians Weckekawk (Anglicized Westcock) from a former grantee, and there, in 1790, he built his house. After its completion he was standing one day at the window of the library with a friend. His thoughts went back to his former home in the pleasant valley of the Connecticut. "Here we are, M——," said he, "on this bleak side of the Bay of Fundy." It was the last expressed regret. The strong man turned resolutely from the past and set manfully to work for his adopted country. During the summer he superintended the draining and dyking of the marshes, turning them into rich meadow-lands. The winter found him in St. John or Fredericton assisting in the organization of the new Province. He was elected Speaker by the first House of Assembly, 1786,

*For this account of the arrival of Amos Botsford I am indebted to the Rev. W. O. Raymond. F. E. M.

and afterwards re-elected by each successive House
until his death, having filled the office of Speaker for
twenty-six years. The following interesting remarks
about him are made by his son's classmate in the
"Memoirs of the Class of 1792, Yale College," by Rev.
T. M. Cooley and Hon. James Cooley : " In consequence
of adhering to the royal cause, he was proscribed by his
country and his property confiscated, yet, such was the
estimation in which he was held by his numerous
friends in Connecticut, that by their influence that
State was induced to grant him the privilege of collect-
ing his debts, to be applied to the education of his
children. Such was his character for integrity that
when he laid his claim for losses before the Honorable
Commissioners appointed by Act of Parliament for
enquiring into the losses and services of American
loyalists, his own statement of the amount of his real
and personal estate was deemed by them sufficient
without further proof." *

The Speaker's son William and his daughter Sarah
were sent back to Connecticut to school. Sarah
returned after a year or two and married Mr. Stephen
Milledge, afterwards High Sheriff of Westmorland.
She settled near her father at Westcock, and became
the mother of one son and five daughters.

William entered Yale College, graduating in 1792.
He then returned to St. John, New Brunswick, and
commenced the study of law. He was admitted to the
Bar in 1795, and soon began to be successful in his
profession, while his genial spirit gathered round him
a large social circle. There are still in existence
several letters written in the years 1796, 1797, 1798, by

* This manuscript memoir is in the possession of **Senator Botsford.**

Elizabeth Upham, a gay, bright girl of that period. They are addressed to her cousin, William Botsford, during his visits to his father in Westmorland. These letters sparkle with wit and good-humoured satire, and contain a description of St. John society by one who mingled in it and enjoyed it thoroughly. The names of Chipman, Hazen, De Wolfe, Murray, White, Jarvis, Botsford, frequently occur, with others, such as Putnam and Bissett, which have long since passed away. We hear of our great-grandmothers, their "Assemblies," their "Gregories" (receptions), their flirtations, their weddings, for "*men may come and men may go, but these go on for ever.*" The following extract from one of these letters shows us the estimation in which young William Botsford was held, and gives us a glimpse of his future wife (Dr. Botsford's mother), a beautiful Miss Hazen, who had just married the old Loyalist Colonel Murray's son. The letter is dated Feb. 19th, 1797, St. John :

"As you seem to have a pretty good idea of female versatility you will not be surprised, dear cousin William, to perceive by the date of this that I am once more, in spite of all wise determinations to the contrary, a visitor in the city."

. . . .

Then follows an account of an assembly in which

"We girls gave an incontestable proof of our good nature by being in high spirits when there was absolutely such a scarcity of beaux that Mrs. Chipman and Miss White got up together in the first dance. I, who drew the first number, sent to ask half-a-dozen gentlemen, and was at last obliged to dance with the manager, and plaguey glad was I to get him. I do not exaggerate when I say that we were all the evening chasing Dingwell, and jostling off the poor old soul's wig in attemps to catch him for a partner.   .   .   .   .   .

We are going to a Gregory at Lowell's this evening; I wish you were to be of the party. Your laugh, the fame of which still lingers among us, and is celebrated by all lovers of mirth, would be a great relief to the stupidity of our young meetings."

But, notwithstanding the scarcity of " Beaux " and the stupidity of the meetings, we find her saying :

"I cannot but feel a little alarmed at the diminution the last six months have made in our number. Many of our apparently most trusty characters have apostatized from their declared faith, and become converts to matrimony. What think you of Miss Gaynor and Miss Irons forsaking the vestal standard in their old age and espousing the fashionable cause? It don't signify, the world is governed by fashion in this point as well as every other. People oftener marry from the dread of being thought singular (I believe) than from any particular fancy for each other. Not but what I suppose there exists such a thing as real love. God forbid that I should think there did not. I have no intention of throwing such a reflection upon the human heart. Indeed, some of the dishes of matrimony which have been cooked lately, I know to be highly seasoned with it. The wedding I was at last summer was a love match altogether, and, I am told, is like to prove a very happy one. Miss Murray (the Honourable R. L. Hazen's mother), I think, we may set down as a traitor of the first magnitude. She acted in direct opposition to the doctrines she preached. Murray's (her brother) marriage took us quite by surprise at last. I have scarcely seen them. They went up the river immediately after my coming to town. They reside with my grandmother for the present. It would do your heart good to see how happy and laughing that good lady looks upon the occasion. Well she may, for, I am sure, if I am not wonderfully blinded by partiality, her son has chosen a most amiable, as well as most lovely woman, for his wife. Her mind, I believe to be as good as her person is charming. Heaven grant that Murray may be always sensible of her merit, and prove himself grateful for the preference so fine a woman has honoured him with. I think him at present rather too boyish and brusque in his manner, but Sally has influence, and the kind of influence that will be most likely to soften him."

A few weeks after this letter was written the "boyish" Murray took cold while driving down the river on the ice. Consumption set in, and, after a short illness, he was laid in an early grave. The following quaint notice appeared in the "St. John Gazette" Friday, May 5th, 1797:

"Died on Wednesday last, universally and justly lamented, after a short confinement with a severe hectic complaint, Thomas Murray, Esq., Attorney-at-Law, and one of the Masters in Chancery in this Province, in the 22nd year of his age."

The widow went to live with her sister, Mrs. Chipman, in the Chipman House, and there her baby boy was born several months after his father's death. Two years were passed in the strictest seclusion, but when for the first time she took her seat in the family pew in Trinity Church it so happened that the popular young lawyer (William Botsford) sat opposite. It was a square pew, more fitted for observation than devotion. That Sunday he met his destiny. When an old man of 86, Judge Botsford pointed out to a granddaughter, with a smile of pleasure, "the place, my dear, where I first saw your grandmother, the beauti-

"THE FAMILY PEW IN TRINITY CHURCH."

THIS PEW (NEAR THE THIRD PILLAR ON THE LEFT HAND) WAS SUBSEQUENTLY OWNED AND OCCUPIED BY
DR. BOTSFORD UNTIL THE CHURCH WAS BURNED IN 1877.

ful Mrs. Murray." His visits at his friend, Judge Chipman's house, became more frequent, and the pretty boy was loaded with balls, tops and other toys before his demure aunt, Mrs. Chipman, divined the object of the young lawyer's attention. Much patience and perseverance were needed; relations did not approve of the match, and three years more passed away before Mrs. Murray consented to become Mrs. William Botsford. They were married in 1802 by Dr. Byles, the Rector of Trinity Church. Wm. Botsford and his wife resided in St. John for several years in the enjoyment of some of life's best gifts—health, competence, friends, and professional success. Three little boys were born, in 1803, 1804, 1806, Hazen, Edwin and Charles. In 1807 a change came. Speaker Botsford's health was failing, though he was not more than 63 years of age. He longed for the companionship of his only son. The property needed attention, and the old gentleman wrote to the young couple urging them to come to the country and make Westcock their home. At the present day we can scarcely realize the sacrifice this involved. Now the whistle of the railway train can be heard from the old homestead, twenty times in the day. St. John is left after an early breakfast, and Westcock is reached before 2 P. M. Then a voyage of several days in a small coasting schooner, or a week's ride through the forest over a bridle path, were the only means of access. But there was no hesitation. The call of duty was felt to be imperative, and in the early summer of 1807 William Botsford, accompanied by his wife and little family, left St. John, and exchanged the animation and bustle of a thriving city for the isolation and tranquility of a country home. Speaker Botsford lived five years to enjoy the society of his son. Two more grandchildren were born in 1807 and 1809, George and Chipman, and on January 26th, 1812, Mrs. Botsford's seventh son, LeBaron, opened his eyes in this changing and changeful world.

During the following summer Speaker Botsford's health failed so rapidly that it was deemed advisable for him to seek medical treatment in St. John. He left his home for the last time, accompanied by his daughter-in-law and her infant. On reaching St. John he became rapidly worse, and died September 14th, 1812. His remains now lie in the Rural Cemetery, close to the tall old monument erected by his son to the Speaker's memory.

Before returning to the country, Mrs. Botsford had her infant baptized by Dr. Byles. It was natural that she should wish that the old clergyman who married her should baptize her child, but she did not know how fitting it was that this one of her sons, whose future life was to be so closely identified with St. John, should be admitted into the church by the Rector of Trinity. The name LeBaron was the maiden name of Mrs. Botsford's mother. Family tradition says it was assumed as a sir-name by one of her ancestors, a French Baron, who fled from the Huguenot persecution in the 17th century, was shipwrecked on the New England coast, where he married and settled. Little LeBaron grew up a bright, joyous boy, with blue eyes, a sweet smile and a merry laugh. Schiller's description of a happy boyhood, when

"The tender cares of a mother's love,
  Guard well life's golden morning,"

was particularly true of the Botsford boys; for owing to their father's long absences on public and professional business, the supervision and training of this large family fell chiefly on the mother. Just after LeBaron's birth, Mr. William Botsford, at his father's death, had to assume the responsibilities of a large landed property. His private and professional occupations might well have formed an excuse for attention devoted only to these claims, but with William Botsford private interests were ever subservient to the public welfare. He personally superintended the laying out and making of roads between the widely scattered settlements, and as an old man he often related with humour the discovery of various tricks which, trusting to his nearsightedness, country contractors endeavoured to practise upon him. One man had merely cut off the ends of the logs in a corduroy road instead of removing them. They were daubed with mud, but did not escape Mr. Botsford's observation, and "the scamp had to do his work honestly before he got his money."

Mr. Botsford took an active part in the militia drill. The Westmorland militia, through his personal interest and energy, being far in advance of those of other counties.

Education received a full share of attention. He was often present at the examinations of the country schools; and, believing with Shakespeare that

"Ignorance is the curse of God; knowledge the wing wherewith we fly to heaven,"

he made many efforts in aid of the Fredericton University, which owes its endowment in great part to Mr.

Botsford's personal exertions, both in and out of the Legislature. Lastly, he was a consistent member and active friend of the Church of England. It cannot be denied that in this respect he met many difficulties. It was very hard to get suitable men for the country parishes of a distant colony, but Mr. Botsford never wavered in his allegiance to the church. When difficulties occurred, he mediated between clergy and laity. He got grants of land from the government for several parishes, and chiefly by his own untiring exertions the little church of St. Ann's was built, not close to his own house, but in a nook in the woods, where it was within reach of church people, both in Sackville and Dorchester. He did all in his power by precept and example to promote the observance of the weekly day of rest and regular attendance on divine worship. To such public-spirited men of the olden time New Brunswick owes much of its present prosperity and success.

While Mr. Botsford's time was thus fully occupied, his wife held the reins of household government with a gentle though firm hand. The tall stately figure commanded respect, the broad fair brow was seldom darkened by a frown, the sweet lips uttered no fretful nor impatient words, but the mother's will was law and even her wishes were obeyed. The fields and woods might resound with noise and shouts, within doors, and especially at table, reigned the respectful silence, which in those days was thought befitting young people. On New Year's day the rule was relaxed, and from early morning till late at night, tin whistles, trumpets and every noise that boyish ingenuity could invent welcomed the New Year.

A large and sudden increase in Mrs. Botsford's

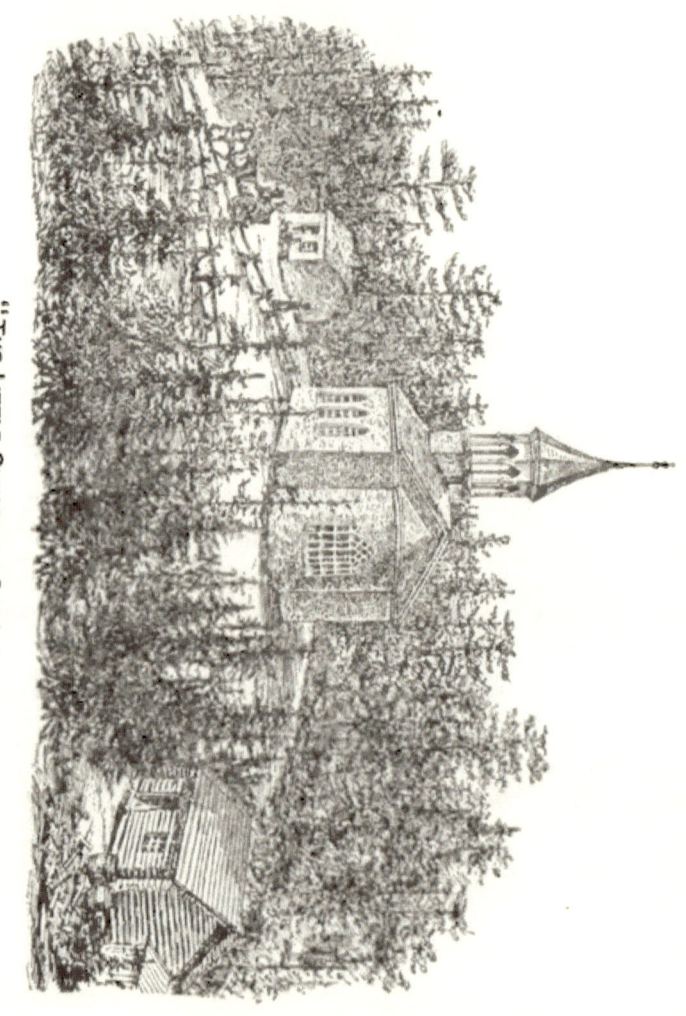

"THE LITTLE CHURCH OF ST. ANN'S."

household cares was made by the introduction into the family of five nieces. Their father, Sheriff Milledge, died from a cold taken during a long winter drive. The widow and only son went to Digby to attend to some law business. As they were landing from the ship in a small boat it was capsized, and they were both drowned. The wail that arose when the poor girls heard the news was heart-rending. Their uncle and aunt did all that was possible to comfort them. Room was made for them at once at Westcock, and there they remained until provided with homes of their own. One of them married Edward Chandler, then, as he often boasted, a penniless but active-brained young cousin, studying law with Mr. Botsford. He died as Governor of the Province.

After LeBaron's birth, two more boys and two girls were added to the family, Bliss, Sarah, Eliza, Blair, and the group was complete. The elder half-brother was absent at school or college, but he kept up active correspondence with his mother. The following boyish letter is one of several written in 1814, just as the great struggle with Napoleon was supposed to be over, and preparations were being made to send the regiments which had been in active service out to the Colonies:

ST. JOHN, Saturday, July 16th, 1814.

Dear Mother:

We arrived here last Saturday after a tedious and uncomfortable navigation. Betsey was so sick that she did not move from her berth from the time of our embarkation until we arrived within Partridge Island. I was pretty well until Thursday, when we had a heavy sea, abundance of fog and no wind, which was enough in all conscience to knock anybody up. You put up enough provision to last a fortnight at least, and as Betsey eat nothing and I nothing after Thursday, there was plenty left.

I found all my friends here well. . . . The vessel goes to-morrow. I have sent by her four cocoanuts, which I hope you will receive safe, though I would not answer for them. I do not know how Betsey did about the basket and jar, as for my part the food in the devilish basket gave me such a nausea, that I would not look at it for a dollar. I have got Eliza's (one of his orphan cousins) whip, bridle and gloves. The whip is good, the bridle tolerable, but as for the gloves, they appear to me to be poor things, but old Lady Nutting told me they were "Ladies' beaver gloves," and you told me to ask her. I found all the good Fellows of the College here. . . . There was a party at Mr. Peters' the first night I came, and happening to meet one of the family I got an invitation and accordingly went. I have been since at Mr. Parker's and Mr. Robinson's, and we had a subscription ball on Tuesday, which was very pleasant, but we had to break up at 12 o'clock, for General and Mrs. S——— are residing at the Coffee House and the old curmudgeon ordered the band off at that hour. Mrs. S——— is a very pretty woman I think, and he is poor, half-starved and insignificant looking. The London fleet has arrived, which makes plenty of bustle about the town. All your friends here expected you down and every person I met asked, " Well, I suppose your mother is down with you," and seemed much surprised when I told them you had not come. I was walking with Mrs. M——— and her two daughters one day and met Dr. N——— who did not know me at first. I bowed to him, and as Mrs. M——— and he, of course, stopped and spoke to each other, I asked if he was going to Westmorland. He said, yes, he was going, and, I thought, very coldly passed on; but after he passed he asked Capt. Coffin (who was with him) who it was, and I heard some one come shouting back " Murray, Murray." I found the Doctor running back, and then he kept me half an hour answering questions, while the whole time I was trying to edge off. . . . They have a number of fine officers here of the 99th, though some of the best went yesterday to Moose Head, of the capture of which I suppose Ayres will give you all information. . . . I will thank you to send by the first vessel a large key I left in the drawer. It belongs to one of my doors at College. You may send it with my shirt and the bag of money I left in the small upper drawer in my room, to which you may add a doubloon if you choose, for I am afraid I shall be in want of money. With my love to all the family.

I am yours affectionately,

JOHN THOS. MURRAY.

P. S.—Grandmother, Aunt Chipman, and all your friends, desire to be particularly remembered to you. They have great hope of seeing Mrs. Fitzgerald (another aunt) shortly, for we find by the newspaper, that two battalions of the 60th are ordered to embark from Bordeaux for America, to one of which the Colonel (afterwards Sir John) belongs, so that she will come with him, I think.   J. T. M.

Murray returned occasionally to Westcock to see his mother and to be the wonder and admiration of his younger brothers, for the pretty boy had become a handsome young fellow, with the courtly grace and debonnair manner of his grandfather, the old Colonel. Murray married in Halifax a Miss Despard, the daughter of an English officer. He soon showed symptoms of his father's delicacy of constitution, and, after spending two years in Italy, he died in early manhood, leaving a widow and three little girls.

The Botsford boys meanwhile grew up healthy and happy. They attended the country school and studied, or played, or quarrelled, as the case might be, with the

country girls. Picnics were made to the "blueberry
plains" in summer, and coasting parties slid down the
snowy hills in winter. The younger boys chased
squirrels; the older ones shot snipe and partridges.
When they outgrew the country school, the Rector of
the parish took them as pupils. The Rev. Christopher
Milner was a sturdy, rough-and-ready Englishman.
He managed to hammer some knowledge into the
boys. He did not, however, inspire them with much
reverence, and innumerable pranks were played by
the mischief-loving, frolicsome lads on their master.

So time passed on with "arrowy swiftness." The
boys' characters began to take shape and to act and react on each other. Hazen grew tall and broad, with a
fair skin, an eagle eye and much frank good nature.
Edwin was thin, taciturn and self-contained. Charles
had a smooth smile and a ready tongue. George, with
easy self-possession, had a sly twinkle in his eye — he
could lead into mischief and yet keep clear himself.
Chip was quiet and grave. LeBaron combined in a
remarkable degree his father's firm conscientiousness,
with his mother's sweetness and consideration for
others. Many stories are told of what was called
boyish obstinacy, which, when controlled by maturer
judgment, became the indomitable firmness of a noble
man. Bliss was solid, very painstaking, but slow.
Blair, the youngest, was full of fun, frolic and quaint
sayings. The characters of the daughters were also
strongly marked. Sarah, afterwards Mrs. R. L.
Hazen, was tall, handsome, imperious, yet she attracted
even when she seemed to repel. Eliza was a pretty
little creature, the pet and favorite of all who knew
her. Such was this remarkable family in the midst of

which Dr. Botsford grew up. Most of them occupied prominent positions in life. All but two have now passed away.

LeBaron's future profession had been settled at a very early age, at least in his own mind. He often related the apparently trivial circumstances that decided it. One evening, when he was about seven years of age, as he was standing by the log fire which roared up the capacious kitchen chimney, a Yorkshire labourer on the place took the child on his knee. "Young maister, what'll thou be when thou's a man?" he said in his broad Yorkshire dialect. The child opened his eyes wide, but did not answer. "I'se knows; thou'll be a doctor. Thou 'ast a healing 'and. Thou's thy mother's seventh son." The short speech in the uncouth dialect was never forgotten. Dr. Botsford often referred to the old Yorkshire labourer as having been, in the Providence of God, the determining cause in the choice of his profession. Whenever his thoughts turned to the future, the idea implanted thus early always recurred.

When he was fourteen years of age his father sent him to Windsor to school, and after remaining there two years he was removed to the Grammar School at Fredericton. The following description of him, on his first arrival, is given by his friend and fellow-student, Dr. Henry A. Hartt, of New York: "I met LeBaron Botsford first one morning in 1826, at the Grammar School in Fredericton. He was playing marbles before the door of Dr. Somerville's embryo college. He had just come from his country home, a tall lad of fourteen, in blue jacket and trousers, fresh and rosy, with a pleasant but serious countenance, and an air of independence remarkable for his age. I immediately inquired who he was, and felt interested in him from that moment. He was put in the class to which I belonged, and we soon became great friends. We sat beside each other at the desk, and studied from the same book, often stopping to talk on all manner of subjects, secular and sacred, and I remember well how, with characteristic suddenness, and apparent sternness, he was wont to bring these confabs to a close by saying: " Stop, Hartt, we must now go on with our lessons."

At school Dr. Botsford was thorough, painstaking, but not rapid. One defect — that of a verbal memory — he often regretted as a serious hindrance, although in future life it probably gave greater originality to his thoughts and compositions. Then, again, the methods of tuition sixty years ago were not as advanced as at present. Educational modes did not yield to individual peculiarities — there was but one system for all — so that it often happened, as it did in Dr. Botsford's case, that teacher and pupil did not understand each other. Great efforts were made to learn certain formularies, while the inquiring mind was seeking light in other directions. The result was not satisfactory. The pupil knew that he was not advancing, and worse still, he became discouraged, and often felt that he could never advance. This is not an imaginary description. Dr. Botsford often spoke of it as his mental attitude on leaving school previous to his entering the University of Fredericton.

His residence at the University did not last long. Dr. J——, the Principal, was an able and erudite man, but he lacked the power of maintaining discipline. Disorders occurred repeatedly. It was thought necessary to make a striking example, and for some slight misdemeanor, such as remaining out one night a few moments beyond closing time, LeBaron and his brother Bliss were rusticated for six months. This was a serious drawback for studious lads. How deeply LeBaron felt it may be inferred from a slight allusion in a letter written fifty years afterwards: "I recollect the case of Bliss and myself too keenly to think such things a bagatelle."

After some consideration, Judge Botsford, for he had been elevated to the Bench in 1824, determined that LeBaron should proceed to Scotland to begin his medical studies at the Glasgow University. He accordingly sailed from St. John for Glasgow, July, 1831.

CHAPTER II.

" Why should we fear youth's draught of joy,
If pure, would sparkle less?"
— *Keble.*

The period of four years spent by LeBaron Botsford
in his medical studies (from the age of nineteen to that
of twenty-three) is, perhaps, one of the most formative
in a man's life. With him it was peculiarly so, for it
was during this time that his religious consciousness
awoke, his religious feelings became deep and strong,
his religious principles took that peculiar shape which
exercised such a dominant influence over his future
life. Hitherto, with his health and buoyant spirits,
life had been like a "long, long summer's day." But
during the many tranquil hours of a sailing voyage
across the Atlantic, deeper feelings were stirred. He
became conscious of the faint pulsations of an inner
life. Very seldom, indeed, did Dr. Botsford unveil his
secret feelings, but he spoke to a friend of this transition state as being one of great despondency. "I
felt," he said, "utterly worthless, as if I could never
be anything, nor do anything; as if I could never
think for myself, but should be led by every one with
whom I came in contact." What gave rise to these
feelings in such a self-reliant, decided nature we cannot
say. Perhaps the best answer is, "The wind bloweth
where it listeth. Thou hearest the sound thereof, but

(36)

canst not tell whence it cometh, nor whither it goeth, so is every one that is born of the Spirit."

At the time of LeBaron's student life in Glasgow, Dr. Chalmers was electrifying the Established Church of Scotland with his vigorous eloquence. He urged upon his hearers with almost apostolic fervour that form of Divine truth known as " evangelical religion." These views have always been held by large numbers in the Church of England, but they come into more prominence at one period of her history than at another. The manly preaching of Dr. Chalmers and his successor in the Tron Church, Dr. Dewer, attracted crowds of students, among them LeBaron Botsford. He had learned the leading truths of Christianity at his mother's knee, but they were lying dormant in his mind until, in the good providence of God, the great preacher's voice roused them into activity. From this time forth consciousness of error and failure, though never lost from sight, was accompanied by a firm faith in the great doctrine of the Atonement and by prayerful trust in the guidance of the Eternal Spirit. On this triple foundation Dr. Botsford's religious life was built. This was the spiritual force from which resulted long years of devotion to God and of unwearied activity for the good of his fellow-men.

We may not try to look too closely into the mysterious workings of the human heart, yet we may say there were three marked characteristics of Dr. Botsford's inner life — his unfeigned humility, his prayerfulness, his interest in the spiritual welfare of others. His *humility* was especially to be noticed in his family prayers, which were usually extemporaneous. The penitential expressions of the Psalms seemed to rise spontaneously to his lips, and, although he heard constantly words of direct or indirect appreciation from others, he never was forgetful of his own shortcomings.

> " God many a spiritual house has rear'd, but never one
> Where lowliness was not laid first, the corner stone."
> — *Archbishop Trench.*

His *prayerfulness* was, owing to his reserve, known but to few. Sometimes an outburst of confidence from a friend would elicit something of the kind in return. On one such occasion he said: "I was very anxious about M——'s child, and all day long, whether in the street or in the house, my heart went up in one constant prayer." His private devotions and daily reading of the Bible were never neglected, and but seldom hurried, even in the height of a busy practice. Sometimes his devotion was so intense that, unconsciously, it became audible, and more than one person has spoken of the earnest, pleading tones of his voice, although the words could not be heard.

This earnestness naturally led him to take great interest in the spiritual welfare of others. When life had become to him an upward journey from doubt and despondency to ever-increasing light and fuller life, he longed to have others share the relief and happiness he felt. His letters to his young friends and relatives in New Brunswick were filled with glowing words, advising, entreating, exhorting. Some of his correspondents were light-hearted and careless; they were amused at the zeal of the young enthusiast. "Old Fight and Pray" was the boyish name by which they designated him. Others who were fighting the same battle, though on different lines, were partly aggrieved. "He writes," they said, "as if we never had a serious thought."

None of these letters have been kept, but one is inserted, written at a much later date. His interest in others was then as deep as ever, but a greater knowledge of himself and of the world, gave a calmer, more argumentative tone to his entreaties:

DEAR ——: One thing has long been a trouble to me, and when I visited you in your illness it was a very, very heavy weight upon me. Years had passed — many years, I may say — and no interchange of thought had taken place on a subject on which I have instinctively felt we were not in accord. My faith is strong in the Scripture revelation of our acceptance and final peace through our Lord Jesus Christ. My impression is that this is looked upon by you in a philosophical aspect, and the whole subject ascribed to the general superstition of the race, and that you have formed your own system in the strength of human intellect. I have no desire to engage in controversial discussion, and yet I must urge a very few suggestions.

The laws in operation in all nature are very exacting. We may run counter to them, but must take the consequences. Stand in the way of gravity, and simple force will crush us. Violate any physical law, and loss of limb or life will be the penalty; and will the great Creator depart from His character (manifested by His laws as unchanging) and permit us with impunity to cast aside His system, which is "peace through our Lord Jesus Christ." "Shall we escapé if we neglect so great salvation?"

As I have stated, my dear ——, no expression of opinion has passed between us, and yet I instinctively feel that in this great point there is between us a wide and, to me, very saddening chasm.

When I saw ——— (a mutual relative) a day or two before his death, as I sat beside his bed, I could no longer be silent, and I put the question: " Do you feel that your peace with God has been granted?" His eye, which had been looking full, clear and intelligent, fell, and his head slightly bent forward. I at once saw that I had mis-shaped my question, that his strong intellect took it in in its full length and breadth, and the assurance was more than he felt justified to give. I repeated my question immediately: " ———, do you think you can trust in the mercy of God through Christ?" The head was raised, the full eye met mine, and slowly, yet firmly, he replied, "I think I can." To me it was a moment of intense interest and great satisfaction. I have often dwelt upon it. Knowing the man, his clear intellect, and his apprehension of all his answer conveyed, I felt it came from his inmost soul. I must not write any more now, may never write again on this subject, but I could not refrain this one time from bringing this to your notice.

Your ——— ——— ———,

LeBaron.

The enthusiasm of LeBaron Botsford in the first fervour of his religious life soon gave rise to mental conflict. He had not, as a lad, had much training in the especial doctrines of his church. Confirmations were infrequent in the widely extended dioceses of Canada. It was not strange, therefore, that Dr. Botsford was at this time strongly inclined to join the Presbyterians, among whom his spiritual life had received such a powerful impulse. Kind friends in the Tron Church opened their houses to the earnest young student. Many gifts of religious books were received and treasured in after years as mementoes of early friendships. Finally, LeBaron wrote to his father on the subject. The old gentleman, whose religious ideas had been fashioned in the High-Churchism of the 18th century, had not much sympathy with this newly awakened fervour. He wrote, however, a kind judicious letter, saying that he should put no obstacle in the way of his son if he wished to follow out his convictions, but he asked him to deliberate carefully before he took any decided step, closing with some forcible arguments in favour of the Church of England. This letter made a deep impression, and after much anxious thought and earnest prayer, LeBaron Botsford determined to remain true to the church of his forefathers. He, however, always retained much brotherly sympathy for Presbyterians and members of other Christian bodies, and he loved to meet and co-operate with them in religious and benevolent associations.

As month after month passed on under circumstances well calculated to intensify his zeal, another question came up for consideration. Should he change the plans he had formed for his future life? He was conscious of an ever increasing desire to devote himself, his life, his all, to the service of God and man. It seemed to him he could do this best by entering the Christian ministry. Again there was a period of doubt and uncertainty, a time of self-questioning and of prayer. At last he decided upon pursuing his medical studies, for he considered he could serve God and his fellow-men as effectually in this profession as in any other. Perhaps more so, for he reflected that a medical man, when called in at the beginning of an illness, might have many quiet opportunities more available for religious purposes than the later period to which clergymen's visits are usually restricted. Then, again, his decision was strengthened by the thought of the disappointment a change in his plans would occasion his father after the expectations which had been raised and the expense incurred. Dr. Botsford seldom returned to a question after it had been once settled, so that from this time we may look upon him as an earnest member of the Church of England, pursuing his studies in the profession he had chosen, not as a means of advancing in life or accumulating money, but chiefly that he might have opportunities of benefiting his fellow-beings in their souls as well as their bodies.

The following undated paper, embodying Dr. Botsford's ideas of the work of a medical man, was found amongst his writings :

"The first step of a physician is to observe the ordinary events of life, and from them draw conclusions, and obtain a knowledge of the laws of nature and of being. Then to grapple with the powers which cause the ceaseless changes of the world, and master their secrets, so that he may say to the lifeless mass, this is my will and it obeys. Then through the study of the Infinite and contemplation of the All-Powerful to be so filled with light and knowledge that he is prepared to go forth to assuage the pains of the suffering, and bring hope and life to the chamber of the dying. Then, if need be (as has been done by many of our brethren), to bend calmly over the prostrate form of countryman or foe, where the battle strife is loudest and death most imminent, or to look with courageous gaze at the coming pestilence, and while others seek a shelter, to stand in the path of the destroyer bent on snatching some victim from its fury. This is, indeed, a high phase of existence."

LeBaron pursued his medical studies carefully and thoroughly, allowing but few things to distract his attention. He has left a record of the classes he attended. It is headed :

" LIST OF CLASSES ATTENDED BY L. B. BOTSFORD."

Session 1831-32.	*Session* 1833-4.
Anatomy,	Midwifery,
Chemistry,	Practice of Medicine,
Surgery,	Materia Medica.
Practical Anatomy.	
Session 1832-3.	*Session* 1834-5.
Anatomy,	Institutions of Medicine,
Practical Anatomy,	Anatomy,
Chemistry,	Chemistry.
Surgery.	

Likewise Botany in 1833, Lectures on the Eye in 1834, with two years hospital attendance, six months clinical surgery and six months of clinical medicine, with three months attendance in the Infirmary Shop.

Dr. Botsford kept the certificate cards of attendance at these various classes, presumably to show his father. Many of them, besides the formal printed notice, have additional lines written by the Professors. Thus Dr. Graham writes : " He was an ardent student and evinced great knowledge of the science." Dr. Weir adds to his card : " He attended my classes with diligence and regularity."

The Professor of Chemistry, at the close of the course, gives a longer written testimonial in these words :

" GLASGOW COLLEGE, 26th April, 1833.

" Mr. LeBaron Botsford attended the Chemistry Class in the College of Glasgow during the sessions 1831-2 and 1832-3, and also the weekly examinations, with the utmost punctuality

c

and attention. His behaviour was perfectly correct, and he highly distinguished himself at the examinations, having obtained in 1832-3 the first prize by the votes of his fellow-students for having acquitted himself with much credit at the examinations.

" Certified by,
" THOMAS THOMSON, M. D.,
" *Professor of Chemistry.*"

To these scanty and brief notices of Dr. Botsford's college life is appended a communication from Dr. H. A. Hartt, the friend and fellow-student mentioned in the previous chapter :

" When I crossed the Atlantic to study medicine, I selected the University of Glasgow, Scotland, solely because LeBaron Botsford was there. He had preceded me at the college by one year ; but we pursued our medical studies together in the University, and dwelt in the same house for three years, and I look back upon them now as among the happiest of my life.

" His nature was conscientious and upright. As a boy he was too proud to lie, or to stoop to any form of meanness. By the power of earnest faith, his native pride disappeared, and in its place came a beautiful humanity which gave him an irrepressible interest in all things noble and good, and led him to embrace in his sympathies all races and conditions of men.

" It was at this time that the insurrection in Jamaica raised the question of West India Emancipation. A great discussion took place throughout the British Isles. Glasgow was the centre of the fight, and a memorable debate was held there between Peter Bothwick, a hired advocate of the Liverpool merchants, and George Thompson, the eloquent champion of freedom. In this controversy Mr. Botsford took a special interest, and soon became a pronounced abolitionist.

" He had a decided talent for drawing, and used to amuse us

with striking caricatures, setting forth the oddities of those with whom we came in contact.

"He was fond of literature, and read extensively even in those early days. But his genius was of a philosophic cast. He loved to look into the causes of phenomena, in the physical; moral and spiritual realms, and to work out the probable results of all that was transpiring in the world around him.

"I find on the inside of a cover, and on a blank half of a page of an old copy of Hume's History of England, two characteristic writings, the only souvenirs of the kind that I have of those times :

"'Hume has gone; but where? Has he become as nothing and entered into that state of annihilation his vain philosophy taught? Can all that once formed man, be contained in a small heap of dust and rest in eternal oblivion? Is there nought to which he could look forward but to rest in the lonely tomb, and to be forever enveloped in the darkness of non-existence? Or has his spirit, indeed, gone to another world? Has the mysterious veil been uplifted? Has the soul of the daring sceptic been ushered into the presence of his God? Methinks I see him, amazed, confounded, doubting, and afraid to doubt. Awful reality surrounded him. Withering before the Majesty of Heaven his spirit takes its flight. Fleeing, but still unable to escape, remorse goads it on. Revolving ages finds but commenced its flight.

"'Hume's ruling passion was love of literary fame. Poor, vain philosophy! Can fame be of use to what does not exist? Still this great philosopher toiled for it. Can any one deny that in doing so this wise man was a contradiction—an absurdity?'"

Dr. Hartt adds with pardonable enthusiasm :

"LeBaron Botsford was one of the most remarkable men I have known on this earth, and if ever the people at large shall be brought up to his standard, the sun of the golden age will rise. From his boyhood he devoted himself to the cause of humanity; he stood like a rock against injustice and wrong; he uniformly set an example of inflexible honour and Christian uprightness. From his inmost soul he abhorred all shams in public and private life. He was ever found an unflinching advocate of what he believed to be truth. In his youth he examined carefully and critically the evidences of the Christian faith, and from that time to the end of his life laughed to scorn the attacks of infidelity on the one hand and the temptations to frivolity and self-indulgence on the other."

These expressions may seem to some to border on exaggeration, but to those who knew Dr. Botsford best, the words of his college friend and fellow-student will not appear too glowing.

CHAPTER III.

Wo Starkes sich und Mildes paarten.
Da gibt es einen guten Klang.
                              — *Schiller.*

The religious and intellectual influences which surrounded LeBaron Botsford during his college life tended, as has been shown, to foster a rapid maturing of his strongly-marked, but hitherto undeveloped character. A third influence, that of society, made a not less powerful impression on the young man.

Before he left New Brunswick his father had refused to accept for him several letters of introduction which influential friends offered to give, as he feared the claims of society would occupy too much of his son's time. He had, however, a few introductions, one to a widow lady, with whom it was hoped he might find a quiet home during his college life. He did so, and much more, for in one of the widow's daughters the young student found his life's companion. Margaret M—— was older than LeBaron, but she did not look it, for she had a petite, plump figure, fair complexion, bright colour, blue eyes, and golden curly hair. She had seen something of society among her mother's friends in Bath, had a piquant, naive manner, and was full of fun, frolic and repartee. Although she was not what is called intellectual, she was well read and conversed brightly and intelligently on the literature and topics of the day. She wrote with facility, her letters

(47)

giving great pleasure to her correspondents, and she read aloud in polished, well-modulated tones, with but a faint trace of Scotch accent. Her voice had been thoroughly trained, but she was shy of singing except when accompanied by her sister. Often, however, in the evening twilight she would sing without accompaniment many old Jacobite songs such as " On hills that were by right his ain he wanders now a stranger," or " Come o'er the seas, Charlie," etc. At these times the interest she felt in the old lost cause gave much pathos to the sweet tones of her rippling voice. In short, she was a charming and fascinating companion. LeBaron soon found himself strongly attracted to the bright, merry girl, while his more mercurial friend, Henry Hartt, was paying quiet attention to her demure little sister, Jesse. Before the young students left Glasgow, the two Scotch " Lassies " had promised that, at some future time, they, accompanied by their mother, would follow their " Laddies " to America.

LeBaron took his surgical degree in 1834, and his medical degree in 1835. He then went to Paris for a few months to complete his studies. Late in the autumn of 1835 he sailed for St. John, thence to Westcock, where he arrived about Christmas.

The following account of his return is taken from the journal of a relative who was staying at Westcock at that time :

" The seventh son, the doctor, was daily expected. It was near Christmas, and all the family were assembled to meet him on his return from Scotland. It was four years since they had seen him. ' I tell you what,' said one of the brothers one evening, ' Le Baron's letters are as good as ser-

mons; let us shew him we know more than he does.' . . .
The doctor arrived a very handsome young man. I looked
at him with interest and wonder. He was on the road to
heaven, which I could not find. Yet he laughed a most
hearty laugh, and danced a Scotch reel with greater glee than
any of us. Several efforts were made that same evening by
his brothers to get LeBaron into a religious argument. I
was much pleased and amused to see how he avoided it, and
with what good humour he turned off the shafts directed
against his opinions. He took refuge by his mother, and
answered her many questions about Scotland.

"The house was now gayer than ever, visitors coming at
all hours to welcome the newly arrived. Not only visitors in
the parlour. The hall and kitchen were filled with patients
from thirty miles round — all sure the doctor would cure
the friends he had known from a child, and that without fee
or charge, so that the doctor's mornings were engaged with
the sick or maimed, and his afternoons in preparing medicine.
His fame soon spread further than he wished, and wonders
were told of the cures he had made. The evenings, when
strangers were not there, were spent in very warm debates
upon religion. LeBaron could no longer avoid it, and
perhaps thought it right to 'let his light shine.' There
were long, earnest and ably supported arguments on the existence of the soul or spirit separate from matter. I listened in
silence, but deeply interested. One evening, after I had said
good night to him at the door of my room, I thought, 'What
will become of me? If I were only a good Christian like
LeBaron!' But I continued in the valley of shadows for two
years before I found peace through the Blood of the Cross.

"LeBaron did not remain long. He said it was necessary
to settle himself somewhere. At Westcock he could get
plenty of practice, but little pay, and there was a Scotch girl
waiting for him till he had found a home."

After many inquiries and repeated consultations

with his father, LeBaron decided on making Woodstock his starting point in life. It was then a pleasant
village, though not half its present size. He moved
there in the early spring of 1836, the people welcoming
warmly the son of the genial old judge. He soon
found comfortable quarters and began the practice of
his profession.

In July of the following year, 1837, the two young
doctors went to New York to meet their brides. They
were quietly married in church July 22nd, and returned at once to New Brunswick. Dr. Hartt settled
in Fredericton. Dr. Botsford took his wife to the home
he had prepared for her at Woodstock.

Life in this pretty village on the St. John river was
to Dr. Botsford a new life full of interest and activities.
It was to him the beginning of many things. There
commenced that unceasing devotion to his profession
which characterized him through life. Day or night,
for forty years, when the call of professional duty
came, he was found ready to respond to it. But once
during that time did he take more than two or
three weeks' vacations during the year. He has
been known to sit down after a long morning's
work with a pleasant luncheon party. A call would
come. "Duty first; pleasure afterwards," he would
say, and leave at once the untasted meal.

It was at Woodstock that his active, energetic habits
of mind and body were at once brought into play.
Springing into the saddle after an early breakfast, he
would ride all day through the settlement and far over
the surrounding country, often not returning until late
in the evening. His fees, like those of many other
young country practitioners, amounting sometimes

only to a small bag of buckwheat meal. If called up at night, he seldom allowed himself a longer rest in the morning. Seven o'clock in summer and eight o'clock in winter were his regular breakfast hours, his theory being that the more light and sunshine the physical frame enjoys the better will a man be both in mind and body.

Then, again, Dr. Botsford began life with habits of strict economy. Sometimes his wife, naturally a little solicitous about his appearance, would lament over his country-cut garments, which showed evident traces of hard usage and repairs. "Never mind," the rector's wife would say, "he looks like Judge Botsford's son whatever he wears."

And so the first winter passed. It was a cold season, far colder than the young Scotch wife anticipated. The cream froze on the breakfast table; nay, the breath froze on the sheets during the night. The little dwelling was far from comfortable and in the early spring Dr. Botsford began to build a cottage. He drew the plans; the workmen were inspired by his energy; it was finished in the autumn, and they moved in before the first snow storm. During the winter the village was enlivened by a detachment of the —— Regiment, which was stationed there for some months. The officers soon found their way to the cottage and enjoyed many pleasant evenings with the cheerful doctor and his bright little wife. "What would you do to amuse yourself if we were not here?" queried a young fellow as he lounged in one morning. "Just what I am doing now" was the quick answer; "making a shirt for my husband."

In the following summer Judge Botsford paid the

young couple a visit. He staid with them while the
court was sitting and was much pleased with LeBaron's
industry and progress. He used to remind Mrs. Botsford in after times of this visit to the pretty cottage.
How he was aroused in the early morning by a
" poultry chorus," and looking out of his window saw
her surrounded by her feathered friends. They were
not only at her feet, but on her shoulders and her head.
They were her pets, her family. No other nestling
had come to the doctor's cottage. Once when Mrs.
Botsford was suffering from a headache, as she was
lying on a sofa, a squaw with baskets peeped in at the
door. Receiving a smile of welcome, she came up to
the sofa and gently lifting the corner of a shawl, "Pap-
poose? sister," she asked. There was no "baby."
This one of God's good gifts was never granted. Dr.
and Mrs. Botsford were both fond of children and
young people. More than one nephew and niece
can testify to the almost parental love, care and
assistance they have received. One nephew remarked
not long before Dr. Botsford's death: "I owe
my earthly existence to my parents, but to my
uncle I owe everything else—my education, my
position, everything I have, or am in the world, I owe
to his kindness." During the last years of Dr.
Botsford's life, after he had been frequently called
upon to sympathize with parents who were grieving
over their suffering or erring children, he would often
say that he was truly thankful that such a source of
happiness and sorrow had not been opened to him.
Sometimes he makes playful allusions to the subject in
his letters. For instance, in writing to one of his
brothers in June, 1881, he says: " H —— is with us, and

has been for a fortnight. She is a very fine girl. F —— returns home on Tuesday, so that we shall have a 'real pleasant' pair of nieces, 'and enjoy the comfort, though a borrowed one.'"

During the winter of 1838 and 1839 there occurred at Woodstock a "revival," namely, one of those mysterious religious movements, which, from primitive times, have been experienced at intervals in the Christian Church. They differ at different periods of the Church's history. They vary according to the intelligence and education of those aroused by them. In mediæval times, crusades, pilgrimages and the various religious "Orders" were the effect of these mass inspirations. Later on the words of such men as Luther, Bossnet, Wesley, Chalmers or Newman were the means of stirring up great tidal waves of religious enthusiasm. And at the present day revivals, under the name of "Missions," are as recognized an agency in the Church of England as among other Christian bodies. This was not the case when Dr. Botsford came in contact with this religious movement among the Methodists at Woodstock. He was at once attracted, and, although he was a regular attendant at the Parish Church (he and his wife being members of the choir), he went to several of the "Revival Meetings" and studied the subject not only in its religious, but also in its scientific aspect. Some years afterwards, when widespread religious movements were taking place in Philadelphia and in the north of Ireland, he read before a meeting of the Evangelical Alliance the following thoughtful paper. Its deductions were drawn from the personal observations and reflections made at this time at Woodstock.

THOUGHTS UPON PHYSICAL MANIFESTATIONS
ACCOMPANYING RELIGIOUS REVIVALS.

The few remarks which I bring under your notice this evening are connected with the subject of the physical manifestations which are apt to disclose themselves in times of more
than ordinary religious movements. I am aware, in doing
this, I am treading on debatable ground, but truth, and truth
only, should be the aim of every Christian heart. Whilst I
would strongly urge the necessity laid upon us to investigate,
I would also acknowledge the difficulty and the responsibility
attending the discussion of a subject which deals with the
soul of man, and the influences of the Holy Spirit upon that
soul. Nevertheless, the responsibility cannot be evaded; the
difficulty must be met.

In the ordinary course of events, when men are turned
from darkness to light, "the still small voice" sinks into the
soul like gently falling dew, producing repentance towards
God and faith in our Lord Jesus Christ. On other occasions,
when the spirit of God works mightily, and many are con-
strained to cry out, "What shall I do to be saved," there are
frequently to be observed bodily disturbances as an attendant,
or as the direct, result of religious influences. As you are
aware, these "bodily exercises" have differed, and do differ,
among various people and in different countries. The question I suggest for your consideration is: "Are they the direct
effects of religious influence; or are they to be considered as
disturbances in the animal frame, the result of mental and
physical laws?" To understand this subject we must, in
some measure, understand the workings of the intellectual
and moral faculties, and their effect upon the rest of the
system. If the intellect is working powerfully, producing
what is called abstraction, then, in proportion to the absorb-
ing character of that abstraction, is there an unconsciousness
of surrounding events. Many instances of this must be familiar. When the moral emotions are called into play, they

exercise an influence in proportion to their intensity upon the intellect and upon the physical frame, at one time paralyzing all effort, at another developing superhuman strength. Who has not seen the poor stricken soul crushed beneath a weight of sorrow, stupified with anguish so bitter that the tears were driven back to their fountain, while the parched eyes stared upon vacancy? And who has not seen the faculties benumbed, the muscles paralyzed, when intense fear overshadowed the soul? There is no doubt, therefore, that moral forces and mental powers do frequently produce overwhelming disturbances in the animal system. These disturbances are in accordance with what may be called laws of our nature.

The history of the human mind bears witness to another fact, namely, the tendency of the individual to develop what is exhibited by the mass. It matters not whether it arises from sympathy, or imitation, or from direct influence, the result is before us in the epidemics which have at times swept over nations and over continents. I can allude to the dancing mania of the middle ages, when thousands were the supposed victims of the bite of the tarentula. The patients fell down senseless and motionless, with difficult breathing and heavy sighing. As these symptoms subsided they became desponding and melancholy. At the sound of music (which was supposed to be the only cure), they began to dance, throwing themselves into every variety of fantastic attitudes. In later times the falling sickness also numbered its thousands, and passed over large tracts of country. To illustrate by a more limited example, I will cite the instance of the school at Bickfort, in Germany, in which, when two girls were seized with epileptic fits, in less than half an hour twenty other cases occurred among the pupils. A peculiarity worthy to be noted attends all such disturbances. It is this: the symptoms assume the shape and direction which are previously suggested to the mind. At one time we have the dancing mania, at another the epileptic, and at another the extraordinary scenes attending the witch hallucination of New England.

These phenomena of mind and body occur not only spontaneously, but they can be produced artificially, and did time permit, instances of a deeply interesting and instructive nature could be made to throw light upon this curious phase of life. On these data I ground the following propositions :

First. Strong mental or moral emotions tend to produce disturbances in the physical frame.

Secondly. These disturbances have frequently developed themselves in the form of epidemics when there has been no admixture of religious influences.

Thirdly. The phenomena take the direction previously suggested to the mind, and become intense in proportion to the result anticipated.

As the above laws are undoubtedly active in man, the next point to consider is — do they continue active in those who are guided by the spirit of God? In other words — do the natural faculties in the religious man continue to be influenced by natural causes? Are we subject to aberrations in our physical and mental workings, though we truly are the children of God? or does the influence of the Holy Spirit supersede natural laws?

We answer — natural causes do certainly act on the children of God. The mind is subject to disease, the body to death, and whilst the Holy Spirit changes the inner man, the natural laws are permitted to hold their sway, so that in the battle of life there is a commingling of the spiritual and the natural, each working in their peculiar sphere and reacting on each other.

We have seen that often the effect of strong emotion is to stupify the mind and paralyze the body. Now I cannot conceive any moral emotion to be as powerful in disturbing the physical frame as the conviction of conscience, when the soul is brought, as it were, into contact with God Himself. On the one hand stands the High and Holy One, of purer eyes than to behold iniquity ; on the other a soul convicted of sin and seeing in the light of God's presence its own utter deformity.

It need not excite wonder that when God thus reveals Himself to His sinful creature, the sense of despair should paralyze both mind and body. If the physical frame can be overwhelmed by emotions proceeding from fear or grief, why not by those which are called into play by religion? In both cases the process is the same. In one case a heavy affliction fills the soul with a sorrow that prostrates; in the other the Holy Spirit produces remorse and repentance so poignant that the outer man is overwhelmed.

I now invite your attention to two places in which a "revival of religion" is producing great results. The first is Philadelphia, which for two years has been the centre of a wondrous work. Day after day the halls have been filled with hearts overflowing with zeal, or with souls stirred to their very depths in their endeavour to enter the straight and narrow way. Week after week, and month after month, does the same God-seeking spirit pervade their assemblies. During the period of this pentecostal visitation, their meetings have been marked with great solemnity, and though sobs may occasionally burst forth from hearts surcharged with sympathy, a deep and holy influence rests upon the gatherings and no bodily contortions or physical phenomena are associated with their emotions.

The second place of which I would speak is the north of Ireland, where the work of God has begun, and thousands are being brought to the knowledge of the truth. As you are, however, aware through the accounts that reach us, many and frequent are the instances in which manifestations of great bodily disturbance accompany these religious awakenings. In view of these facts, I submit for your consideration the following conclusions:

First. A great and continued revival may take place without any disturbance of the physical system accompanying it.

Secondly. Spiritual and mental emotions act with equal power on the human system, and produce the same results.

Thirdly. The phenomena of these physical disturbances, assuming a peculiar form in each place, manifest a tendency to develop in natural epidemics.

Fourthly. Man being subject to infirmity, it is more in accordance with truth to ascribe these " bodily exercises " to natural laws than to the direct agency of the Holy Spirit.

I have considered it my duty, gentlemen, to bring these thoughts before you. I am aware that a great responsibility rests upon us. As rational beings we are called upon to discern between good and evil, and while it is incumbent on us to ascribe all glory to the Eternal Spirit for His mighty works of grace, we must also beware lest we fill our censers with "unsanctified incense."

CHAPTER IV.

Plying their daily task with busier feet
Because their secret souls a holy strain repeat.
— *Keble.*

Dr. Botsford, though comfortably settled in his new cottage, and making his way successfully in country practice, was not destined to remain long at Woodstock. Friends in St. John wrote that there was a good opening in the city for an energetic young medical man, and they urged Dr. Botsford to take advantage of it. His friend Dr. Hartt, who paid him a short visit at this time, gave strong advice in the same direction. After a little hesitation, the change was decided upon. There is no record of the motives which prompted this important step. No doubt in this, as in other decisive moments of his life, Dr. Botsford sought God's good guidance and then made use of his natural powers of judgment and foresight. He had that innate consciousness of power at once the guarantee and means of success which urges its possessor forward to wider fields of action. Probably one of the strongest motives which influenced the home-loving man was the desire to avoid those long absences so trying to the young wife which country practice naturally entailed. There was great regret among his Woodstock friends when his decision became known. An address was presented to him, accompanied by a handsome silver snuff-box with the following inscription: " Presented to LeBaron

D (59)

Botsford, M. D., on his departure from Woodstock, by a few of his most intimate friends, as a token of their high respect and esteem for him as a physician and member of society, 1839."

On reaching St. John, Dr. Botsford took lodgings in Charlotte street, thence he removed to Horsfield street. During his first winter in town he was much occupied by attendance on his sister Eliza, who had been brought from Westcock in the last stages of consumption. Nothing could be done to prolong the sweet young life, yet her brother's daily visits were a comfort to both body and mind. After some months of suffering she passed away in perfect peace.

In May, 1841, after having been in St. John two years, Dr. Botsford moved to the well-known house in Wellington Row, and the place and the sphere of his life-work was settled for all the future of his earthly years. His energy, which branched out in after life in so many different directions, was at first wholly absorbed in the duties of his profession. It was uphill work, for he began, as all young doctors must, with poor, non-paying patients. He had, it is true, many connections in town, whose practice he eventually secured; but old family doctors cannot, and ought not, to be superseded at once by a young practitioner, even though he be a cousin. One of the first to hold out to the young doctor a helping hand was a wealthy relative*, to whose munificence the Church of England in New Brunswick is so much indebted. He told his young cousin to draw upon him yearly for a certain sum as long as it was needed. The offer was accepted

---

* The late Chief Justice Chipman.

with frank gratitude, and for three years Dr. Botsford
drew half the amount mentioned. With this exception
he was dependent on his own exertions, for after the
liberal education he had received, he did not wish to
call upon his father for aid. The same prudent economy with which he began life at Woodstock was continued in the city. His household was a model of
primitive simplicity even in those days, less ostentatious
than our own. Bills were not allowed to accumulate.
For many years he did not keep a horse and but seldom
hired one, his long walks at this time contributing
much to the health which he enjoyed in after years.
His day's work was regularly planned, and if, during
the morning, a visit was forgotten, he patiently retraced
his steps in the afternoon, "to teach his memory a
lesson." Sometimes after a long day's work, when
resting in the twilight, a message which ought to have
been sent hours before, would summon him to a house
which he had passed during the day. His wife's
anxious words would be met with "Never mind,
Maggie, we are all inconsiderate in some directions,"
and swallowing his evening meal, he would hasten
away.

It was thus by hard-working, unwearied industry
Dr. Botsford succeeded in laying the foundation of a
solid practice among the business men of St. John.
He had many elements of character which attracted
their confidence. His straightforward sincerity was
very apparent. Anything approaching to what is
called humbug was foreign to his nature. He disliked
to employ slight deception, even when professionally
necessary. For instance, when a child died in a house
where there was a babe a week old, to avoid giving

the mother a fatal shock, her questions about the dead child had to be answered, and the doctor had to pass through a certain door in order to keep up the illusion of visiting the child. Any such circumstance, often so unavoidable in the profession, was a great trial to him. He was very reticent about his patients, carefully avoiding allusions to the gravity of an illness lest he should seem to desire to enhance the importance of the cure; all such contrivances which strong professional competition almost forces upon men were unknown or unpracticed by him.

A friend writes since his death: "In the midst of the shams and hypocrisies by which we are surrounded, it is an unspeakable satisfaction and joy to be able to point to even one man and say with absolute confidence, 'Behold an Israelite indeed in whom there is no guile.'"

There was no assumption of dignity, the transparent simplicity of his character shining out in all the details of his profession. Then, again, his punctuality was proverbial. In professional business or social engagements he was always "on time." Consideration for others, he used to say, ought to prompt us to avoid delay. These characteristics of industry, economy, sincerity, and punctuality, in addition to his professional skill, might be considered the basis of his life's success. The details given may seem trivial and unimportant, but they are proofs of a substantial foundation upon which much life-work may be built. In Dr. Botsford's character there were, however, two elements which gave peculiar and additional power to his other traits—his *personal magnetism*, and *sympathy*. Perhaps these are but the objective and subjective forms of the same thing. His personal magnetism influenced the patient, his sympathy seemed to assume the sufferer's burden, in order to understand and lighten it. This double characteristic may be considered Dr. Botsford's chief "power-winning, love-winning" peculiarity. His sympathy was intense, and often very exhausting. At one time, when he had been absent two days, his wife and niece went to see him, and give some important messages. When he came into the room, he said in answer to inquiries, that mother and child were both doing well, then covering his face with his hands, he sobbed aloud, quite overcome by his sympathy with the suffering he had witnessed, and this was not at the beginning of his practice, but after fifteen years might be supposed to have made him tolerably familiar with such scenes.

At another time a patient, after many years of married life, gave birth to a daughter. When the doctor had finished his professional services, he sat down by the bedside of the happy mother, and read the 103rd Psalm. Sometimes his sympathy took a very practical form. He was called, for instance, to a patient who had just entered a new house. Nothing was ready when baby came. The doctor, after attending to his professional duties, assisted in putting up the bedstead, and making the bed.

His personal magnetism was both consciously and unconsciously exercised. At the beginning of his professional career in Woodstock he first became cognizant of the phenomena of animal magnetism, or hypnotism, as it is now called, and was conscious of his magnetic power over others. He felt his way cautiously, as was his wont, but the more he observed and experimented, the more he became convinced of the reality of the phenomena. He was fully aware of the mystery and uncertainty that enshrouded the subject, of the deception that could be so easily practiced by the magnetizer and the patient. Yet, he soon felt assured that a power did exist under the name of magnetism or mesmerism, which could be employed for the benefit of others. He had no hesitation in making use of this power in his practice, and by means of it more than one sufferer was restored to health. These were exceptional cases; generally he used his magnetic influence to relieve temporary pain, sometimes to the astonishment of patient and nurse. For instance, after being sent for twice to soothe a sufferer, the nurse exclaimed as he was leaving, "Oh, doctor, if we could only keep your hand." As he advanced in life, he used his direct magnetic power but rarely, and when questioned on the subject, he said, that it occupied much time and exhausted his vital energy.

His unconscious personal magnetism was universally acknowledged, but difficult to describe. As a medical friend writes: "A large proportion of the things which went to make up our estimation of Dr. Botsford were not such as taken by themselves could make a like estimate in the mind of another. There were a thousand and one things impossible to enumerate, the genial manner, the pleasing countenance, in fact the *tout ensemble* of our dear friend which combined to form the attractive power." Probably his tall, athletic, well-proportioned frame had its influence. His entrance into a sick-room has often been compared to sunshine. As a young man, the first notice of a professional visit would be Dr. Botsford's cheery laugh as he encountered a friend in the hall; then he would mount two stairs at a time, his quick, elastic tread would be heard along the corridor, and when he stood beside the bedside with his bright smile and beaming eye, his very presence seemed to radiate life and health. A few months after he had entered into rest, a dying friend was asked if she were comfortable, " Oh yes, but I do so weary to see Dr. Botsford come in."

It would be thought presumptuous for a non-professional to venture to describe the peculiarities of Dr. Botsford's medical treatment, and in a memoir intended for general readers it is not necessary. Yet we all know that marked men in every profession, taught by experience, influenced by their own individuality, gradually develop a certain system of work to which they partly owe their success, but which can never be satisfactorily copied by another. Therefore a record of Dr. Botsford's life would not be complete without giving some general outlines of his medical treatment.

In the first place, his opinion of an illness, the diagnosis of a case, to speak technically, was slowly and carefully made, and always leaned to the favorable side if possible, so that if Dr. Botsford's opinion was unfavorable, he was seldom mistaken.

Then, again, he never gave any large quantity of medicine, even when it was customary to do so. His principle was to watch nature, and assist her. His basis of operation, the stomach and diet. " What have you been eating?" was often the first question asked of a sick person, and many said that Dr. Botsford starved his patients. But his general success encouraged him in this peculiarity. He himself was most abstemious, and as he advanced in years, he became

more fully convinced of the truth of his favorite saying, "That more disease is engendered by over-feeding
than by want of food."

Although he was near-sighted, he was successful in
surgical cases. His touch was peculiarly gentle; he
seemed to be able with his smooth, soft fingers to
handle inflamed or wounded parts without giving pain;
he was skilful in any mechanical device that might be
required to relieve, and was continually planning
peculiar-shaped cases for broken limbs. During the
last years of his life he contrived a frame by which a
patient might be raised so as to make his bed. Of
course, there are many such arrangements, but the
peculiar excellence of Dr. Botsford's bed is that by
loosening the head and foot rests, the whole bed re-
laxes and forms an easy instead of a tightly stretched
surface for the patient. The bed was tried in the
Marine Hospital, and in the "Home for Aged
Females" in St. John, with success. When urged to
patent it, he said, that if it was of any benefit to
sufferers, he did not wish to restrict its use. He sent,
however, a model to London with a description, which
was published in the Lancet, January 2nd, 1886.*

In one department Dr. Botsford was unusually successful—in attending mothers at the birth of their
children. It is believed that at the close of his forty
years practice, he could say with truth, that he had
never, in such cases, lost one patient. All who experienced his services at those times were unanimous
in their praise of his kindness, sympathy and skill.

His manner to his patients was, as has been said,

* See Appendix.

full of gentleness and sympathy, but at the same time it was most decided. He never took his patients into his confidence; he required from them absolute trust and submission. Sometimes he may have seemed to carry this very far, but in a general way his plan worked well. One day, on leaving the room of a new patient, he met an attendant carrying a rich delicacy, "Is that for —— ?" "Yes, sir." The doctor returned to his patient and explained that he expected attention to his directions, as well as to his prescriptions. Tears followed. He then said that unless she could make up her mind to obey him, she must look elsewhere for a medical attendant. After a little hesitation she agreed to submit, and though she had been a sufferer for years, she was, in a few months, restored to health. "Doctor," a sick man would say, "I am not one particle better this morning." The doctor, after an examination, would seat himself at the bedside, look straight into his patient's eyes and say, "You are better —I can see it—trust me. In a few hours you will feel that I am right." "Mind acts on mind." Yes, and mind acts on matter also. As Dr. Botsford advanced in age and experience, he became more and more conscious of the power of mind over matter, and he sought by the force of his own personality to rouse and stimulate his patients. He seemed to anticipate this modern idea which, much as it has been caricatured by the exaggerations of "mind science," has nevertheless its foundation on facts. Dr. Botsford's views on this subject were given in a paper read before the New Brunswick Medical Association. We select some extracts suited to general readers. The paper is entitled

MIND A FACTOR IN DISEASE.

There is no one factor among the many which tend to induce disease, or to remove it, more powerful than the influence of mind; and yet there is no fact more persistently overlooked in our medical treatment.

This may be attributed to the number of palpable causes which take so much time to master; also to the unpalpable or uncertain character of the mental forces.

I need not say anything about hysterical phenomena, which are protean in character and simulate almost every disease. I wish to direct your attention to organic or functional derangement. We are all aware of the effect of sudden emotion upon functional action—how the heart's action may be arrested or the digestion paralyzed. These results, though involuntary, arise from the mind disturbing the circulation of the blood. And if such effects are produced *without* the conscious direction of the nervous centres, why may not similar and more varied results follow when the will directs and moves nervous force to expected results? I have but to allude to the sickness which follows an army when demoralized by defeat. In our professional work we have all seen the effect of this principle—how readily those patients who are hopeful and have confidence in their medical man will respond to medicine; on the other hand, how the desponding and the distrustful often baffle our best and wisest efforts. I have always disliked to come into contact with the latter class of patients. It is evident we should look for good or bad results in our patients just as their minds are led to look for them. Not that all patients will respond, for there is as wide a difference in the impressibility of people as there is in their other powers, imagination, music, benevolence, veneration. . . . I have no doubt but that the success which sometimes attends patent medicines can be traced to the strong expectations created by recommendations and advertisements. In the early days of magnetism, tractors were in vogue and were apparently efficacious. But a shrewd observer who doubted quietly introduced wooden shams made to resemble the real magnets, and with them produced similar results. The bubble burst. Tractors fell at once into disrepute — results anticipated no longer followed. The real force at work beneath the phenomena was not recognized, and consequently not used. I am inclined to think that in devotion to palpable remedies we overlook the subtler energies of the system, and lose much of our power in battling with disease.

Sydney Smith sarcastically remarks that a medical man reminds him of a "person thrusting a needle among the wheels of a watch to correct its action; failing with one thrust, he tries another push among the wheels; so the medical man, finding no healing from his first dose, tries another and then another." In this way electricity is often used. It is a subtle agent, and can interfere with the processes of life, but who can tell *when* it should be used and *how* it should be used except by experience ? Systems of medicine rise and fall. The power of a drug is at one time thought supreme, at another time its use is neglected. New remedies in favor today give place to others to-morrow. One need not take a Rip Van Winkle sleep to wake up to a new order of things in the medical world. Not a year passes but new land-marks meet the eye, some to point out what has been erroneous, some, however, to remain a witness to a steady, though it be a slow, progress. My remarks thus far have been confined to the *subjective* forces in the human system — those which show the action of the mind upon the body. Are there any facts which tend to show that mental or physical force can be projected from the individual so as to produce results upon other minds ? In connection with this part of the paper I will give an account of what fell under my own observation. If I had been the only witness, I could readily believe that I might have been the dupe of my own fancy, and that I might have been perhaps in that biological condition when the subjective working of the brain is received as objective realities. There were, however, several persons present who were well capable of judging, and who never showed any biological tendencies. More than thirty years ago I knew a young man, Robert Trainor by name, a journeyman painter, who was a good subject for biological experiments. As such he was frequently operated upon by a club of investigators much interested in the subject of hypnotism. One set of experiments was made with a man, a native of Carleton, deaf and dumb from his birth. When Trainor was hypnotised, he directed the experiments upon Beatty, of Carleton, who was easily thrown into a hypnotic state, and began to utter uncouth sounds. Trainor stated that Beatty could be made to speak, and that the first words that he would speak would be his (Trainor's) name. One evening, when several gentlemen were present, the usual course was pursued, and the efforts to stimulate the deaf-mute were continued for some time. Beatty began to make uncouth sounds, which presently assumed syllabic form, until the words "Rob Trainor, Robert Trainor," were articulated a number of times as clearly and as distinctly as could be done by mortal man. The case required persistent effort, the novelty wore off, the persons in charge ceased their efforts, and the experiments were discontinued. Beatty lost what little benefit had been received, and returned to his deaf and dumb condition. During the experiments Trainor was not in contact with Beatty, and if any influence was exerted, it must have been of a mental or nervous character. To suppose that Beatty's brain was the source of the cerebration which developed articulation in his untrained vocal muscles, or to suppose that Trainor, through Beatty's brain, called into play his power of speech, involves more difficulty than to suppose that Trainor acted directly on the man's vocal organization. This is the simplest explanation, and is strengthened by the fact that the efforts to make sounds increased as long as the experiments were continued.

I am perfectly aware, gentlemen, that in submitting this statement to you, I must be ready to meet the ridicule of some, to be considered a deluded crank by others.

I am, satisfied, however, that this fact is one only among many similar in character. These facts when investigated, their natural causes determined, and their conditions better known, will prevent delusions based on ignorance from misleading people, and blinding even men of genius.

A little more light upon these obscure psychical phenomena, and a little less dogmatic philosophy will cause the wild vagaries of modern spiritualism, the pretentious assumptions of mental scientism, and many crude theories to scatter and disappear.

There is one other characteristic of Dr. Botsford which must not be omitted in this chapter—his unfailing courtesy, and gentlemanly bearing towards younger practitioners. The following is only one out of many cases which occurred. He was sent for to see a sick person. On entering the house, he inquired if any other medical man was in attendance. "Oh, yes, Dr. —— has been visiting here, but he is young; we think he does not know much; we wish you to take charge of the case." "Indeed, I can do nothing of the kind," was the answer, "send for Dr. ——; I will meet and consult with him." So Dr. —— came and matters were arranged. Dr. ——, who became afterwards a well known physician, but was then struggling into practice, thanked Dr. Botsford warmly, and said he had not often met such kind consideration. At the same time it is not the intention of this memoir to represent Dr. Botsford as uninfluenced by the ordinary feelings and impulses of human nature, perhaps few stood more unyieldingly on his dignity. He claimed very strongly what he considered his right, and resented most indignantly any interference with his patients, or his practice.

CHAPTER V.

> We faintly hear, we dimly see
> In differing phrase we pray
> But, dim or clear, we own in Thee
> The Lord, the Life, the Way.
>
> — *Whittier.*

The deep religious tone which Dr. Botsford's character acquired in Scotland, has already been mentioned. When he settled in St. John he had reached that period of life (twenty-seven years) when an earnest man's inner sentiments more visibly influence his outer life and lead him to take an active part in the religious and benevolent movements around him. Dr. Botsford became a regular attendant at Trinity Church, a vestryman,* and an intimate friend of the rector, the Rev. J. D. W. Gray.

Dr. Gray had been assistant minister in Trinity Parish since 1826, but he succeeded his father as rector soon after Dr. Botsford's arrival in St. John. He was a noble type of an evangelical clergyman, then a novel character in St. John, and not quite acceptable to the easy-going Church people of the period. Dr. Gray's sonorous voice made Trinity resound Sunday after Sunday with earnest appeals to " flee from the wrath to come; " " to forsake the world ; " " to let their light shine." He denounced cards and dancing as " worldly

---

* He continued to be a member of the vestry for thirty years.

(72)

amusements." His preparations of candidates for confirmation was very strict. He made demands on the purses of his congregation for missionary and Bible societies; demands unknown before. Colonists were accustomed to receive, not to confer, benefits. Dr. Gray went further. Trinity had pews. Public opinion had been, and was still altogether in their favor. Bishop Inglis writes: "It gave me no small concern to learn that the pews in Kingston Church were all held in common. I never knew an instance of this in England or America. . . . . The worst characters might come to sit themselves down by the most religious and respectable in the parish. . . . . What could occasion such an innovation? I earnestly recommend to your consideration the removal of this strange arrangement." But the injurious limitations of the pew system made themselves felt. During the lifetime of Dr. Gray's father a small free church (Grace Church, Portland) had been erected. When Dr. Gray became rector, after much opposition Trinity was opened free on Sunday evening. The sleepy afternoon prayers were changed into a bright six o'clock service, not arranged exactly according to our "advanced" ideas, but still a vast improvement on the old style. Great was the dissatisfaction in many quarters. "Any one," it was said, "who wished to attend church could certainly go in the afternoon." "The prayer books would be injured." "The young people merely went in the evening to walk home together." Dr. Gray, however, persevered. The evening services became popular, and were attended by large numbers of people, attracted not merely by the fine anthem which then usually *closed* the service, but by Dr. Gray's earnest, intellectual sermons. There are few now to remember the power with which the deep tones of his rich voice fell on the ear, making even his abstruse and philosophical arguments attractive to ordinary hearers. A Sunday school had been established by Dr. Gray when he first came to the parish in 1826, an innovation considered quite unnecessary except for poor children, but a band of devout men and women gathered round the rector, and in 1847 a large school-house was built.* In those days there were no leaflets or teacher's assistants. Dr. Gray himself drew up yearly a system of Bible and Prayer Book lessons for his young people.

For some time Dr. Gray struggled through great difficulties. Instances occurred when a neighbouring clergyman would be called in to attend an invalid in the parish, Dr. Gray being absolutely refused entrance into the sick room, lest his earnestness should alarm the sufferer. Through all these trials Dr. Botsford stood by his friend. It was at this time that his church ideas took definite shape, he was confirmed, and henceforth, though he was always ready to join other Christian bodies in any good work, yet he was prepared when attacked to do battle for his church, her liturgy, her articles, according to his reading of them.

*The school was first opened in the Madras School buildings, north side of King square. Among the first teachers were L. H. DeVeber, George Sears, Sarah deBlois and Isabella Kinnear. One of the scholars was J. W. Lawrence. At the death of Dr. Gray, 1868, Beverly Robinson had been connected with the school over a third of a century. In 1855 Henry B. Nichols, a scholar and teacher, was ordained a Deacon. and 1856 a Priest. In 1862 he left for England to prepare for missionary work. His field was Burmah. He died 1864 from brain fever, The first missionary of the Church of England from New Brunswick to find a grave in heathen lands. J. W. LAWRENCE.

After a time Dr. Gray became one of the most esteemed, and one of the most popular men in the city, and religious thought and feeling moved on smoothly and quietly in the new channels. But

> "God's universe may know no rest
> We must go on forever changing
> Through endless shapes forever ranging
> And rest we only seem to see."
> — *Goethe.*

St. John was not to prove an exception to this rule. It was not possible that the colonies could escape the influence of the great "Oxford movement" which in the mother country was stirring men's minds to their very depths. As has been well said by Sir Charles Eastlake:

"A remarkable change was gradually taking place in the convictions of English Churchmen, which resulted in a movement known under various names at various stages of its progress, really representing a tendency to invest the church with higher spiritual functions, and to secure for it a more imposing and symbolical form of worship."

The first or at least the first prominent exponent among us of this new movement was our present beloved Diocesan, the Metropolitan of Canada. He came to us in 1845, in the fullness of his intellectual powers, with his decided Church views, his cultivated literary taste, and his English habits and manners. When his quiet voice, so sweet, and yet so penetrating, was heard in our pulpits, it was soon discovered that the new opinions which were being promulgated on the other side of the Atlantic had reached our shores. Before long there was another storm in the ecclesi-

E

astical atmosphere, and this time it extended from St.
John throughout the Province. "Apostolical Suc-
cession," "Baptismal Regeneration," were the watch-
words of debate. Those who had been formerly
"innovators" now found their position reversed.
They were on the defensive. In opposition to the new
movement, Dr. Gray and several of his friends issued a
weekly newspaper called the *Church Witness*. It was
on the whole ably conducted, but was strong and sometimes fierce in its opposition. Dr. Botsford gave it
great financial support, and often contributed to its
columns. His character was one of much firmness,
and the principles which he held so strongly, and
maintained so persistently, were held and maintained
to the end of his life. Again, and again, he descended
into the arena to do battle for what he considered "the
truth." But, could he now return to us from where

"Beyond these voices there is peace,"

he would be the last to desire that the details of those
past controversies should be revived. Even before he
left us he saw other ideas looming in the distance,
ideas which, he felt, were more dangerous than
"Sacramentarian tendencies" or "Ritual innovations."
The famous "Essays and Reviews" were published,
and ten years after the *Church Witness* was established.
The following significant passage, probably from his
own pen, is found in one of its editorials: "No one
who has watched the progress of religious controversy
during the last ten or fifteen years can have failed to
observe how greatly the ground of it has shifted in the
course of that period. The question was formerly of
particular doctrines, of forms of discipline and belief;

and the appeal on either side was confidently made to
Holy Scripture as a decisive authority. Now the question in debate has changed. The main controversy is
no longer what is the teaching of Scripture? but
what is the value of its teaching? What is the authority of Scripture itself?" Allusion is then made to
the "Essays and Reviews," to Colenso, to Huxley—
the paragraph closes thus: "The Bible has passed
through many severe trials, and survived them all. It
will survive the present assaults, and come forth
stamped anew with the Divine Signet that it is the
Word of God, which will live and abide forever."
—[*Church Witness*, November 12, 1862.

In the latter years of Dr. Botsford's life the wide
prevalence of the sceptical views alluded to in the
above paragraph was frequently forced upon his attention, especially in travelling in the United States.
During these journeys he constantly entered into conversation with those around him, particularly with young
men, endeavouring to draw out opinions and quietly
to instruct or influence. One instance can be recalled.
It was on the deck of a New York and Savannah
steamer, as under a bright Southern sun it ploughed
its way through a heavy sea off Cape Hatteras. A
group of men of "all sorts and conditions" were
gathered round the "English doctor," who seemed so
much younger than his white hair betokened. Various
subjects were discussed—politics, natural philosophy,
art. Dr. Botsford, in an almost Socratic fashion, questioned and cross-questioned as was his wont. Natural
philosophy led up to religion. The Mosaic records
were mentioned. "Surely, doctor," exclaimed one
of the group, a Harvard man, "you are too wise

to give any credence to those old Jewish writings."
For an instant Dr. Botsford was startled by this sudden
and unexpected challenge, but after a moment of self-
recollection he answered: " Why should I not ? " and
then proceeded in his favourite inductive method to
demonstrate the claim Holy Scripture has upon our
belief, to show the reasonableness of Christian truth
and the contradictions involved in scepticism. Hours
passed away. Twilight crept over the ocean before
the discussion was ended; and so much was Dr. Botsford interested in one of his fellow-travellers, that
earnest letters were written months afterwards to him
at Harvard College, with what results the future only
can tell.

The untenableness and contradictions of scepticism
were favourite subjects with Dr. Botsford. He often
touched upon them in his addresses to the Bible
Society and the Natural History Society. He read two
lectures on Scepticism before the Young Men's Christian Association. He also wrote with great care and
much thought a short paper entitled, " The Super-
natural Based Upon Scientific Induction," which, after
receiving a note of encouragement from Dr. McCosh,
of Princeton, New Jersey, he published. It will be
found in the Appendix.

It may be supposed, with Dr. Botsford's strong religious convictions, he would soon be claimed as a
worker by the various religious organizations which
are endeavouring to further the cause of truth in the
world. The New Brunswick Auxiliary of the British
and Foreign Bible Society, the Young Men's Christian
Association, the Evangelical Alliance, the Church
Missionary Society, the Colonial and Continental

Church Society, all shared in various degrees his interest, his work and his financial support. Of these, the British and Foreign Bible Society stood foremost in his estimation. Soon after he settled in St. John he became an active member, Chief Justice Parker then being President, and the Honorable W. B. Kinnear one of the Vice-Presidents. At the death of the Chief Justice Mr. Kinnear became President. He occupied the position but three years, and, at his death, in February, 1868, Dr. Botsford, who had been for many years a Vice-President, was requested to take the Presidency.* He at once declined, and all his friends could say, or the members of the Society could urge, was of no avail to change his opinion. For a time the position was vacant. In the spring he spent a Sunday in Philadelphia, when a "winged word" of that prince of preachers, the present Bishop of Massachusetts, Dr. Phillips Brooks, was the means of influencing him to accept the responsibility and distinction from which he shrank with so much humility. "The opportunity for service is God's call to it," and, feeling this, he no longer hesitated. When he was President† with what eager interest did he fulfill even the smallest duties of his office. It was a pleasure to him to have the

* The following note on the subject was received from the late T. W. Daniel, Esq., shortly before his death:

Dec. 11, 1891.

I see by the 48th report of our Auxiliary that Honble. W. B. Kinnear died Feb. 21st, 1868, and that on the 3rd of March, at the Regular Meeting of the Committee, Dr. Botsford was duly elected President. Mr. Kinnear had been Vice-President for forty years during the presidency of Chief Justice Parker. T. W. DANIEL.

† Dr. Botsford continued President for twenty years, from 1868 until his death.

monthly meeting of the Executive Committee at his house. In his cosy parlour there must be a bright fire, good light, comfortable seats for the earnest men who met to talk over this work. Then when the annual meeting approached, with what care were the resolutions drawn up, the speakers selected, the hymns chosen. On the evening of the anniversary, he would look round in the Mechanics' Institute with satisfaction on the well-filled platform, the crowded house, all interested in the same great cause—the distribution among the nations of the earth of the Book of Books. His speeches as President were generally read. Once or twice his annual address was extempore, and it was then observed that he spoke with more fire and energy, but not possessing a good verbal memory, he generally preferred writing out what he wished to say beforehand. He varied the subject of his speeches as much as possible, and he always tried to make them brief. One address contained an account of the Rev. H. Lansdell's distribution of Bibles among Siberian prisoners; another touched on the popular craze about Budha, and the comparison often instituted between the sacred books of the Buddhist and the Holy Scripture. From the annual address made in 1883, the following passage on the intellectual influence of the Bible, and the Bible Society, is selected:

"It is impossible to estimate the influence which this Society is now exercising upon the civilization of the world. Independent of the vitalizing force of the moral principles inculcated in the Bible, this Society, according to Max Muller (no mean authority), has, by its numerous translations of the Scriptures, conduced largely to the elevation of the race. The bare fact that a mass of writings such as our common Bible contains has been translated into 250 languages or dialects, stamps this Society as a power in the mental work of the world. And when we further take into consideration that this amount of work is carried on by educated men, we must admit the claim of the British and Foreign Bible Society to a high position among the intellectual forces of the century. But not only have these translations been made into languages whose written characters were already formed, but they have in many instances entailed upon the men engaged in the work the necessity of originating a written language when no method previously existed for communicating knowledge. Such a preparation for any people must be regarded as an important factor in the problem of civilization. And were there no other claim for the existence of the Bible Society, this one alone will be regarded by thinking people a sufficient reason for the support of this noble institution. These are far from being its strongest claims. There are reasons of much greater weight, as much greater as the moral transcends the intellectual; and a still higher phase of life is opened up to us by the book it circulates. Upon the spiritual condition of man does the permanency of his moral and intellectual attainments depend.

"Without an authoritative criterion there cannot be a sound foundation for moral laws, and no guarantee for intellectual progress. No doubt nations have risen to a certain height, and others may rise, but they must fall back into a moral chaos, and their civilization break down beneath the load of corruption which besets humanity. The surface of the earth is strewn with the wrecks of the nations which have perished.

"Such has been the case on this continent. Mexico rose to eminence in wealth, in commerce, in the conveniences of life, in luxuries — but she had no standard of morals. And who cannot recall the historian's description of that dreadful night when the boom of the monster gong fell upon the ears of the Spanish prisoners who knew that the first beams of the morning sun would witness their bodies stretched upon the stone of sacrifice—their breasts cut open, their hearts torn out, and, whilst still palpitating, thrown upon the burning altar. And yet a handful of hardy soldiers under Cortes blotted out an empire which had culminated in effeminacy and was stained with the blood of human sacrifices. In the old world Egypt embodied her once elevated thoughts in forms and symbols; bowed before them in adoration, and buried her centuries of civilization deeper than the sands which cover the monuments of her greatness. The kingdoms of Asia were once civilized and prominent among men, but now the stranger digs among the ruins of empires and can scarcely recognize the sites of their overturned capitals. And China, the most persistent of the nations, has been stagnated for centuries, and is covered with gross idolatry. Such has been the experience of the world when there has been no criterion for truth, no authority to stamp its demands; when every man formed his own standard of right and wrong. In the very nature of things this must be. For the laws which govern human actions, as well as the material universe, will shape the destiny of men, as well as the rise and fall of nations. Is there then no hope for man, even though his intellect be lifted up to great attainments? None; unless a light comes from an external source, and unless there exists a spiritual force which shall influence his principles of action, hold out pure motives for conduct, and help him to attain a higher plane of life."

Occasionally Dr. Botsford attended anniversary meetings in country places. He was in Sackville in 1886, and in his address said: "I feel it a duty and a privilege to be present at this meeting in my native place. . . . Almost sixty years have passed since I left my native county to fight the battle of life. I return to the old scenes, but the old familiar faces are not here. Another generation has entered the field.

I appear before you to express my belief, my growing belief in that blessed Word of God which the Bible Society is endeavouring to disseminate through the world. Believing the Bible, I also believe in its importance, as the only rule of life, the source of liberty, and of all right government." To these earnest words Dr. Botsford's private life bore witness. He read and studied his Bible diligently—it was filled with pencil marks to assist his memory. As may be supposed, he was a generous contributor to the funds of the Bible Society, though at the anniversaries his donation was generally put in the plate in several notes to avoid ostentation. When the various churches appointed collectors, he did the work on behalf of Trinity Church. Nor did he forget the New Brunswick Auxiliary of the British and Foreign Bible Society in his will. His last annual address was made at the Anniversary Meeting of 1888, about three weeks before his death. It is here given from his manuscript:

" We are privileged to meet once more on this, our anniversary, to hear and consider the claims of the B. & F. B. Society, and to express our gratitude to the Giver of all for its continued success. Some one may ask, Why do you assemble year after year? What is your object? Is its importance not sufficiently acknowledged? I would reply that its importance can hardly be over-estimated; it is yearly assuming greater dimensions. At the same time such is the tendency of every-day life to shut out all else, that it is necessary to stir up men to consider these high and growing claims, that they may apprehend and do the work which is required at their hands.

" It is not for us to question why this should be so; why He who could reveal Himself without human agency to every soul of man does not do so; why in His wisdom He has seen fit to exalt man to be a co-worker with Himself; why we cannot throw off the responsibility He has laid upon us; and why He has constituted us our brothers' keepers.

"Agency is the principle by and through which the Ruler of the Universe condescends to work, not only in the physical world, but also in our every-day life, where man must be taught before he can perform its ordinary duties — must sow before he can reap. Labour in some form or other is a necessary ingredient in progress, and to produce results we must be stimulated to labour by our necessities or by a sense of duty. It is a principle which permeates all society, and when acted upon produces a corresponding reward. So in the spiritual world, our Heavenly Father has associated results with work. He has laid upon man the responsibility of using spiritual forces to benefit his fellow-men. Thus in the old dispensation, the Jews had the lively oracles of God committed to their charge, and they were commanded 'to teach them to their children,' 'to write them upon the door-posts of their houses and upon their gates.' Then when the fulness of time had come, and the Gospel of the Kingdom was to be proclaimed, chosen men were ordained to make known this revelation of the Messiah to be the witnesses of this life and death, and to commit all to writing (as in the former dispensation), so that the truth might descend from generation to generation, to be a permanent record of the Divine Will.

" Now, whilst we fully recognize the necessity of a human agency to preach personally, and to instruct men in the truth ; whilst we acknowledge that preaching is a great and ordained method by which men are led to receive the truth, and are built up in the truth, we are also as fully convinced of the supreme importance of sending the *written* Word to every inhabitant of this earth.

"There are many, very many instances, recorded in the reports of the Society in which, without human teaching, the

Word of God, under the Holy Spirit, has led souls to a knowledge of God's mercy, the atonement of Christ. On the other hand, many, like the Ethiopean Eunuch when reading the Scriptures, require another Philip to explain the meaning of the Word that they may understand it.

"To print and distribute the Word of God is absolutely necessary, not merely for the people which do not have it, but for the nations which profess Christianity. It is necessary also that men who have entered upon the Christian life should be furnished with it, that they may increase in wisdom and spiritual understanding by a constant personal contact with the Word of God.

"The necessity for such a contact to keep the truth alive has perhaps never been more clearly demonstrated than in the case of the Nestorian Church and its mission to the Chinese people. Christianity was carried by that church into China 1250 years ago. But the only evidence as yet known that such was the case is derived from a remarkable monument upon which was written an account of its introduction and its progress.

"This tablet is of granite. It is nine feet high and over three feet broad. The inscription, in Chinese, consists of 1800 words or characters. A small part has statements which are in the Syriac. The Chinese writing consists of a statement of the Christian doctrines introduced, the government of the church, also a general history of its progress.

"This granite tablet was unearthed about 250 years ago by some Chinese labourers who were digging a foundation for a house. At present it is standing in the grounds, and amid the ruins of a Buddhist temple in a row of Buddhist tablets.

"According to the inscription the monument was erected in the year 781. 'It was set up on a Sunday, the seventh day of the first month in the second year of King Chung, of the T'ang dynasty.' The text was written by Sii Sin Yen, Secretary of the Imperial Council.

"It states that in the year 635 Christianity was introduced, that it rapidly extended among the people, and that illustrious churches were erected in every province. It enumerates the chief Christian doctrines. That the sacred books, twenty-seven in number (same number in our New Testament canon) were translated in the imperial library. That the Sovereign investigated the subject in his private apartments, and gave special orders for its dissemination. The following are a few sentences taken from his proclamation: 'Having examined the principles of this religion, we find them to be purely excellent and natural. Investigating its originating source, we find it has taken its rise from the establishment of important truths; its ritual is free from perplexing expressions; its principles will survive when its frame-work is forgot; it is beneficial to all creatures; it is advantageous to mankind. Let it be published throughout the Empire.' Thus Christianity was introduced into China 1250 years ago. It flourished for a century and a half as stated on this remarkable monument. But there has not been found as yet any record to show how it was thoroughly blotted from the face of the country. This tablet is the sole proof of its existence and general prevalence. It is, however, possible that histories connected with the period, and it may be copies of the translated Scriptures, may yet be disinterred from the archives of that singular people, for it is expressly stated that such were ordered to be made by the King. If the art of printing had been known in those days, as it is now, there would, without doubt, have been a large number of the sacred books struck off, and being brought into contact with many individual Christians, the truths contained in them would have been treasured up, and would have produced more permanent results.

"This striking, nay startling fact in history, should deeply impress us with the necessity of such a society as the British and Foreign Bible Society, and the duty laid upon us to further its aim, which is to furnish this great gift, the Word of God, to every man, in every nation, and in his own language.

"Without the living Word (which is the Word of the Spirit) individuals may lose sight of the truth. Communities drift away from it. Nations lapse into spiritual ignorance, and church organizations, as in China, prove inefficient to keep alive the knowledge of the true God."

The next society with which Dr. Botsford heartily co-operated, was the Young Men's Christian Association. He deemed it was doing an important work among the young men in the city. For several years he filled the position of President, and occupied a seat in the Board of Management for a much longer period. He took even deeper interest in the more spiritual side of the work. For many years he taught a Bible Class in the Y. M. C. A. on Sunday afternoon. Thirty or forty young men were often present. He prepared for this Bible Class very thoroughly, as anxious and puzzling questions were often asked, but so great was the doctor's earnestness, that neither trifling nor flippant remarks were made by the most thoughtless present. Many youths in after life looked back to those Sunday afternoons as to a time when permanent religious impressions had been received, and firm resolves made to lead a life regulated by high Christian principle. Dr. Botsford lectured repeatedly before the Y. M. C. A. on religious, intellectual and moral subjects. One address to men only, on drinking, gambling, and other vices, is said to have been most judicious and instructive. He maintained his interest in the Young Men's Christian Association to the end of his life, and remembered it in his will.

The meetings of the Evangelical Alliance were

always attended by Dr. Botsford with great regularity. When President of the St. John Branch he went as delegate from St. John to the World's meeting of the Alliance which was held in New York in September, 1873.* He enjoyed the discussions on Evolution and other great topics of the day, and he met and conversed with the Dean of Canterbury (Dr. Payne Smith), Dr. McCosh, of Princeton University, Dr. Parker, the eminent Congregationalist divine from London, Henry Ward Beecher, Dr. Christlieb from Germany, and other celebrities who were present.

Dr. Botsford aided with zeal in the efforts of the Alliance in St. John for a better observance of the Lord's day, and other good works. He especially enjoyed the yearly week of prayer held in January, and usually presided over one of the noonday meetings. Many spoke of the devotional earnestness with which he conducted the prayers and praises of the worshippers. The broad benevolence of his religious opinions found free scope at such times. It is true, not many of his own church could see their way to attend these meetings, but some, like his valued friend, the late Rev. G. M. Armstrong, found satisfaction and profit in so doing. In such things one may not judge another. There are many now, as in the olden time, who would forbid "because he followeth not with us." But, distinct and clear, comes to us from the Master the reproving command, "Forbid him not, for he that is not against us is for us." (Luke ix., 30.)

Dr. Botsford was an active member of the Local Committee of the Colonial and Continental Church Society,

---

* He was accompanied by Mr. J. E. Irvine, and several other delegates from St. John.

and later in life President of the St. John Branch of the Church Missionary Society. Other good works were assisted by him of which little record remains, as he had a special dislike to see his name, or even his initials, in subscription lists. He tried to act out the principle of not letting the left hand know "what the right hand doeth."

His attitude as regards the temperance movement was peculiar. Accustomed in his father's house to see wine always on the dinner table, he probably gave no consideration to the subject until he began to practice in St. John. Then sad cases of self-indulgence were encountered, and the sorrow and suffering caused in many families by intemperance forced themselves upon his attention. When the temperance question began to be strongly agitated in St. John he was at first inclined to join the movement, but the admixture of politics, which soon took place, repelled him. He never took the pledge. Many may regret this, but it can be stated that he gave his influence in other ways to the temperance cause. He refused to be present at scenes of conviviality. He never joined in public dinners, the first thing of the kind he attended being a temperance dinner given to Sir Leonard Tilley in 1874. He was most cautious in prescribing stimulants to his patients, and, as the importance of the question increased in his estimation, he banished wine altogether from his own table.

His abstinence from the use of tobacco might be mentioned here. He said he felt the habit growing upon him. He feared he should become its slave; so, in the first year of his St. John life, he gave it up. It was a struggle at first. The desire sometimes recurred

to him in dreams, but he finally conquered what he
was wont to term a " pernicious and degrading habit."
When the Anti-Tobacco Society was established in St.
John he became a member, and a few days before his
death he was engaged in preparing an address to
be delivered at the annual meeting of that society.

Thus was Dr. Botsford actively engaged in further-
ing various plans, and in assisting many organizations
for the help and benefit of others.

CHAPTER VI.

We all are changed by slow degrees,
All but the basis of the soul.
— *Tennyson.*

After the first ten years had been passed in the busy
activities of professional life, Dr. Botsford was recognized as one of the leading physicians of the city. He
was, as has been remarked, a man of " strong views
and decided convictions " in all directions; therefore
it is not strange that we find it said of him : " At this
time (1849-1850) he was a leading figure in our political
affairs, although he never sought representative
honours. His appointment in 1857 to a public position
(that of medical attendant to the Kent Marine Hospital)
withdrew him to some extent from active participation
in public affairs, but he was a man whose intellect never
dulled, and whose interest in the world around him
never slackened." (*Globe*, Jan. 31st, 1888.) He was
at the time of which we are speaking a Liberal.
When, in 1867, the isolated Provinces of British North
America were to be united, when the Dominion of
Canada was to take her place as an influential member
of our colonial empire, then occurred many changes.
Conservatives, who were Anti-Confederates, joined
hands with former opponents, and Liberals, who ap-
proved of the wide-reaching policy of the measure,
went over to the Conservative ranks. Among the

F   (91)

latter was Dr. Botsford. From the first he took great
interest in the movement. He writes to his brother
Edwin, under date January 25th, 1865: "There will
be a stirring time here until the elections are over. I
can form no idea of affairs from anything I see or hear.
I am strong for Confederation, and will not be found
on the fence." To the end of his life he continued to
note with pleasure the various benefits which he
thought had been brought about by Confederation. A
friend (the Honorable John Boyd) writes: "His
politics were pronounced, but he had warm friends in
both parties. He was an all round, many-sided, good
man." The attitude of Dr. Botsford's mind during the
latter years of his life regarding politics is probably expressed in the following sentences from a letter written
to one of his brothers on the eve of an election : "I have
my predilections, as a matter of course. At the same
time I hope that the men best calculated to hold the reins
may get them."

In 1848, Judge Botsford, who, on account of his
deafness, had retired from the Bench, came to St.
John, and spent two winters under his son's roof.
The old gentleman was much pleased with the success which Dr. Botsford had attained in his profession, and with the evident esteem in which he was
held by his fellow-citizens. Judge Botsford was accompanied by his wife. The dignified and handsome old
lady, who was aunt or cousin to so many in St. John,
held what might be called daily "receptions" in the
pretty room assigned for her use. Young people would
gather round her while the afternoon sun lighted
up the tall figure, and the sweet face so serene
in the calm beauty of old age. At the close of the

second winter Mrs. Botsford went to spend a few
weeks with her daughter, Mrs. R. L. Hazen. She
took a severe cold, and after a short illness entered
into rest May, 1850. It was a source of great satisfaction to Dr. Botsford that he could be with his
mother during the closing hours of her life, and his
thoughtful care alleviated much suffering. After her
death Judge Botsford longed for the quiet of his country home. He returned to Westcock almost immediately, accompanied by one of his grand-daughters (the
eldest child of his stepson Murray), who had just returned from Europe, where the widow had resided near
her mother since Mr. Murray's death.

As time went on alternate clouds and sunshine passed
over St. John. Dr. Botsford, like a good citizen, rejoiced in its prosperity, and sympathized in its adverse
circumstances. In 1851, the waterworks for the city
were finished. The event was duly celebrated. Sir
Edmund Head, the Lieutenant-Governor, turned on
the water. Cannons were fired. There were great
rejoicings, an exhibition and a trade procession. The
city had hitherto been supplied with drinking water
from the carts of water carriers, who sold the water at
"a penny a bucket." The introduction of a supply
of good water into the city was of great importance,
especially in the eyes of one who, like Dr. Botsford,
thought, wrote, and lectured repeatedly on Hygiene
and Sanitary Laws. One of his medical lectures on
Hygiene will be found in the Appendix.

The spring of 1853 saw the commencement of the
Intercolonial Railroad, the first railroad in New Bruns-
wick. The sod was turned with great ceremony by
Lady Head, and the scene was as impressive as crowds,

banners and bands could make it. The hills on each side of "The Valley" were literally black with enthusiastic spectators, and shout after shout went up as Lady Head raised the first turf with her silver spade. Dr. Botsford took much interest in the proceedings, and when, after the National Anthem, one of the bands played Old Hundred, his devotional nature was touched. He spoke of it afterwards as one of the solemn moments of his life. He recognized the importance of the event in the history of his province, and the appropriateness of this tribute to the unseen Ruler of the Universe. He was in touch with all that betokened improvement and progress, and would not on this occasion allow himself to be discouraged by a pessimistic friend, who prophesied that the railroad would not be built; that, if it were built, it would not pay; but that probably the sleepers might be taken up and a good post road secured for practical purposes. No one, not even Dr. Botsford, with his sanguine hopes, could then foresee that in less than forty years 1,400 miles of railroad would have been built in New Brunswick.

In 1854 St. John was visited by the Asiatic Cholera. It raged from July to the end of August, and the mortality was very great, 1,500 persons, men, women and children, falling victims to the epidemic. All the physicians and clergy of the city had their time and strength severely taxed. Doctor Botsford, with his healthy, powerful physique, was able to endure immense fatigue. He was unremitting in his attentions to the sick and dying. Day after day was spent in scenes of sadness and horror, generally in the poorest quarters of the city. The calls for him at his house were incessant. The only way he could obtain rest was by remaining an hour or two with his friends, Mr. and Mrs. James McMillan, who considerately offered him the use of a room. He often recalled their kindness to him at this trying time. During these fearful weeks much experience was gained. It is believed that at first Dr. Botsford was not inclined to think the epidemic contagious. He was soon convinced of the contrary, and with his usual frank sincerity he did not hesitate to avow his change of opinion.

One memento of that sad time was the establishment of the " Protestant Orphan Asylum." An appeal for such an institution was made in the *Church Witness* (Nov. 1st, 1854) by the city clergy, headed by the Rev. Dr. Gray. On the 12th of November, a meeting was held at the Mechanics' Institute to consider the question of an orphanage. Resolutions were passed and speeches made by clergymen and laymen. Among the latter Dr. Botsford's name occurs. When the project was carried out, and the Protestant Orphan Asylum was incorporated at the next session of the Legislature, Dr. Botsford was one of the twenty-two corporators named in the Act. He always took great interest in the institution, and even during the busiest periods of his life he visited it occasionally. He and Mrs. Botsford were present at the large meeting which assembled at the Orphanage on the evening of November 17th, 1881, to celebrate its rebuilding and reopening after its destruction by the " Great Fire " of 1877. On that evening $1,500 were raised by the friends of the institution to pay off its last indebtedness. The idea of the collection originated with Mr. S. T. King, who headed the list with $100. All present responded gen-

erously to the appeal, Mrs. Botsford subscribing $50.
During the leisure of his latter days, Dr. Botsford and
his wife visited the Orphanage frequently, and at
Christmas, donations of toys and sugar plums glad-
dened the little ones. At such times a few cheery
words would bring the circle of young faces closer
round their kind friend, who would then talk to them,
and by simple questions draw out their childish ideas
and impress what he was saying, while his own simplicity of nature thoroughly enjoyed this contact with
the freshness and joyousness of childhood. With his
usual consideration he never left without saying a
friendly word of encouragement to the worthy matron.
He assisted the Asylum financially during his lifetime,
and at his death he left it heir to the sixth part of his
estate.

There was also another institution in which Dr.
Botsford was deeply interested, "The Boys' Industrial
School." This school, mainly through the efforts of its
President, Mr. H. W. Frith, was maintained in efficient
working order for ten years. As it was situated in
Carleton, Dr. Botsford could not often find time to
visit it, but he was a liberal contributor to its funds.
He had some years before adopted a plan of systematic
giving. A tenth of his income was devoted to religious
and benevolent purposes, and, in his usual methodical
way, this tenth was equally sub-divided among four or
five objects. One of these objects was the Bible Society, another the "Boys' Industrial School," and when
on one occasion the president remarked on the frequency of the contributions, Dr. Botsford said, he was
"only giving the school its dues." There were not
many as interested in this object as he was, and con-

sequently, after the president and directors had struggled on for ten years amid difficulty, the school had to be given up, much to the regret of those who felt that every city needs a reformatory, or an industrial school, or some institution of a similar nature.*

In 1857, Dr. Botsford added to his professional work by accepting the appointment of visiting physician to the Kent Marine Hospital. He had, in 1850, refused the charge of the Lunatic Asylum in Carleton, but when, on the death of Dr. Boyd, who had been for many years the visiting physician at the Marine Hospital, his position was offered to Dr. Botsford, he accepted it, as he had assisted Dr. Boyd for some time previously, and he knew and liked the work. Henceforth a daily visit to the hospital became part of the routine of his life. The Marine Hospital was established by the Imperial Government in 1822, and was named after the Duke of Kent. It was at this time a low wooden building with no "modern improvements," but the ground about it was laid out as a garden, and afforded fresh air and sunshine to the convalescents. Most of the widely-scattered races of the globe are represented in the motley groups of invalid sailors, who come and go in the Kent Marine Hospital, English, Scotch, Irish, Swedes, Norwegians, Dutch; Germans from the shores of the Baltic; Italians and Spaniards from the Mediterranean; Japanese, Chinese, Negroes. Sometimes, in his leisure moments, the doctor's ready pencil would sketch in the blank pages

---

* While these pages are passing through the press, it has been learned that Lady Tilley has made a move towards establishing a "Boys' Reformatory" in St. John. It is to be hoped that this effort will receive the cordial sympathy and efficient aid which it deserves.

of his Physician's Diary the facial peculiarities of
the different nationalities. Sometimes his sense of the
ridiculous would be touched, his merry laugh would
echo through the ward and awaken a sympathetic
smile on many a suffering face. For instance, one
day he was vainly trying to speak professionally
with an Italian sailor — French and Latin had been
tried in vain — when a "bright little Jap" came
to the rescue, and acted as interpreter between the
English doctor and the puzzled foreigner. There was
much opportunity in this institution for the exercise of
Dr. Botsford's characteristic benevolence and sympathy.
Vessels would come into our port in the depth of
winter, encrusted with ice and with many sad cases of
frost-bitten sailors. One instance recurs to memory.
A vessel was wrecked off Grand Manan. Many of
the crew perished. The three that survived were
exposed all night on the rocks without shelter, the
thermometer below zero. When they reached the
hospital all was done that skill or kindness could
devise. Two lost parts of their feet. The third, a
colored man, had both legs amputated. Artificial
limbs were procured, but the shock to the system had
been so terrible that it was many months before the
poor fellow could leave the hospital. Sometimes fearful accident cases would be brought in, falls from the
mast or rigging, often much aggravated by the distance
travelled before the hospital could be reached. One
case was an almost dying sailor put ashore by a vessel
at St. Martins, and jolted in a wagon all the way to
St. John. The doctor, hoping against hope, watched
day after day over the poor fellow with the solicitude
of a mother over her son, until finally Mrs. Botsford

heard with sympathetic gladness that the injured man was creeping back to life. And in the midst of all the medical care, higher interests were never forgotten. Words of reproof, or comfort, or warning, would be spoken here and there as occasion offered. One or two, out of many instances, may be given. One day as the doctor entered the corridor off the ward, he was met by a convalescent patient, who said that when he had been allowed to go out the previous evening, temptation had met him which he could not resist, that he had been drinking, that he was truly sorry, and longed to be able to reform. The doctor answered with kindness and decision; he told the man in strong words the utter ruin of soul and body to which he was exposing himself, and advised him as his only means of safety to abstain totally from anything of an intoxicating nature. At another time, after going his rounds in the wards, he noticed in a private room the deep shadows of heartsickness and hopelessness upon the face of an invalid. Seating himself by the young man, he spoke to him of sorrow and suffering, and the effect they are intended to have upon the characters of men. He alluded to the all-protecting care of "Our Father" in heaven, and as "these loving echoes of the Master's tone" fell on the ear, the young face grew brighter, and the weary, hopeless look began to pass away. The bells were ringing for church. "Now," said the doctor, with a kindly smile as he was leaving, "I have preached *you* a sermon. Now I must go and hear one preached to me." Christmas is always well remembered by sailors. It was an especially pleasant time at the Marine Hospital during the latter years of Dr. Botsford's life, when the Ladies

Hospital Committee of the Church of England Institute began to give a Christmas supper to the inmates of the hospital. After stipulating that nothing very injurious to invalids should be set before the men, the doctor would enter with great zest into the proceedings. When beef, turkey, jelly, etc., had been fully discussed, a cabinet organ would be drawn into the hall, and then the sailors would join heartily in their favorite songs, "Pull for the Shore," "Let Your Lower Lights be Burning," and other hymns. Sometimes a Swede or Norwegian would sing a Christmas hymn in his own language. Then, after a few words of advice from their Chaplain, Mr. Spencer, and from the President of the Institute, Canon Brigstocke, "these entertainments," as the sailors called them, were closed by singing the Doxology, in which the doctor would join with heart and voice. The sailors often said that in other ports they had good Christmas dinners, but only in St. John did they enjoy "good entertainments."

After repeated solicitations, the Dominion Government determined on replacing the old wooden structure which represented the Marine Hospital by a handsome brick building. Dr. Botsford was deeply interested in its erection. He visited the principal hospitals in the United States, that he might get ideas as to the best mode of construction, heating, ventilation. He examined the windows, fireplaces, bedsteads and mattresses, and the result has been one of the most commodious and well-planned buildings (for its size) on the continent. Before leaving this subject it might be added that, though Dr. Botsford's manner to the sailors was frank, hearty and almost jovial, yet he was a strict disciplinarian, and if, in defiance of the rules, an old salt would smoke in his "bunk," as he called his bed, instead of in the room allotted for that purpose, or if an injudicious friend would bring mince-pies to a fever patient, Dr. Botsford could be stern, indignant and righteously angry. His manner to the employees of the hospital was always very considerate. He assisted them in difficulties and upheld their authority, smoothing away any unpleasantness by his bright, genial manner.

Some time after Dr. Botsford's appointment to the Marine Hospital, he was asked to take an interest in an effort to erect a General Public Hospital. In the *Church Witness*, dated November 23, 1859, the following paragraph occurs:

"The *News* and other journals are advocating with much energy the erection of a hospital in this city. It is admitted now, we believe, by every reflecting citizen that such an institution is indispensable. The only question is how the work shall be accomplished. A few years ago Dr. William Bayard, with the most praiseworthy zeal, obtained subscriptions to a large amount towards it, and an appeal was made to the Legislature for aid, which proved to be unsuccessful, and nothing further was done. We trust Dr. Bayard will again take the matter up, as the public mind is now fully prepared to act. The Legislature should unquestionably aid the undertaking, at all events, at its commencement, but it should be maintained by local taxation, if the subscriptions of our wealthy citizens should prove insufficient for the purpose."

Dr. Bayard did "again take the matter up," and through his exertions, aided by others, the General Public Hospital was built and opened in June, 1865.

Dr. Bayard became President, and a medical staff was appointed, consisting of Dr. Botsford, Dr. Harding, Dr. Steeves, Dr. Edwin Bayard, Dr. Keator, Dr. J. W. Smith.   Dr. Botsford continued an active member of this medical staff for three years.   He then sent in his resignation, March, 1868.

CHAPTER VII

THE FIRST HOLIDAY—THE NATURAL HISTORY SOCIETY.

Thus the men
Whom Nature's works instruct with God Himself
Hold converse; grow familiar day by day
With His conceptions; act upon His plan
And form to His the relish of their souls.
—*Akenside.*

Dr. Botsford had passed his fifty-first birthday before he allowed himself a well-earned holiday of three months' duration. The last few years of this busy period of his life had brought many changes, both at home and abroad. The Crimean war had been fought to its close of sorrow and triumph. The Indian mutiny had stirred our sympathies, and our churches had resounded with the litanied petition, "*Especially for our suffering fellow-countrymen in the East: we beseech Thee to hear us, good Lord.*" The year 1860 had seen the railroad opened from Moncton to St. John, and had also brought the Prince of Wales to our shores. It was a gala day for St. John when, in the bright summer sunshine, the young heir to the throne drove from Reed's Point through cheering crowds to the old Chipman House, where his grandfather, the Duke of Kent, had been entertained long years before. Dr. and Mrs. Botsford saw the procession from a relative's house on Chipman's Hill, and Dr. Botsford's voice led the ringing cheer that greeted the Prince as he passed.

In the spring of 1861 a gun fired from Fort Sumter announced the beginning of the American Civil War,

(103)

and Canadians watched with eager interest and divided sympathies the progress of the bitter contest. The excitement was increased during the following winter by the arrival of an unusual number of regiments from the mother country. These troops were welcomed with great enthusiasm, and officers and men were entertained on their way through St. John to Upper Canada with right royal hospitality. At one large supper given to a recently arrived regiment, the Bishop of the Diocese was present and was asked to address the men. The crowd was so great that it was almost impossible either to see or hear His Lordship. Dr. Botsford, perceiving the difficulty, contrived with prompt ingenuity to erect a stand, from which the Bishop's voice could be distinctly heard by the large assembly.

The doctor's views on the Slavery question had been settled, as we have seen, during his college life at Glasgow. Writing in October, 1857, to his friend Dr. Hartt (now a resident in New York), Dr. Botsford expresses his ideas on the subject.

" The American nation have deliberately sinned in the face of light. Supposing the continuance of slavery to be for their interest, they give no heed to the warning of inspiration, ' Woe to you that are rich. Behold the hire of labourers who have reaped your fields, which is of you kept back by fraud, crieth, and the cries of them have entered into the ears of the Lord of Sabaoth.' The nation says it is for our interest to support a slave system of government. Our interest requires that things should be maintained as they are. They will find that God is stronger than they."

These are stern words, but Dr. Botsford felt strongly on the subject, and no one rejoiced more than he did when, at the close of the war, the United States was freed from the curse of slavery.

In the autumn of 1861 Judge Botsford's eldest son, Hazen, died at Westcock, after an illness of a few months. Dr. Botsford visited his brother as frequently as possible, and was with him at the end. This trial was followed by a long cold winter of arduous work. When spring came he found that rest and relaxation were needed, and suggested to his wife that they should again visit England and Scotland. The doctor's first preparation for his outing was to calculate the expense. Then he placed an equal sum in the hands of the Vestry of Trinity Church for the benefit of destitute orphans. He said that before spending so much on his own pleasure, he wished to do something for others. He and Mrs. Botsford crossed the Atlantic in a Cunard steamer, early in May, 1862. They enjoyed the voyage, as neither of them knew what it was to be sea-sick. It is supposed that one of the main objects of Dr. Botsford's trip was to see the second International Exhibition, which was opened May, 1862. He visited it several times. He was also much interested in the Industrial and Mechanical exhibits at the Sydenham Crystal Palace. We may conclude that he did a large amount of sight-seeing in London, from a remark made by him some years afterwards, "Oh, it requires the strength of an elephant to see sights in London." His experience in the great Metropolis of our Empire was interest and fatigue, and it was not until he reached Scotland that his real holiday began. Although Mrs. Botsford had been absent from her native land for more than twenty-five years, she had kept up an active correspondence with many friends and relatives in

Edinburgh, from whom she and her husband received
a warm welcome. Dr. Botsford felt at home in the
intellectual atmosphere of the Scotch capital, and a
good deal of attention was paid to the " fine-looking,
intelligent colonial doctor."

It is to be regretted that no letters nor papers can be
found, recording Dr. Botsford's ideas on the progress
of medical science since his last visit to Edinburgh,
twenty-five years previously. There is no doubt that
he had abundant opportunities for observation in his
intercourse with medical men, and in his visits to various hospitals. For instance, a St. John medical student
in Edinburgh at that time, writes :

" I was a dresser in the Infirmary, Edinburgh, in 1862,
under Professor Syme, and while acting in that capacity, Dr.
Botsford came in one summer's morning with the professor.
I recognized him, and after the walk was finished, went up
and introduced myself."

Before leaving Scotland, Dr. Botsford took an intensely enjoyable trip through the Highlands. He had
a great appreciation of fine scenery, and he often spoke
of the indescribable awe which almost overpowered
him when, while travelling through the Trosachs, a
veil of mist lifted, and he saw the giant forms of the
mountains looming up around and above him.

In August he returned to St. John with renewed
health and vigour, to take up his daily routine of
work, or as he expressed it, "to go into harness
again."

It was about this time that a fresh object of interest
claimed his attention, " The Natural History Society of
New Brunswick," and to it he devoted more and more

of his time and thoughts. His work in connection with it is thus alluded to in the seventh Bulletin of the Society:

"Dr. L. B. Botsford has been at the head of this Society since its organization, except for a short time during the middle term of its existence. Among the many benevolent activities in which he was engaged, it received a large share of his attention. He entered heartily into all its aims and objects, and was always ready to support and encourage any project to extend its usefulness.

"For a quarter of a century our late President maintained his warm interest in this Society, attending its meetings with the regularity and promptness for which he was noted, and by his facility in public affairs, his ready tact and genial manners, added greatly to the interest of the meetings.

"Always ready during his lifetime to aid it with his means, as well as with his influence, the Society acknowledges with gratitude that at his death its prospective wants were not forgotten by him."

Dr. Botsford was strongly impressed with the importance and usefulness of a Natural History Society. In one address he says:

"An association of men forming a society for the study of Natural History, is a necessity in any community, if that community is to keep abreast of the tide of knowledge which is sweeping over the nations of the earth."

In another address he says:

"One of the objects of this Society is to lead its members to broad and pleasant fields of enjoyment, to stimulate their faculties to a healthy activity, and to add to the general as well as to the individual welfare. . . . Certainly if knowledge is power, and the working of the mind is in itself

G

a source of happiness, then the study of one or more
branches of Natural History will lead to a higher standard
of existence, even should the experience be confined to the
individual. This, however, will be much furthered by interchange of thoughts with others similarly engaged. . . .
However varied the construction of human minds may be,
each mind can find a subject in the various studies of Natural History which will commend itself to its peculiar powers
and afford a pure and elevating pleasure. A higher plane of
existence will be attained ; higher aspirations will be roused
until the highest attainments are reached. Man, from the
cradle to the grave, must have employment. Without employment the weariness of life will seek to bury itself in folly
or vice."

The Natural History Society of New Brunswick was
formed in 1862, and the following brief sketch of its
rise and progress, given by Dr. Botsford in his last
annual address, will not be thought out of place by
those who know how closely he identified himself with
its interests :

"The twenty-fifth anniversary of the Natural History Society of New Brunswick has passed, and the history of our
Society does not differ from that of similar institutions. Its
experience has been like that of others the world over.

"The law of progression is not always one of continuous advance. Night and day alternate in all things. Individuals,
communities, cities, peoples and nations have their ebb and
flow, and why not societies? And such has been the experience of the New Brunswick Natural History Society in this
city.

"January 29th, 1862, a meeting was held in the Mechanics'
Institute, for the purpose of forming a society for the culti-
vation of natural science. Forty-two persons were present.

At that meeting the following resolutions were carried unanimously :

"1st. That a scientific association should be formed, and that it be called 'The Natural History Society of New Brunswick.'

"2nd. That it shall be one of the efforts of this society to form a collection of books of a scientific character for the use of the members.

"3rd. That it shall be another special aim of the society to form in connection with it, such a collection of specimens in the different branches of scientific research as shall fully illustrate the natural history of this Province and, as far as possible, that of other countries.

"4th. That in order to carry these views into effect a committee be appointed to prepare a constitution for the society.

"The committee consisted of H. W. Frith, William Jack, M. H. Perley, W. P. Dole, R. P. Starr, L. B. Botsford, and G. F. Matthew.

"February 5th, the committee submitted their report, the constitution and by-laws were adopted, and the society adjourned to meet February 14th to elect office-bearers.

"On the 14th the following were elected : L. B. Botsford, President; M. H. Perley, Vice-President; R. P. Starr, Recording Secretary; H. W. Frith, Corresponding Secretary; G. F. Matthew, Curator and Librarian ; W. P. Dole, W. Jack and C. F. Hartt, Members of the Council. At the first meeting thirty-two members were enrolled, and soon after eight others. Meetings were held once a fortnight, with an average attendance of twenty-five.

"At the annual meeting, January, 1863, the roll consisted of two honorary, ten corresponding, and sixty-nine ordinary members. Of the latter nine had been admitted during the year.

"Messrs. Hartt, Matthew, Starr, Payne and Hegan, members of the Steinhammer Club, gave their valuable collection to the society.   Dr. C. K. Fiske donated a valuable collection of aquatic birds.   Measures were taken to secure to the society the very valuable collection of Devonian Fossils made by Mr. C. F. Hartt.

"In 1864 there were in the Museum 10,000 minerals and fossils, 2,000 marine invertebrate, 750 insects, 500 plants and 30 birds.   Mr. H. F. Perley gave a collection of minerals, illustrating the gold formation of Nova Scotia.

"In 1868 the Society concluded to secure another place for their meetings and their collection.   The basement of the Grammar School, Germain street, was occupied.   The change did not prove advantageous.   The room was too small; it was gloomy and uncomfortable; its dampness threatened to injure the collections.   Arrangements were then made with the Directors of the Mechanics' Institute.   During two years only five meetings of the society were held, and from 1874 to 1880 the society slept a quiet sleep.   In March, 1880, a meeting to resuscitate it was convened.   The members present were W. Jack, Esq., President; Dr. Inches, Dr. Hamilton, G. F. Matthew and R. P. Starr.   New energy was infused by the election of twelve members.   Regular meetings of the council and society have been held from that time to the present, and the tide of prosperity has continued.

"In 1881 arrangements were made to occupy our present quarters.   These have been kindly granted us by the City Corporation.   This same year another step in advance was taken, and lady associate members were introduced, very much to the benefit of the Natural History Society.

"Mr. G. U. Hay presented the Museum with 400 specimens of the native plants of the Province.   These were supplemented by a number from Mr. W. R. Chalmers and Mr. I. A. Jack.   In 1882 our first Bulletin was issued, in which were valuable original papers by members of the society.   This year were added to our collection 146 specimens of birds.

"During this year, 1882, Mr. Chamberlain gave several

free lectures on Ornithology to the pupils of the public schools. Other members of the society, Dr. Coleman, Dr. Allison and Mr. Best, gave lectures on different subjects.

"The summer field camp was commenced in 1883. It has continued its meetings, and yearly adds to the success of the society. The practical knowledge acquired proves it to be beneficial and almost a necessity for our progress. Donations of the food fishes in our waters were received from Mr. P. Campbell, and many specimens of insects collected near St. John by Mr. Herbert Gould. In 1884 Mr. G. F. Matthew presented his herbarium of over 2,000 species of foreign plants.

"The society has been incorporated, and has a proper seal to stamp our acts. It is evidently now firmly established. Our Bulletin is yearly issued, and reflects great credit upon the society. It is especially intended for contributions showing original research. At the request of the Royal Society of Canada delegates have been yearly sent to represent this institution at their annual meetings.

"The Provincial Government now gives us an annual grant, and this enables us to extend our usefulness.

"During the summer vacation, a class composed of the teachers in our public schools availed themselves of lectures given by members of this society. These lectures were the more instructive, as they were illustrated by the abundant material in our museum. It is proposed to extend this course in the future.

"During this winter a series of lectures upon different branches of Natural History was inaugurated, and will be delivered by members of the society.

"Such is a brief outline of the Natural History Society, embracing a period of twenty-five years. It has passed through the difficulties which generally attend the formation and growth of similar institutions, and we feel confident that it has entered upon a wider field of usefulness.

"It has not a numerous membership, and its field is limited, and yet there are some on our little roll of names well known elsewhere, and who have secured a place for themselves in the prominent ranks of science."

The social element of the Natural History Society, as manifested in the annual conversazione, gave great pleasure to Dr. Botsford. In one of his addresses at these gatherings, he says:

"Many will perhaps wonder how we members of a grave society can descend from our position among the abstractions, and associate the study of science with a merry meeting such as we hope to enjoy to-night. Ladies and gentlemen, philosophy despises no one relationship of being, physical, moral or intellectual, and our gathering to-night, springing out of the social relationships of life, is as truly connected with philosophy, as are the midnight studies of the metaphysician."

In another address he speaks of the influence of women in the Natural History Society:

"We have departed from the old constitution, and a new order of members has been established, which innovation I am satisfied will be attended with the best results. I allude to the lady associates. We know from the very nature of things that society must be benefitted and its civilization advanced when woman takes her position with a duly cultivated brain. . . . It is, then, with great satisfaction that I perceive that our Natural History Society boasts of having on its roll a goodly number of associate members, who, becoming engaged in scientific pursuits, get their intellects sharpened, and their brains developed, and thus to both men and women an impetus is given towards the rational development of our common nature."

A description of the conversazione in 1882, will give a general idea of these pleasant gatherings:

" The conversazione of the Natural History Society, which was held last evening, was one of the most brilliant affairs of the season. All the rooms of the society were tastefully decorated, and by 8 o'clock they were thronged by a large number of ladies and gentlemen, who evinced great interest in the proceedings. On entering the first of the series of rooms, it was found to be devoted to entomological specimens, plants, and a number of rare butterflies and moths. In an adjoining room is an interesting collection of fossils. On a table in this room were arranged several microscopes. These were a centre of considerable attraction during the evening. The main room was devoted principally to ornithology, mineralogy and the invertebrates. The President read an address reviewing the work of the society during the past year. Several carefully prepared and interesting papers were read by members of the society. Ice cream and other refreshments were served by the ladies' committee, shortly before 10 o'clock, when this successful and enjoyable meeting came to a close."

On these occasions, after reading his address, Dr. Botsford would move about among the guests, with a kind word for one, a pleasant smile for another, or a hearty laugh as something amusing struck his fancy. His tall figure could be seen by all as he walked through the rooms, forgetful of self, and only anxious that all should be amused, interested and instructed. His addresses were always very carefully prepared. Several have been quoted, but one of the most characteristic, that on the Human Thumb, is given in full in the Appendix.

Then there were field-days, when the Natural His-

tory Society and their friends, would spend many
hours on the sea-shore or in the country. A spot was
always chosen where the fossils and flora offered objects of interest. After luncheon various groups would
be formed. Some would follow Mr. Matthew in the
study of geology; some would accompany Mr. Hay
to study botany. On all these occasions the President
was the central figure, taking even more than his
share of the fatigue and responsibility necessarily attending the organizing and superintending of these
expeditions.

In fact he was interested and took part in all the
work of our Natural History Society in every direction. He felt that it was but in its infancy; he looked
confidently forward to its large growth, and he closed
his last annual address as President, delivered but a
fortnight before his death, in these hopeful words:

"Not only do I wish that great success may attend the
future of the society, but I feel assured that such will be the
case. You have material that would secure a prominent
position to any society, and I have no doubt that a first rank
will be maintained by the Natural History Society of New
Brunswick among those of the Dominion."

CHAPTER VIII.

Grow old along with me,
The best is yet to be,
The last of life, for which
The first was made.
— *Browning.*

Between the years 1860 and 1870 Dr. Botsford was
called upon to part with several much-loved relatives.
In 1864 his father died at the ripe age of ninety-one.
Judge Botsford had resided at Westcock since his
wife's death, his two eldest sons and his step-grand-
daughter, Miss M——, being his companions. His
was an ideal old age. He enjoyed the full use of
his faculties, both of mind and body, except that his
deafness prevented his joining in general conversation,
although he heard easily when addressed in a clear,
distinct voice. He was much in the open air, in the
pretty grounds round his house. He would walk up
and down beside the hawthorn hedge, of which he
was so proud, or he would wander among the apple
trees in the orchard, or watch the progress of the
flower-beds. One large square was given up to roses
of the hundred-leaf kind. He would linger beside
them, enjoying their fragrance and beauty, with all the
zest of youth. Sometimes a bushel basket of full-
blown roses would be gathered from that bed in one
morning, for rose-water distilled from these flowers

(115)

was one of the Judge's favourite perfumes. In the
autumn dahlias were his delight. He would watch
while their glowing flowers were piled into bouquets
for the table or the mantel-piece, according to the then
prevailing fashion. Often he would examine his rasp-
berry, currant and gooseberry bushes, or watch his
pears, green-gages and damsons as they ripened, giving
constant directions about them, for much care and work
are necessary in this northern climate to secure the
supply of delicious fruit for which Westcock was
famous.

The house kept up its reputation for hospitality.
Nothing delighted the old Judge more than to have
his rooms filled with relatives and guests from St.
John, Fredericton, and Boston. His daughter, Mrs.
R. L. Hazen, and her children, generally spent two or
three summer months with him. Dr. Botsford and
his brothers would meet for a few days to enjoy the
country air, to talk over old times, and tell school
stories. Young people came and went, and Westcock
echoed with the cheerful voices of a second generation of Hazens and Botsfords.

> "All are scattered now and fled,
>   Some are married and some are dead."

In the winter, when the guests had departed and
the marshes were one wide expanse of dazzling snow,
the Judge would spend the morning in his library.
The sunshine streamed in over the flowering plants
which filled the low, old-fashioned window seats. The
newest books and leading magazines were found on
the table, and here the old gentleman, in his ninety-
first year, would read hour after hour without glasses.

In the evening he enjoyed a rubber of whist, or talked over some articles in the reviews, his wonderful memory going back over points in history and literature with legal accuracy. So Judge Botsford walked slowly down his long decline of life. In 1863 he had a heavy attack of illness from which his great vitality enabled him partially to recover. Then there was a relapse, and he finally lay down to die, his last conscious look and smile resting on a beautiful bunch of flowers at his bedside. Thus passed from among us one of New Brunswick's remarkable men.* His remains rest in the St. John Rural Cemetery, near the monument which he had erected in memory of his father, Speaker Botsford. The following lines, which he much admired and often quoted, are singularly appropriate to himself:

> "So live that when thy summons comes to join
> The innumerable caravan which moves
> To that mysterious realm where each shall take
> His chamber in the silent halls of death.
> Thou go not, like the quarry slave at night,
> Scourged to his dungeon, but sustained and soothed
> By an unfaltering trust, approach thy grave
> Like one that wraps the drapery of his couch
> About him, and lies down to pleasant dreams."
> — *Bryant's Thanatopsis.*

After the Judge's death, Dr. and Mrs. Botsford invited Miss M—— to make their house her home.

---

* Judge Botsford was born in 1773. At the age of nineteen he took his degree at Yale. At twenty-two he was admitted to the Bar in St. John. At thirty-four he was appointed Judge of the Vice-Admiralty Court. At thirty-nine he represented the County of Westmorland. At forty-four he was appointed Solicitor General, and was elected Speaker of the House. He was continued in the office by re-election until, at the age of fifty, he was appointed Judge of the Supreme Court. He resigned at the age of seventy-two, in 1845.

The constant intercourse, the interchange of thought thus afforded, ripened into a warm and lasting friendship. Miss M——'s eyes were never very strong, and at one time it was feared that she would become blind. Her uncle bestowed much care and attention upon her, and mainly, through his skill, her eyesight, after a cessation from all work for two years, was restored. During that time Mrs. Botsford devoted hour after hour to reading aloud, and the doctor, even in the height of his busy practice, always contrived to reserve one hour daily to read to her some book on science, history or metaphysics, which formed the basis afterwards of many interesting "talks." Such kindness could not fail to call forth warm feelings of gratitude and affection. The niece became almost, if not altogether, a daughter to the childless pair. Mrs. Botsford, in declining years and feeble health, leaned more and more upon her. Dr. Botsford looked to her for sympathy in his intellectual pursuits. She became his companion in travel; she superintended his household after Mrs. Botsford's death, and when he, too, passed away, she has endeavoured to perpetuate his memory by becoming his biographer.

In the autumn of 1866 Mrs. Botsford's meek and gentle mother entered into her rest. She had resided with Mrs. Botsford almost ever since her younger daughter had gone to New York. Dr. Botsford's manner to his mother-in-law was wonderfully courteous and reverential, and she, on her part, almost idolized her kind son-in-law, who, ever since his own mother's death, addressed her as "mother," and sought to gratify her slightest wish.

A few months after Mrs. Main's death, Dr. Botsford's

sister, Mrs. R. L. Hazen, and his brother Chipman, passed away also to the " Shadowless Land," 1867.

At this time Mrs. Botsford began a journal, from which we give some extracts in order to show the phase of St. John social life in which she and her husband participated. They were not seen at balls, dances nor card parties. Those who followed Dr. Gray's lead generally refrained from these " worldly amusements." But there was constant social intercourse. Friends met every week, sometimes oftener, in pleasant parties, where they had a little music, a fair amount of talking, and a good supper. Those who remember these evenings know how enjoyable they were. Mrs. Botsford especially made a model hostess. She had a pretty speech, a bright compliment, or a little hit for each of her guests, while Dr. Botsford's hearty laugh and mirthful manner enlivened everything. Mrs. Botsford's journal abounds with such notices as these: " I had my clerical party last night, which passed off very pleasantly; every one seemed to enjoy it." Again: " Had my party for the two brides; very good music and nice supper, though I say it. Both brides looked very well." Mrs. Gilchrist (" Prudie," as the doctor called her), and Mrs. William Lawton, by their musical talent, added greatly to the pleasure of Mrs. Botsford's parties. We read: "April 9th (1872). At Mrs. W. J——k's party last night, and a pleasant one it was; met a great many nice people; got home at 1 o'clock." Again: "Spent a pleasant evening at Mrs. L——'s; met —— and ——, from Montreal; fine music; had a most agreeable evening; got home at midnight." The following entry shows some energy: "Thursday, January 6th. I went to the Bible Society meeting,

and was delighted with my dear husband's short address; also liked Mr. H. W. F——th very much; he
is a good man. I heard another speech that I did not
like at all. I came away with Miss A——, dressed,
and went to Mrs. J. McM——'s party; drove home at
twelve."

Then there were larger gatherings. We read: "Aug.
10th (1872). We were last night at Mrs. B——'s
(Hon. John Boyd); a very large party; a number of
lawyers, doctors and clergy; the Lieutenant Governor,
several Senators and M. P.'s. The band played all the
evening; got home at 1.30 a. m.; splendid supper; two
hundred guests." Again: "Spent last evening at Rockwood; quite a large party; dear good Mr. Kellogg was
there; we had some capital music; about fifty guests.
My doctor had nice conversation with several clergymen and others." There are also occasional notices of
dinner parties and lunches. "Went to lunch with
Mr. and Mrs. R. T. Clinch; met Rev. George Hill and
Miss Hill, from Halifax, and several other pleasant
people." Again: "Aug. 6th (1873). Lunched with a
great many medical men at Dr. W. Bayard's; very
pleasant." Also: "Lunched at Newlands with our
new rector (Rev. F. H. J. Brigstocke); a large party.
Watched some of the guests walking on snow-shoes;
bright and pleasant." * Then she writes: "We went
to dinner at Mrs. R. DeV.'s; spent quite a pleasant
evening; fifteen guests; got home about 11 p. m."
Then, "Dined at Dr. Waddell's at 7 o'clock, March

---

* The Rev. J. W. D. Gray resigned from ill-health in 1867; he was
succeeded by Rev. James Hill. On his resignation in 1873, the Rev.
F. H. J. Brigstocke, from England, was chosen as rector of Trinity
Church.

18th, his birthday, and a very pleasant party we had. Drove home by moonlight; not cold." Then, "Dined at Mr. R. F. Hazen's; got home at 11.30, much pleased." Sometimes the notices are longer, as June 28th: "Last evening I went with L. B. and the Senator (Botsford) to the most elegant dinner of thirty-two at Mrs. B.'s (Hon. Isaac Burpee). The whole was in perfect keeping; appointments as good as possible; attendance excellent. It was the most stylish dinner I have been at in this country; seven courses, well cooked and well served. My dear husband and I really enjoyed the evening."

These selections from Mrs. Botsford's journal have been made promiscuously.' Many other names occur more or less frequently, for Dr. and Mrs. Botsford had a large circle of friends; but the most numerous visits mentioned are those to Rockwood and Rothesay. Whenever Dr. Botsford felt that he needed a little relaxation from his professional cares, it was at Rockwood (the residence of T. W. Daniel, Esq.), or at Rothesay, that he sought it. Always passionately fond of beautiful scenery, he enjoyed the wide view at Rockwood over the city, harbour and bay beyond. From some favourite seat in the grounds he would watch the sunset clouds while he discoursed gravely with his host and hostess, or exchanged playful banter with the younger members of the family, with whom he was a prime favourite. On these visits Mrs. Botsford generally accompanied him, and no entry in her journal occurs more frequently than "We drove to Rockwood and spent a pleasant afternoon and evening." To Rothesay, being more distant, he usually went alone and staid all night at Mr. H——'s or Mr.

Ch. F——'s. From the high position of these houses he loved to look at the twilight shadows as they fell over the Clifton hills and the beautiful Kennebeccasis. There was generally a rubber of whist in the evening, over which his merry laugh would be often heard. He retired early, and rising at six the next morning, would roam in the woods until breakfast time. One shaded path is still called " The Doctor's Walk." In summer a lovely bunch of flowers for Mrs. Botsford was always ready for him, and we find frequently in the journal: " L. B. returned from Rothesay with a beautiful bouquet for me from Mrs. H——." Dr. Botsford often speaks in his letters of the extreme kindness of his Rothesay friends. Indeed, he was received there, and elsewhere, with such a warm welcome, that it was often a genuine surprise to him, all unconscious as he was of the attractive power of his own love and kindness. " He that hath friends must show himself friendly," is as true now as when it was uttered three thousand years ago.

Dr. Botsford was, in appearance and feeling, still in the prime of life, although he was approaching his sixtieth year. He was always fond of travelling, and he now began to indulge in it frequently, as he felt the necessity of more rest and recreation than he had hitherto allowed himself. For some years many of his journeys were taken in connection with the meetings of the " Canadian Medical Association." This society was organized in Quebec in the autumn of 1867. A medical friend (Dr. Charles Johnston) tells us :

" The first annual meeting was held in Montreal in September, 1868. Dr. Botsford, Dr. Harding, myself, and other physicians, whose names I cannot remember, were present, going to Portland by steamer, and taking the Grand Trunk Railway for Montreal. We all staid at St. Lawrence Hall. The meeting was a great success, was largely attended, and closed with a conversazione at McGill College. At that meeting Dr. Tupper (Sir Charles Tupper) was President, and I am of the opinion Dr. Botsford was chosen Vice-President for New Brunswick."

He probably attended the second annual meeting in 1869. The third annual meeting was held in Ottawa in 1870, and Dr. Botsford's first visit to Niagara was made on his way thither. He left St. John for New York, accompanied by his wife, his niece, Miss M., and a young friend. After a short visit to New York, they went up the Hudson to Albany, thence by rail to Niagara, where they staid at the Clifton Hotel on Saturday and Sunday. Dr. Botsford's intense enjoyment can be better imagined than described. He seemed to be irresistibly attracted to the " Falls." He stood beside them at sunrise, at noon, in the moonlight. He was never weary of listening to the rush and roar of the moving mass of waters. He expressed his feelings in the following enthusiastic words, which a friend not inaptly calls a prose poem : ·

" I sat speechless beside the surging turmoil of Niagara. Dumb while drinking in the wonders of the great cataract. The imagination wandered to the far regions from whence its waters flowed ; to the southern bounds of the wide sea-lakes ; to their northern slopes ; to the distant lands of the setting sun, whence came the commingling floods gathering their forces to leap in untold volumes over the rock-barriers to the stony masses beneath, whilst day and night, and night and day, the mist ascends in clouds to the heavens, a perpetual witness of wondrous power. And as I gazed, there came over

H

me the blessed thought of Him whose hand formed it all, who was the express image of the Father's glory, the manifestation of that Father's love, who, coming forth out of the Infinite, manifests all *that* love in Himself, and bursting over the rocky barriers of sinful humanity, falls with such force on the stony hearts of men that, like the mist of the great cataract, evermore, day and night, there rises towards heaven the incense cloud of prayer, whilst amid the cloud the assuring bow of God's love appears. And as I gazed the love of Christ filled all my heart with wondrous power. My eyes grew dim with the tears of a great joy, for His love was forcing the incense of praise from the very depths of my soul."

On Monday the party left for Toronto, thence by boat through the "Thousand Isles," to Kingston. Dr. Botsford, of course, was out of his stateroom long before sunrise, that he might not lose the beautiful scenery through which we were passing. From Kingston to Ottawa by rail. There the third annual meeting of the Canadian Medical Association opened September 14th. Dr. Botsford attended the meetings assiduously, and took great interest and active part in the debates. His pleasant, hearty manner soon made him a favourite, and he gained several warm friends, especially Dr. David, Dr. Hingston (Mayor of Montreal in 1875), and Dr. Marsden.

Mrs. Botsford's journal gives this account of the trip :

"We steamed from New York up the most beautiful Hudson to Albany; got into a sleeping car for the first time. By daylight were passing through rich cultivated lands. Met conversible people. While crossing the railway bridge at Niagara, I stood on the platform with L. B., F. M. and F. S. The scene was awfully grand. No one thing I had ever seen or felt, brought so strongly before me the wonderful power of the Most High. As soon as possible we got a carriage, drove to Goat Island, the Rapids, saw everything, returned very tired. Next morning, Sunday, September 11th, the doctor, F. M. and F. S., went across the bridge to church, and heard Bishop Odenheimer. In the evening we went to a little, country-looking, retired church, heard a beautiful service and a plain, short sermon. We got back to the hotel before ten, viewing the Falls all the way, and feeling the spray in our faces. Next morning, still splendid weather, left for Ottawa. Were there nearly four days and saw everything — the Houses of Parliament, Rideau Hall, the Chaudiere Falls. We left Ottawa for Montreal; went about there as much as we could, seeing everything. Had to leave Saturday night. Staid at Island Pond on Sunday. No church, no service of any kind. L. B. went to a Sunday School; taught a large class of boys and young men. Off the next morning to Portland; took the ' New England' to St. John."

In the spring of 1871, Dr. Botsford spent a few weeks in Philadelphia, in order to shake off a heavy attack of influenza, and he has left no record of his attendance at the Medical Association that autumn. In 1872, the annual meeting of the Association was held at Montreal in September. We find Dr. Botsford there, taking part in the discussions, and also joining heartily in the dinner which closed the proceedings. He was quite hoarse the next morning from the vigorous manner in which he cheered the speakers. On his way home he staid for a day or two at Quebec. He visited the Citadel, and looked in silent admiration on what has been called one of the four greatest views in the world. He and his niece went over the historic battlefield, saw the falls of Montmorenci, and returned to St. John by the St. Lawrence, the Gulf and the Shediac railroad.

In 1873 the Canadian Medical Association met at St. John, where a large lunch was given to their guests by the St. John medical men, in the grounds of the Lunatic Asylum, on the Carleton Heights. There were also several private entertainments, one at Dr. Bayard's being particularly pleasant.

In 1874 the Association met, August 5th, at Niagara Falls, and soon after Dr. Botsford's arrival, a friend remarked to him : " We have dropped your name from the nominating committee. It is our intention to nominate *you* as President." This was accordingly done, and Dr. Botsford was elected. The whole proceeding took him by surprise, but he could not help feeling gratified by the honour conferred. He was also requested to represent the Canadian Association at the twenty-sixth annual meeting of the American Medical Association, which was to be held in Louisville, Ky., the following spring.

Dr. Botsford looked forward through the winter to this trip with much pleasant anticipation. He started from St. John April 29th. The party consisted of himself, his niece, Dr. Steeves and Mr. Walker. Passing through Boston and New York, they crossed the Alleghanies, descending their western slopes amid beautiful scenery to Pittsburg. At the various stations medical men boarded the train, and a large and merry party was formed bound for Louisville. Many prominent physicians from various States were there, Dr. Gross of Philadelphia and his son among them. Repartee and fun, merry jokes and " quips and jests " were the order of the day, and Dr. Botsford's hearty laugh was frequently heard above the buzz of conversation. Cincinnati was reached on Saturday night. Most of the party took the Sunday steamer for Louisville, but Dr. Botsford and his niece remained in Cincinnati, attended church morning and evening, and spent part of Monday in sight-seeing. We tried the elevator cars, which were then a novelty, and we also went over a large brewery. In the afternoon we embarked on the " Ohio " for Louisville. The early spring foliage and Kentucky blue grass clothed the hills on either side, but twilight had closed over the lovely landscape before we reached our destination. The next morning the Association began its sessions. The following extract is from the columns of the Louisville *Courier-Journal*, dated Wednesday, May 5th, 1875 :

"The opening session of the twenty-sixth annual meeting of the American Medical Association was convened in Public Library Hall, yesterday morning. Convention assembled at 11.30. There were between four and five hundred delegates present, and it can be truly said that a body of finer, and more intellectual-looking men have never assembled in this city. The meeting was called to order by Dr. Richardson, and the proceedings were opened with prayer by Rev. Dr. Lamar. Dr. Tuor, the former President of the Association, then stepped forward and introduced Dr. W. R. Bolling, of Tennessee, the present presiding officer. Dr. Bolling took the chair, and announced that the first business would be the report of Committee of Arrangements. Dr. E. Richardson, the Chairman of the Committee, advanced to the front of the stage and delivered an address of welcome. He then presented the report, and the list of delegates was read. Dr. Davis, of Chicago, announced that Dr. Botsford, President of the Canadian Medical Association, was present, and moved that he be invited to a seat on the platform. The motion was carried, and upon complying, Dr. Botsford addressed the convention as follows:

"' *Gentlemen*, I have been called upon by your President to address you upon this occasion. The fewer words I say the more acceptable, no doubt, they will be. As you are aware, the country which I have the honour to represent, extends along your Northern border, touching the Atlantic on the East and the Pacific on the West. I have come to learn the principles which have secured your success—a success manifest from the assemblage which I see before me. We Canadians are as yet few in numbers, scattered over a large surface, but we are making an effort to advance the interests of our profession. As yet we cannot be said to show great results, but we trust before long to' prove ourselves worthy competitors in the arena, not of conflict, but of emulation, prepared to maintain the principles which are the foundation of our profession, and to foster as benefactors of the race all that may conduce to the well-being of humanity. For without arrogating to medical men undue prominence, I think I may claim for them an amount of self-denial and sympathy for their fellow-beings not to be surpassed or equalled in any profession.'

" Dr. Haley, of Texas, said he wished Canada the same good luck that had attended Texas—annexation to this country medically and politically."

The remainder of this morning session was occupied by the eloquent address of the President, Dr. Bolling, of Tennessee. In closing he made the following allusion to Dr. Gross, of Philadelphia, and to Dr. Yandell, a retired physician of Louisville :

" One, S. D. Gross, whose fame has filled the world, stands in a green old age like the statue of a demigod, raised on the apex of its monumental shaft, far above all surrounding things, pointing to an earlier day star than greets the vision of ordinary mortality; and another, L. P. Yandell, happy in the memories of a well spent life, lingers in the peaceful en. joyment of that subdued enchanting twilight of life, between the sunset and the deeper gloaming."

As there was but one session, the rest of the day being devoted to committees, we were driven in the afternoon four miles out of town, to visit Mr. John McFerran's Stock Farm. Very beautiful were the creatures, horses, mares, and colts which were led or trotted past us for inspection. In the evening a splendid reception was given at our hotel (the Galt House) by the physicians of Louisville to their visitors. It was a magnificent affair—2,000 invitations. There were quantities of flowers, lots of pretty women, most elegant dress and good music. The variety of costume was amusing. By the side of some rich creations of Worth's genius, or the gauzy ball-room robes of the period, would be seen the prim black silk of a doctor's wife from some quiet New England town, or a stylish tourist outfit from New York. The next day public attention and curiosity were much occupied with Dr. Gross and his lecture on " The Lost Art." Many conjectures were hazarded as to what this lost art might be, and the name of the lecturer, as well as curiosity about his subject, gathered a large audience of both sexes. Dr. Gross began by telling us that fashion not only ruled our dress, but also our ailments and their remedies. He gave a short popular sketch of the history of medicine. He then named " Bleeding " as the lost art. He said his subject was " Blood Letting as a Therapeutic Agent." He regretted that this remedy had been so completely abandoned, and proceeded to

point out the cases in which he supposed bleeding
might be beneficial. The interest of a lecture does not
depend upon its subject, but upon the way in which
that subject is handled, and the old doctor contrived to
make even this unattractive theme interesting to all.
When Dr. Gross had concluded his lecture, for which
he was heartily thanked, the following communication
from the Canadian Association was read and referred
to the Committee on Nominations :

MONTREAL, April 10th, 1875.

To W. H. Atkinson, Secretary American Medical Association :

As the time is approaching for the meeting of the American
Medical Association, I have the pleasure in forwarding a copy
of a resolution unanimously adopted at the last meeting of
the Canadian Medical Association, held at Niagara Falls on
the 5th and 6th of August, 1874, and request you will kindly
bring it to the notice of your Association.

The Canadian Medical Association will meet this year at
Halifax, on the first Wednesday in August, and we shall be
much pleased at meeting, as heretofore, delegates from your
Association. I think it more than probable that our Association will be represented at your meeting by at least two of our
members, one of whom will be the president.

S. H. DOUD, *Secretary.*

The resolutions are as follows :

" That in the consideration of the best interests of medical
science, it is desirable that a medical conference should take
place between the American and Canadian Medical Associations, at some central point, to be determined upon, and that
the American Medical Association be advised as to the desir-
ability of such a conference, for the purpose of becoming
more intimately acquainted and of affording an opportunity

for the discussion of medical and surgical subjects on a common basis.

"That the need of such a conference being determined upon, it would be desirable that the Secretary of the Canadian Medical Association notify the various local medical societies, so that our Dominion might take part in a manner worthy of the occasion, and in keeping with the best interests of medical science."

The afternoon of Wednesday, March 5th, was devoted to sight-seeing in Louisville, and in the evening we attended four receptions given by leading citizens of the city in honour of the Association. One of these receptions was at Dr. Yandell's, to whom Dr. Bolling alluded in his opening address. Another was at the mansion of Mr. and Mrs. James Trabue. There we were told by a friend that our hostess had been a reigning belle in Louisville for fifty years. This did not seem incredible, when we looked at the sprightly old lady in her white lace dress, her bare neck and arms flashing with diamonds. Her reception boudoir was lighted with wax candles, and after receiving a few words of cordial greeting, we passed from that soft light to the more brilliant parlours and supper room beyond.

After we had enjoyed these hospitalities, we left Louisville at midnight, for, although Dr. Botsford was interested in the medical discussions, and enjoyed the society of his professional brethren at the Association, his time was limited, and he felt that his stay must not be prolonged. The next point of interest was the "Mammoth Cave," which we reached by rail and a fatiguing stage drive at noon the next day. Guides were engaged, we entered the rock archway, and began

our wonderful walk below the earth. Soon the "black-
ness of darkness" shrouded us, and we could only see
by the torches of the guides that we were passing
through "columned aisles," surrounded by beautiful
and fantastic shapes. Occasionally a rocket would be
sent off to show us the "fretted roof," arching far
above us. Sometimes we had to clamber on hands
and knees through a narrow passage, which would
gradually widen into a noble hall of more wondrous
beauty than any passed through before. At one time
we heard rushing waters near us, and stood upon a
bridge looking down into the "bottomless abyss,"
listening to the echo of a stone which seemed to roll
down, down, down forever. At last we reached the
dim, silent lake; the water was too high for us to embark on it, but we saw the little boat floating on the dark
water, and it recalled the myth of Charon, the ghost
ferryman. We returned to the surface of the earth.
It was night, and we retired to rest to wander again in
dreams through the Mammoth Cave. The next day
we passed through Louisville and Indianapolis to St.
Louis. Saturday was spent in driving through the
streets and looking at the merchant palaces of the
"Queen of the West." We visited the botanical
gardens, steamed across the Mississippi at the foot of
the famous Lindell Bridge, which spans the wide
breadth of the "Father of Waters" with five light
graceful arches. On Sunday we attended St. George's
twice; heard for church music most beautiful quartette
and solo singing, which Dr. Botsford enjoyed, as he did
also Dr. Holland's intellectual and imaginative sermons,
which seemed to set the mind adrift on the ocean of
thought. Monday was a long day across the rolling

prairie to Chicago. A few hours sight-seeing there, and then through Detroit, Toronto and Niagara to Boston and Milton. On Sunday we went into Boston to worship in Trinity, and to hear one of Phillips Brooks' grandest sermons. It was Whitsunday, and the subject "The Power and Presence of the Holy Spirit in the World." The congregation listened in breathless silence. It seemed in the solemn stillness that prevailed as if the Eternal Spirit were indeed present in an especial manner, "brooding," as of old, over the vast assembly, and revealing Himself to men through the utterances of His gifted servant. Bishop Brooks always takes advantage of these Festival days to emphasize the distinctive doctrines of the "Holy Catholic Church." On Tuesday Dr. Botsford reached his own home, after what he called in one of his letters "a most pleasant trip, in which I saw many things, and was absent but just three weeks."

The eighth anniversary of the Canadian Medical Association was held at Halifax, August, 1875, Dr. Botsford being then the President. We close this chapter by giving a full account of this meeting, including some passages from the President's Address, as reported in the *Morning Chronicle*, Halifax, August 5th, 1875.

CANADIAN MEDICAL ASSOCIATION.

The annual meeting of the Canadian Medical Association commenced in this city, yesterday morning, in the Young Men's Christian Association Hall. The meeting was called to order at 11.30 by the President, Dr. Botsford, of St. John. There were present besides Dr. Botsford, Drs. Tupper, Thorburn, Hodder, Walker, White, Robillard, Muir, Monroe,

Hamilton, Roseburg, Harding, Atherton, Ryan, DeWolf, Lawson, Flemming, Jennings, Farrell, Johnston, Peppard, Burgess, Moren, Campbell, McMillan, Hingston (Mayor of Montreal), David, Gordon, Oldright, Christie, Dawson, Kerr, Sanford, Clay, R. S. Black, J. F Black, Parker, and others.

Dr. Pineo, of the United States Marine Service (a native of Nova Scotia), and Dr. Tyler, of Boston, were introduced to the meeting. They were cordially received and made a few remarks.

Dr. David, of Montreal, Secretary, read the minutes of the Association's last meeting, which were confirmed. Drs. Baxter and Sharpe, of Moncton, N. B.; Fleming, of Sackville, N. B.; Carr, of Londonderry; Burgess, of Cheverie, Hants; Peppard, of Great Village; and Lawson, Woodill, Campbell, Walsh, Clay, and Dodge, of Halifax, were elected members of the Association.

Letters were read from Professor Gross (Philadelphia), Marsden (Montreal), and Trenham, expressing regret for their inability to be present.

Dr. Hodder, of Toronto, made a few remarks on medical education. He thought the system of education in Ontario was excellent, and, if it were possible, that one standard and system should be adopted throughout the Dominion. He would like to have the matter referred to a committee from all parts of the Dominion. The duty of this Society was to elevate the standard of the medical profession in order to put down quacks and other illegal practitioners.

Dr. Oldright, of Toronto, said he thought that students should be examined yearly, and that practical work should be added to the examinations.

Dr. Pineo presented four volumes of reports of the U. S. Marine Hospital Association, and the thanks of the meeting were tendered to him for the same.

THE PRESIDENT'S ADDRESS.

Dr. Botsford then delivered his address, as follows:

GENTLEMEN, —

In the order of business it is now my duty to address you on this our eighth anniversary. With one exception the Association has held its meetings in the Provinces of Quebec and Ontario. On this occasion we have the pleasure of assembling in one of the oldest cities of the Maritime Provinces, which with its noble harbour adorns the Atlantic coast of the Dominion. Perhaps the day is not distant when a session of this same Association will be held on that other shore where the waters of the Pacific wash its Western boundary.

Those among us whose heads are nearing their resting place may not see this event, much less the gatherings of our profession in those intermediate regions which must one day become the home of millions; but you who have commenced the battle of life, when you take your stand between the present and the future, you will witness vast changes, and in the meetings of the "Canada Medical Association" will find yourselves surrounded with brethren, coming from the different quarters of the Dominion — from the Pacific coast, with its genial winters, from the valleys of the Saskatchewan and Assiniboine, from the prairies of Manitoba, from the old homestead provinces of Ontario and Quebec, from these Provinces by the sea, and you will reap the benefits which such meetings are so well calculated to confer, for they will embrace the experience of the profession under varying climates and under many conditions. And, gentlemen, we must not be discouraged by seeming failures. These are incidental to the commencement of all such institutions. The time will come when full success will crown our efforts, and our Association will be commensurate with our nation. We must have our evening as well as morning to constitute a perfect day. We cannot measure the results by present benefits. They will assume proportions which will surpass the anticipations of the most ardent. For no matter how extensive the experience of the individual practitioner, how close his observation, how powerful his mental capacity, he will, if confined to one locality, become cramped by its limits, and his professional growth may be checked by the incrustation of routine so apt to settle upon us all. Throw the same person into contact with genial minds from other regions, and he will enter upon new fields of thought, and receive as well as impart new suggestions. This has been the case in other departments of culture, and will prove true in this. When professional brethren meet, each member, from his contact with disease under varying circumstances, will bring to light some new experience, and at the same time will carry away that detailed by others, each having some special opportunities in the wide field of observation; whilst the most cultivated will be benefitted even in their own special direction by the critical shrewdness of those who may be their inferiors in their specialty, yet their equals, if not their superiors, in other departments of the profession.

Another result will be the modifying influence which will be exercised upon the profession. The too hasty will be held in check by the naturally conservative, whilst the latter will be stimulated to new life by the impulsive energies of the former. All will be stirred up from a sluggish routine which dislikes to have its calm disturbed, and will be induced to enter upon that strict investigation and careful line of thought so necessary to all progress.

By such collisions of mind may we not hope that there will arise some check to fashion, which has lessened, and still lessens, the influence of the profession. No one can deny the prevalence of fashion. Not merely in the past, when dogmatism prevailed in proportion to existing ignorance, but even now in our own times. The evil is ever ready to come to the surface.

No doubt a few active or powerful minds lead to such results. By their force they set the new system in motion, and the mass follow; and "the followers of a sect are always more inclined than the founders to push systematic opinions to the most absurd extreme;" "and if we are to believe the recorded results of therapeutic research, conducted under complicated conditions, we shall be obliged to admit that the same diseases have equally well been cured by the interposition of the gods — by witchery and priestcraft — by the most sanguinary and antiphlogistic and by the most mild and expectant treatment; by remedies founded on the rational pathology of the disease; by the administration of infinitessimal parts of nothing; by peppermint water and bread pills. Each and all of these diverse plans of treatment have had their advocates, who bring forward in their favour accumulated masses of evidence."

There can be no effect without a cause. But the difficulty is to determine, amid the complicated actions of the human body, what is the cause which makes efficient the varying systems of treatment. Men become the subject of disease, and under *every* system throw off the morbid state and resume a healthy condition. Many a medicine has been used and proved apparently successful in the hands of the regular practitioner, but the thorough empiric can also parade the cures which have attended his panacea. And both the regular and the empiric have succeeded, not because their remedies were beneficial in themselves (in many cases they may have been injurious) but independently of the means used. We have, therefore, to look for a reason why this should be. Why judicious means shall fail in the hands of one man, and why inert, or it may be injudicious medication, shall be attended with favourable results in the hands of another. It is a common experience to witness the eventual failure of the theories, or of the medicines which have been initiated by strong and ardent minds because they are unphilosophically based, yet the success which has attended theories demonstrates the necessity of looking for some principle beyond mere physical agencies, some underlying cause for the success which follows the same or varying treatment. It may be urged that the *vis medicatrix* explains the difficulty; but that power has been present in the same case in which the philosophical attendant has failed, and the inert globule has afterwards succeeded. We are, therefore, compelled in many cases to look further for the efficient cause; one which aids the ignorant empiric as much as it does the regular practitioner; one which stimulates the force of the system to renewed activity and to a healthy termination; one which is more than a natural tendency to a sound state; one which exercises a curative power when called into play, and residing in the mind and proceeding from it aids the physician, who enlists in his favour a strong anticipation more potent in certain temperaments than well adapted drugs. This is no new idea. It is one we all recognize, yet one we continually overlook. We are so engaged in the contest with disease — so bent upon effecting results by the power of medicine — that we are practical sceptics as to the enormous force which the mind exercises not only over the functions of the organs, but over the structure of the organs and tissues themselves.

This is an aspect of our profession which demands our consideration; for though it has been well determined that the mind is often seriously affected by the condition of the body, it is questionable whether the body is not as much influenced by the mind, and that changes may thus be brought about even in the tissues themselves. If this is so, it will give one solution why recoveries occur under the same or varying systems of treatment, when the *vis medicatrix* cannot be regarded as the cause. There is a class of cases which gives efficacy to, and confirms each peculiar system of treatment in the estimation of its followers; and it will be futile to reason

with any one as to the merits of his system, if he is *conscious*
that he has been relieved when using it. We can only do so
by going behind the system and showing that there is a cause
which is operative, though not generally acknowledged—a
cause capable of producing results of a wondrous character,
and, when recognized, sufficient to reconcile to sound philosophy what now appears a mass of contradictions.

I do not say that the class of persons on whom the mind is
capable of producing such results is very numerous; but it
is numerous enough to make the results a disturbing element in our medical progress, to such an extent as seriously
to affect the laity in their belief, and the profession itself in
its certainty. . . . But, however subtle the principles
which are operative, they can be mastered by a rigid system
of investigation, and as soon as the phenomena become tangi-
ble they will not long escape the penetrating power of the
medical mind.

Facts, no matter how incompatible with our previous experience and theories, ought to be faithfully registered, and
when a sufficient number has been accumulated, then some
one will rise to the emergency and establish the law of their
production.

Medical science has always required patient research, and
never more so than at the present time. Its foundations are
based upon the laws of being, and these laws are bound up
with, and modify every change in the organism. And as
there is no domain of nature but what may throw light upon
our path, the amount of knowledge requisite to become a well
grounded member of the profession will steadily increase.
And if the scientists who can stand on the firm earth, and
have to deal with matter in its more simple combinations,
have still before them vexed problems and long years of
patient research, how much greater must be the endurance
of the physician who has to determine his certainties amid
the shifting sands of life, where the varying phases are all

I

but infinite and the organic forces and mental powers assume protean shapes.

In May Dr. Steeves and I went to Louisville to attend the meeting of the American Medical Association. We were most kindly received, and they have responded by appointing six of their number to be present at our session. There is evidence that the meetings of their Association are producing a very beneficial result upon the whole profession in that country. Not only is the tone of the profession raised by the mixing of the leaders and veterans with the general body, but its culture and intellectual attainments force upon the public a truer estimate of its importance.

In closing, Dr. Botsford said : There is one subject which I would submit to the Association for its consideration, and that is, the want of a registration of births, deaths and marriages. In some of the Provinces it does not exist, and it will be for you to decide whether a memorial from this Association to the general government will tend to hasten that most to be desired action of the Dominion legislature.

Dr. Tupper moved a vote of thanks to Dr. Botsford for his address, and heartily seconded the suggestions in regard to the importance of vital statistics.

Dr. Hodder seconded Dr. Tupper's motion. He thought the matter of vital statistics should be undertaken entirely by the Government.

The vote of thanks was unanimously tendered to Dr. Botsford.

Drs. Tupper, Parker, Wickwire, Robillard, Thornburn, Hingston, Harding and Oldright, were appointed a committee to nominate officers.

The meeting then adjourned until two p. m.

AFTERNOON SESSION.

The meeting was called to order at half-past two p. m.

Several wax specimens of diseases were exhibited by Dr. Black, of Halifax.

Dr. Botsford then read a paper on "Sanitary Science;" also one on "The Climatology of New Brunswick and its Relation to Disease."

Dr. Parker moved that a committee be appointed to request the Dominion Government to take up the whole subject of vital statistics. Referring to the drainage of houses, he said he was perfectly satisfied that many cases of typhoid fever had resulted from this source.

Dr. Hingston, of Montreal, referring to climatology and vital statistics, suggested that a medical man from each of the larger cities should be appointed to draw up a memorial for the Government. He thought that compulsory vaccination could not be carried out.

Dr. Oldright read a paper on "The Ventilation of Drains," which elicited a discussion in which Drs. Farrel, Pineo, Walsh, Jennings, Christie, Hamilton and Warner took part.

Dr. Farrell then read a paper on "Surgical Cleanliness," which was discussed by Dr. Parker and others.

Dr. Hodder moved a resolution to the effect that two members of the Association, together with the local secretaries, be appointed a committee to wait upon or memorialize the Dominion Government with regard to the establishment of one general system of education.

The meeting then adjourned.

EVENING SESSION.

The meeting opened at eight o'clock.

A paper was read by Dr. Dodge on some cases of eye disease. Dr. Bent, of Truro, read a paper on a case of bent knee joint, which contained many practical points. Dr. Hingston made some very terse remarks on disease of the joints. A discussion ensued on this disease, and was continued for some time. Dr. Roseborough read a paper on some of the more common diseases of the eye, as met with in private practice.

TO-DAY'S PROGRAMME.

It is probable that the business of the Association will be finished to-day. The medical men of this city are sparing no pains to make the visit of their brethren from abroad an enjoyable one. At noon the steamer "Goliah" will take the party for an excursion on the harbour, Basin, and N. W. Arm. The Admiral's flag ship "Bellerophon," and the Mount Hope Insane Asylum, will be visited, and at the latter the party will be entertained at dinner. During the cruise a stoppage will also be made at Point Pleasant, to witness the Halifax Field Battery's practice. To-night a ball will be given by Dr. W. J. Almon, at his residence in Hollis street, in honour of the visitors. In the evening a concert in the Public Gardens will enable them to judge of the efforts made by the Corporation to provide healthy enjoyment for our citizens.

CHAPTER IX.

"But suffering is my work and worship now."
— *Richter.*

The year 1875 was an era in Dr. Botsford's life. At its commencement he may be said to have attained the apex of his career. He had not only worked his way in his profession in his native Province, so that he now stood among the foremost medical men here, but he had been acknowledged by the Canadian Medical Association, as one worthy to stand at its head. He was esteemed by his fellow-citizens, and was prominent in most of their benevolent and religious organizations. He was not wealthy, yet, by his own exertions, added to the small inheritance derived from his father and mother, he had laid up as capital that moderate sum which, at the outset of his life, was the limit of his wishes. His sixty-fourth year was nearly completed; he had a good constitution, and was full of vigour. To all human probability many years of active life and work lay before him, when suddenly he was touched by one of those swift strokes to which the medical profession is so exposed. He was laid for months on a bed of suffering, and when he rose from it he knew that his regular work as a medical man must be given up for ever.

It was a case of pyæmia, or blood poison. He had been called upon to attend a brother physician suffering from this terrible malady, and in lancing an abscess it

(143)

is supposed some of the virus or poison touched a scratch in the forefinger of Dr. Botsford's right hand. He was at the same time visiting a severe case of puerperal, or childbed fever. In his anxiety to save the patient, he "worked over her," to use his own expression, for an hour, inhaling the feverish atmosphere. This he considered aggravated his own attack. For some days he did not feel well, though he went about as usual, but one chill, damp November morning, after being out for an hour or two, he returned and lay down on his bed, to endure for the next seven months a terrible struggle between life and death. Mrs. Botsford's entry in her journal is : "Monday, Nov. 22nd. The doctor not very well." "Tuesday, 23rd. The doctor breakfasted and went out as usual. Soon returned. He appeared quite ill and complained of great pain in his right hand. I sent for Dr. Harding. The doctor seems quite feverish. Cannot eat anything." In a few days Dr. MacLaren was called in. The inflammation increased and extended up the arm. One night he called his niece to him and said : "F——, I do not think that my frame will bear this attack. I was not sure for a while what it was, but I know now, and I doubt if I can stand it." His niece was much startled, not having been fully aware of the serious nature of the illness, but she tried to speak hopefully, suggesting that it was nervousness which made him feel depressed, and doubtful of recovery. He said, "Perhaps so," and never, during the long course of his illness, did he again allude to the subject.

In the beginning of December, young Dr. Hartt, Mrs. Botsford's nephew, came from New York to assist in nursing. He staid for three weeks. "Harry is such a comfort," says the journal. The inflammation, after passing up the right arm, quickly extended to the left, forming several dreadful abscesses. Mrs. Botsford writes: "December 24th. My dear, patient sufferer's arm was opened above the elbow; it was severely painful, and he said, 'Thank God, that is over.' His medical attendants are unremittingly kind and attentive, and such universal sympathy." After Dr. Hartt left, many kind friends offered to sit up at night until a nurse could be found—a difficult thing to do. Finally Marshall, an old soldier, was engaged. He proved a most faithful attendant. He took the night watches; but Mrs. Botsford seldom left the room day or night, sleeping on a sofa at the foot of the bed, while Marshall kept watch at the head. Her journal at this time contains frequent allusions to the number of people who called to inquire for her husband; to the kind messages she was constantly receiving; to the jellies, fruits, wines, flowers, which were daily sent by loving friends, who appeared to think they could not do enough to show their interest and their sympathy. Very few were allowed to see him. His clerical friends, Canon Brigstocke (the Rector of Trinity) or Mr. George Armstrong (the Rector of St. Mark's) would be admitted for a few moments to read a verse or two and say a short prayer; but all excitement had to be carefully avoided. His brothers George and Blair came down whenever they could spare time, and would sit up at night, so as to give Marshall a rest. Thus day after day, and night after night, passed on in patient suffering on the one hand, and in wearing anxiety on the other. Regular as clock-work the two medical men came at nine in the morning and at seven at night to dress the right hand, which had to be lanced several times, and the left arm, which, from a little below the shoulder to a little above the wrist, was one dreadful running sore. The patient was perfectly helpless; he could not even use his handkerchief, nor brush his teeth, nor do anything for himself, and this was a great trial to one of his neat, personal habits. The pain in the arm was very severe, and it was difficult to find an easy position for it until the doctor himself suggested that a rest should be suspended from the ceiling, upon which the arm was laid. At length the first symptoms of healing appeared—" granulation " the doctors called it—and the patient was reported as progressing. The journal says : " January 12th. The doctor declares he has not felt so well as he does to-day since his illness began. Mr. Daniel brought him some tomatoes from the greenhouse, and some beautiful flowers; both were a treat. He saw Mr. Daniel for a minute, and Charles Drury; took his food, and feels comfortable."

" Thursday, 13th. Still the same; very weak, and oh! so thin."

" Sunday, 16th. Getting on, but so very slowly."

" Wednesday, 26th. The doctor's birthday. George came down. The arm not quite so well. I wish I could *see* the doctor gaining strength, which I have not done yet. It may be that strength cannot come till the arm has done discharging, which it does very freely. He was much tired to-day and is very weak."

The doctor had now been confined to bed for three months; his hand and arm were improving, but he did not seem to be gaining strength. He had been up for a short time one or two days, and felt so exhausted afterwards that he was unwilling to renew the effort. Mrs. Botsford writes: "Had his room changed. The doctors carried him into the drawing-room; it is a much more cheerful room, and we had a spring-bed put in, on which I trust he may rest comfortably." One morning, in the beginning of March, his feet were observed to be swollen; the same symptom gradually showed itself in various parts of the body, and when it reached the neck a terrible attack came on. The journal says: "March 7th. Awful day for me; the doctor appeared so well before I laid down, but Marshall called me at three o'clock, as L. B. was alarmingly worse. I sent immediately for Dr. M——; Dr. H—— was out of town. Then I sent to the hotel for George. I do not think Dr. M—— had any hope whatever." Dr. Botsford was at this time unconscious, in convulsions, foaming at the mouth. The swelling had so affected his face that not even his nearest friends could have recognized him. It is difficult to say how we lived through the next three weeks. The doctor talked incessantly and incoherently. He did not know his wife, and it was pitiful to hear him hour after hour entreating his niece to let him "go home; I shall be so much better at home." One seemed almost willing to breathe the prayer, "Let Thy servant depart in peace."

When this change in Dr. Botsford's illness became known in town, the inquiries at the door were so incessant that the medical men had to put up a bulletin on the hall door three times a day. Old and young showed their interest in the sufferer. The first question when business men met in the street was, "Have you heard how Dr. Botsford is this morning?" One of his patients said to her little daughter, "What were you doing so long alone in your room?" "I was asking God to make our dear doctor well." And hers was not the only intercession. Sunday after Sunday Dr. Botsford was prayed for in Trinity Church, and after his most wonderful recovery it was said that he must have been prayed back to life by the supplications of Trinity congregation.

The delirium was succeeded by a heavy death-like sleep, which could hardly be distinguished from "coma." On Monday, 13th, a week after the attack, the journal says "Sleeping heavily, stertorous breathing, almost without a ray of hope." That day, while his wife and niece were sitting beside him, the heavy breathing suddenly ceased, and the quieter breathing which succeeded was almost imperceptible. Mrs. Botsford exclaimed, "F——, he is gone!" but a faint pulse at the wrist showed that he was still with us, and the next day the journal says: "Sleeping quietly; not coma; the slightest shade of hope." And so alternate hope and fear went on for a fortnight longer, and even then the entry is, "Much the same; physicians say no worse." Marshall, poor fellow, was quite worn out, and was replaced by two men, who relieved each other by turns. The journal says: "The men are both good nurses and seem very faithful. F—— does much. I think her dear uncle likes her to be near him. How thankful I feel that she is here."

When Dr. Hartt, in New York, heard of this last attack, and of the little probability there was that his friend's strength would hold out, he "dropped everything," to use his own phrase, and although a very busy man, he rushed to St. John, telegraphing to the doctors to meet him in consultation as soon as he arrived. The conference lasted two hours, and when concluded, Dr. Hartt said in his impulsive, sanguine fashion, " Dr. Botsford will get well. I do not see why he should die." This was some encouragement, but three weeks more of anxiety were passed before Mrs. Botsford could write: " Easter Sunday, April 16th. The doctor improving slowly." The next week: "L. B. waked, asked me to read the psalms of the morning for him. The doctors came. Said he was going on well. Boils still discharging and painful." A week later: "April 30th. After breakfast had a little church at home. We read the service together. Then F—— read a chapter of Farrar's Life of Christ, and dear L. B. said he quite enjoyed the day." At length, on 11th of May, Mrs. Botsford writes joyfully: " Carried down stairs on a swinging chair of his own contrivance."

"May 14th. Out in Hamm's barouche. Is gaining strength, though very slowly. He wishes to go to Halifax this week. The medical men are saying all they can to dissuade him from going so soon, but I know he will go." And go he did. Many friends met him in the station. He was lifted into a Pullman, the bed arranged, and the easy, swaying motion of the car put him into a healthy, refreshing sleep soon after the train started. The journal says: " We reached Halifax early the next morning and drove to Elm Bank. Mr. Walker had a bed ready in the drawing-room, as the doctor could not go upstairs; indeed every possible kindness was shown us during our six weeks' stay." About the end of June he returned to St. John, not very strong, nor capable of much exertion, but no longer an invalid. The terrible illness, lasting from the 23rd of November

to the middle of the following June, had been borne
with the most astonishing fortitude and patience. His
nurses cannot recall one fretful word during his conscious hours. It was necessary frequently to lance the
gatherings, and in his " supersensitive state " this gave
great pain — only once he uttered a sharp cry. At
such times he would like to have a gentle hand press
his head, and his lips would move in secret prayer.
During the first part of his illness the dressing of the
fearful abscesses occupied the medical men fully an
hour every morning and evening. He was often much
exhausted, but it was all borne with cheerful composure.
Sometimes a quiet joke would come to the surface,
and he never failed to acknowledge the extreme kindness and attention of his physicians. In his weakest
hours, when reading fatigued him, he would like a
psalm or hymn repeated, often asking for the 23rd
Psalm. His favourite hymns were "Rock of Ages,"
" Art Thou Weary," and "Abide with Me."

Upon Dr. Botsford's return to St. John he was able
to attend church, and Mrs. Botsford's feelings of thankfulness, when they sat again together in the old pew,
may be better imagined than described. Her husband's recovery seemed almost like a resurrection.
They were very early, and Dr. Botsford whispered :
" I think I will go and speak to the rector." She
looked, saw his eyes were full of tears, and merely
pressed his hand. When he got to the vestry his
emotion nearly overcame him; he could only utter a
few inarticulate sounds. Canon B—— saw at once
how much he was moved. " I suppose, Dr. Botsford,
you wish to return thanks for your recovery." Dr.
Botsford bowed an assent, and left the vestry, lest he

should lose control of his feelings. It was some time after he returned to his pew before his emotion subsided, and many a heart in Trinity Church that morning united in the thanksgiving, and felt grateful that God had spared his servant's life, and had granted him a few more years in which to do his Master's work. Dr. Botsford remained a short time in the city, then he went out to Rothesay and spent a fortnight with his kind friends, Mr. and Mrs. H——. Every change seemed to give him additional energy. From Rothesay he went to Milton, six miles out of Boston, where Miss M—— was spending the summer with her sister, Mrs. R——. The journal says: "The doctor very much enjoyed his visit to Milton; all so kind. Mr. R—— drove him out frequently, and he took lovely country walks." From Milton he went on to New York, where he remained five weeks, the guest of his friend, Dr. Hartt. While there he received the following letter from Dr. Gross:

PHILADELPHIA, August 8, 1876.

Dear Doctor Botsford:

Upon my return home a few days ago, I had the pleasure of finding your kind letter of the 22nd ultimo. I need not tell you how sincerely rejoiced I am at your recovery after so terrible an attack of pyæmia. You must, indeed, have been at death's door. You are, of course, a sensible man, and, therefore, fully able to take care of yourself without any warning on my part. Keep away from this city as long as you can. We are again suffering frightfully from the heat. Do not fail to be here at the opening of the International Medical Congress, and at the meeting of our "Conference" on the previous Saturday. We need your presence. By that time we shall certainly have pleasant weather. When you write to Mr. Walker, thank him kindly for his invitation. If I am ever so fortunate as to visit Halifax, it will afford me great pleasure to spend a few days under his hospitable roof. God bless you!

Yours very truly,

S. D. Gross.

Dr. Botsford did not attend the Medical Congress, as suggested in the above note. His strength was not equal to the exertion ; but he did make a short visit to the "Centennial Exhibition" with his niece, and by means of rolling chairs was able to visit most objects of interest in the "great show." The machinery department especially attracted his attention. In the autumn he returned to St. John with his wife and niece to take up again the life which had been so wonderfully restored to him.

He looked at this time the picture of health. His bright colour and clear complexion had returned. There was no trace of weakness in his figure or bearing. He was rather stouter than he had been before his illness, yet his medical friends told him, and his own knowledge confirmed the dictum, that traces of the disease remained in his system, and that strenuous work and excitement must be avoided. He himself told his niece that, though he felt perfectly well, he knew that his vital force was weakened, and that, it at any time his lungs, digestion or heart were attacked by disease, he would have but little power of resistance. He formed his plans accordingly. His daily visits to the Marine Hospital were resumed, but his patients, to their often expressed regret, had to be told that his general practice was given up. There were a few old friends whose entreaties he could not resist, but even then, if a long illness threatened, he felt that his strength could not stand any continuous strain, and generally requested that the case might be handed over to some other medical man, and he absolutely refused all night work.

It was at first feared by his friends that he would miss the interest and occupation of a large practice. But it was not so. He had, it is true, stepped suddenly from the burden and heat of the day to the "afternoon" of life, but his active, energetic spirit soon found many objects to take up his attention and much to do for his fellow-beings during the twelve years of life yet allotted to him. He was always fond of reading. Besides his medical works and periodicals, he had gone through a few scientific books, but now, for the first time in his busy life, he had leisure to devote to general literature. History, travel, but especially biography, gave him great pleasure. He often said, after reading a life like that of Louis Agassiz, of Lord Lawrence, of Bishop Hannington, or of Henry Fawcett, that he felt as if he had made another friend. His reading was not merely for his own amusement; the thoughts thus acquired were reproduced in various shapes in conversation or in his lectures before the Y. M. C. A., and often in annual addresses before the different organizations with which he was connected. Thus occupied, he was more at home than formerly—a great pleasure to Mrs. Botsford, whose health of late years, never very strong, had been much weakened by the anxiety and fatigue of the preceding winter. We find such frequent entries in her journal: "I have had much pain in my gouty

foot; often feel weary and stupid now; not good for
much." Yet her buoyant disposition enabled her to
make the best of everything, and it was a perpetual
delight to her to watch her husband's improvement in
health and strength. She writes: "April 25th. The
doctor is getting stronger. I am not able to go out
this week, and feel weary and sick and stupid, but so
happy to see my husband getting stronger." She
chronicles the pleasant "high teas" which had now in
St. John generally taken the place of the more cere-
monious dinner parties, and observes at the end of a
week: "We have been out two evenings this week,
and the doctor does not seem tired."

To his other evening engagements Dr. Botsford now
added the meetings of a literary association of about
forty members, calling themselves "The Eclectic
Reading Club." The literary and social evenings
arranged every month by this Club were much enjoyed
by the doctor. Six readings or recitations were usually
given at each meeting by different members in turn,
Dr. Botsford's readings being very popular, as he made
his selections carefully, and read in a clear, distinct
voice. At the annual meeting of the Club he was
elected President, and contributed not a little to its
continued success and progress. He felt that it supplied a need in St. John society by furnishing a social
gathering for persons of intellectual culture and taste.
Mrs. Botsford was not often able to attend the meetings, but she was always glad to welcome the Club to
her own house, and enjoyed getting up a nice supper
for the benefit of the members.

And thus the year 1877 found Dr. Botsford, though
retired from general practice, yet still busily engaged.

There was work connected with the Bible Society, with the Natural History Society, with the Evangelical Alliance, and with various other societies of which he was a member. His morning walk to the Marine Hospital was the prelude to the day, followed perhaps by one or two medical visits. Sometimes he would go in for a few minutes to the Girls' High School, where the principal, Mrs. Carr (Mrs. deSoyres), always felt his presence to be an incentive and a stimulus. Occasionally he would make a short address to the pupils on some popular scientific subject, or give them a plain "talk" upon Hygiene. A book or his pen filled up his leisure hours. Once more his tall figure was seen, and his ringing laugh was heard day after day in the streets of St. John. "Do not forget Dr. Botsford's hilarity," was the advice given to the writer of this memoir. "I told him once that he must be the happiest man in the world, for he was always humming some lively tune when he came into my office."

His sixty-fifth birthday, January 26th, 1877, Mrs. Botsford celebrated by giving a little luncheon party of twelve. There were the doctor's three clerical friends, the Rectors of Trinity, St. Mark's, and St. Paul's; his two faithful physicians, Dr. H—— and Dr. M——; his cousin, Mr. Drury; two lawyer friends, Mr. W. M. J—— and Mr. Ch. W——; and Mr. T. W. Daniel. The journal says: "It was a nice, pleasant, and very harmonious luncheon at half-past one; they did not leave till four."

The first sad event of the new year was the death of Dr. Botsford's good friend, Mr. Walker, of Elm Bank, whose kindness and attention during both the doctor's illness and convalescence had been very great. Dr.

K

Botsford went twice to Halifax to see him. The journal says: "Never can I forget what Mr. Walker did for my husband, who feels this very much. L. B—— was with Mr. Walker, at his own urgent request, till shortly before his death, and came home so worn out, and looking so weary, I felt almost alarmed at his appearance. He said he felt unable to stay longer." Mr. Walker died shortly after Dr. Botsford left, and his remains were brought to St. John for interment.

During the whole winter the journal contains frequent notices of Dr. Botsford's increasing vigour: "Sunday the doctor was at the Marine Hospital, and *twice* at Trinity. How delighted I was to be with him in dear old Trinity again. First-rate sermons both times, and so earnestly delivered." On May 21st: "Splendid day; the doctor went with Dr. Harding in his new boat as far as Pisarinco; had a lovely sail. I wish he could get away in this very fine weather." About a fortnight after this was written, the doctor did get away on a little trip with his niece and his friends, Canon and Mrs. DeVeber. They were to visit the northern part of New Brunswick—the Metapedia and the Restigouche.

We left in the train on the 11th of June, a lovely day. Dr. Botsford was in the best of spirits, laughing and talking with the passengers in the car. "Was that an old friend with whom you have been chatting so merrily for the last half hour?" asked Dr. Botsford's grave and reserved fellow-traveller, Canon DeV. "I never saw the man in my life before," was the answer, "but I liked his face and felt inclined to exchange thoughts with him." At the Junction, while waiting for a "Special" to take us to Chatham, an employee of the road, a long-headed sceptical Scotchman, was using some strong language in Dr. Botsford's hearing. The latter felt he could not hold his peace, but the reproof was given so kindly that no offence was taken, and the result was a religio-metaphysical discussion which lasted till the "Special" was ready. The next day we proceeded via Campbellton to the Metapedia, where we staid, as all travellers then did, at "Dan Fraser's." The doctor revelled in the glorious scenery, and, in his newly acquired strength, he climbed the hills around to get the best views, and thrashed through the underbrush with the most astonishing vigour. One day was devoted to floating down the Restigouche in canoes paddled by Indians, and Dr. Botsford sat almost speechless with delight as we glided swiftly and quietly down the clear stream, while the hills on either side seemed to enfold us in beauty. From the Metapedia we returned to Bathurst on the Nipisiguit, along the banks of which we had a lovely drive. At the little country inn at Bathurst, a characteristic incident occurred. When we arrived, as the meek, quiet landlady was showing us our rooms, her tipsy husband appeared, and reeling up to Dr. Botsford began to talk about the old Judge, how often he had staid with him, etc. With some difficulty the poor mortified wife persuaded her husband to leave the room, but not before Dr. Botsford had got thoroughly indignant and excited. He walked up and down, talking about temperance, wondering why men would make fools of themselves, and he could not calm down until his niece opened an old melodeon, and played some favourite hymns. The next day we left for Moncton, where the party separated. Dr. Botsford went to Halifax to meet Mrs. Botsford. The rest of the party returned to the city, no one imagining that before they met again the following week, the " Great Fire " would have swept over St. John, and laid the greater part of it in ruins.

The story of the St. John fire has been so often told that it seems unnecessary to repeat it here, as it did not form part of Dr. Botsford's personal experience. Those who were then in St. John have the terrible scenes photographed in their memories. Those who were absent can never, by the aid of any description, fully imagine its horror. It came upon us with such swift rapidity as almost to paralyze exertion. A suffocating pall of black smoke and ashes hung low over the city ; the howling of the wind and the terrific roar of the flames were appalling. The most substantial stone houses burnt like wooden shanties, huge granite blocks curling up in the intense heat and blazing like sheets of cardboard. House after house, street after street, square after square, were enveloped in fire, until from the harbour the city seemed one vast glowing furnace. Dr. Botsford's house stood in a comparatively safe part of the city, and was soon filled with furniture, plate and valuables from other houses. His niece knew how anxious he would be that all possible assistance should be given, so that beds were made up and bread prepared, as the bakeries were all burnt or burning. At one time it was feared that even this part of the city would be included in the conflagration, but, by a merciful Providence, the wind changed, and the flames were blown towards the harbour.

Dr. Botsford did not hear of this terrible calamity

until the next morning, just as he was leaving Halifax for St. John. By that time the fury of the flames had spent itself, but two-thirds of the city lay in ashes. Churches, banks, shops, public institutions were in ruins. The principal streets were so choked with *debris* and masonry that they were almost impassable. Fifteen millions' worth of property had been destroyed, and twenty-five thousand people were homeless and houseless. Dr. Botsford had intended to make a visit in Sackville, but he came direct to St. John, hearing at every station additional details of the great destruction, and by the time he reached his home he could form some idea of the work that lay before him. Relief committees were at once organized to distribute wisely the provisions and clothing which were so quickly and so generously poured into St. John—not only from Fredericton, and different parts of the Province, but from the United States. Portland sent a relief train immediately, and Boston was not far behindhand. Large sums of money were also most generously contributed in the States and elsewhere, and every effort was made to alleviate the distress. Dr. Botsford was on both the General Relief Committee and the Special Church of England Relief Committee, the meetings of the latter being held at his house. Only those who have had the experience know what an amount of labour and responsibility such work implies. Dr. Botsford stood the strain wonderfully well. For three weeks it was incessant toil from early morning till late at night—toil of both hands and brains, but especially the latter. It was thought the fatigue and excitement would be too much for Mrs. Botsford, so, at her husband's request, she

remained several weeks with her Halifax friends.
Meantime, **Dr.** Botsford kept open house—twelve,
fifteen, sometimes eighteen, friends or acquaintances
dined with him every day.   Besides the work on the
General Relief Committee at the Rink, and that in
connection with the Church of England Committee, a
large Needlework Society was organized in St. Mark's
school-room and in the Mechanics' Institute, where
numbers of young girls, thrown out of employment,
were engaged and paid to make up undergarments
and cotton dresses for those who had only saved from
the fire the clothes in which they were dressed.

When Mrs. Botsford returned she writes: "The most
awful conflagration !   Our venerated church and all the
public buildings swept away.   I drove over part of the
city to-day, and did not know in what street I was.
Everything that can be done is doing for the relief of
the sufferers.   Our own home has been open to any
in want of a dinner, and the Church of England Committees are held here every day from three till five.
I hope my dear husband's strength may hold out, and
that he may be able to do what is so needful.   He
has for the past four weeks been very busy—helping,
cheering, managing.   He is chairman of the Church
of England Committee.   He is very active, and so
much interested, that he will not allow himself to
rest."   Again: "Friday, July 27th.   The doctor and
I have been busy all day about the people's clothing."

After a while the streets were cleared, gangs of busy
workmen passed to and fro, the tap of the hammer
and the click of workmen's tools were heard from one
end of the city to the other, men began to take heart,
and by October the doctor was able to write this hope-

ful letter to his brother, the Senator. The letter shows how closely Dr. Botsford watched and observed the progress of the buildings in the city, and how much he was interested in its welfare:

ST. JOHN, Oct. 8th, 1877.

My Dear Edwin:

I did not answer your letter written on the eve of your going north. . . . We are progressing in the way of building. I think I may say there are now 280 brick stores in process of construction. Many have the brick work finished and the roofs on, and many more are well advanced, and about 120 dwelling houses of brick. Each store I count as one, though in some buildings there are two or three. I suppose you may put down $6,000 as the average cost of each; that is certainly a low estimate, so that you can form an idea of what is doing. There are about 450 wooden buildings, one-third of them shanties or ells, the remainder better buildings than those which were burnt; average cost of each say $1,200. The cost of what is now undertaken cannot fall short of two and a half millions, a pretty big sum. The churches alone are a heavy item. Centenary, $60,000; St. Andrew's, $40,000; St. David's perhaps the same; St. Malachi's, $25,000; Victoria School, $45,000; Trinity, not yet decided, will not fall short probably of $50,000; Baptist, Germain Street, $40,000. Dock street, now widened, has the west side mostly roofed; the east side not much done on account of delay in widening. How are the "Jacky snipes" this autumn?   Your affectionate brother,

L. B. BOTSFORD.

And thus closed the year 1877, so fateful for St. John and St. John citizens.

CHAPTER X.

"Grief walks the earth, and sits down at the feet of each by turns."
— *Æschylus.*

At this time Mrs. Botstord's journal contains frequent allusions to her health, which was evidently failing. She felt deeply the loss of a much-loved niece in New York, Maggie H——, who died the week before Christmas, just after the birth of her first baby. Mrs. Botsford wished to go to her "poor afflicted sister, but I am weak and weary, and not able to do so. I have written her to visit me; the change would do her good." Mrs. Hartt was not strong enough to travel in the cold weather, and the sisters did not meet till the following summer.

The winter was spent quietly. While the doctor was out in the morning at the hospital, Mrs. Botsford, if she were able, would take a walk with Miss M——. In the afternoon, while her husband attended his committee meetings, or looked at the papers in the News Room, she would have pleasant chats with her visitors, for a day seldom passed without her receiving several "calls." In the evening, friends would come in to play bagatelle with the doctor; or, if they were alone, he would read aloud. She often mentions spending a quiet evening, with a few other people, at a friend's house, but she did not feel able to attend larger gatherings. On Sunday she always made an effort, even if not very strong, to go to church with the doctor, either

(162)

to the " Stone Church," or to the Madras school-room,
where Trinity congregation now worshipped. As for
the doctor's health, he was wonderfully well, and
stouter than he had ever been, weighing 188 lbs.
This was probably owing to the milk diet, which he
continued to take until every trace of the disease had
disappeared.

When the long, chilly spring of 1878 opened, Dr.
Botsford took a slight cold, and this, combined with
what he called a " migratory" feeling, induced him to
think of another trip. This time it was to be towards
the South. Mrs. Botsford was not strong enough to
accompany him, but young Dr. R. L. Botsford, the son
of his brother Bliss, came to stay with her and to take
charge of the Marine Hospital. Miss M——'s sister,
E—— M——, and her friend, Miss L. M. Towne,
from Philadelphia, had been engaged for many years in
educational, temperance and missionary work among
the freedmen of South Carolina, and when it was known
that Dr. Botsford contemplated a trip to the South, Miss
Towne kindly invited him and his niece to visit Frogmore, the pretty home she had made for herself in the
Island of St. Helena.

We left St. John on a dull, chilly Thursday in April.
Little patches of dirty snow could be seen in the streets.
It was a decided case of " Winter lingering in the lap
of spring." When we caught sight of Mount Katahdin
on our way to Portland, it was glittering, white as an
Alpine peak. During our few hours' stay in Boston
we went to hear one of Phillips Brooks' Friday Lent
lectures. Dr. Botsford never lost an opportunity of
listening to that earnest and intellectual preacher.
Trinity was full to overflowing on this week-day after-

noon, and there were more men than women in the
congregation. We left the same evening for New
York, where, after spending an hour or two with Dr.
and Mrs. Hartt, we embarked for Charleston, crossing
the bar and landing there on Tuesday morning. The
transformation scene appeared magical. We had stepped suddenly from winter to summer. Trees were in
leaf, shrubs in blossom; the air was balmy with the
breath of flowers, and clustering roses in full bloom
were climbing over windows, porches and houses.
When we went to the hotel, which was built round
a large inner square, filled with tropical plants, the
waiter brought us, as an appetizer for breakfast, a
plate of fresh strawberries. Two days were spent in
Charleston. We drove about the city and out into
the country beyond. The luxuriance of vegetation
was marvellous. For miles along each side of the
road the Cherokee rose, with its large white flowers,
and their golden centres, threw its sprays over the
hedges. It was literally

> "One boundless bloom, one white and golden shower
> Of mingled blossom!"

We were certainly in the South. The dusky faces far
outnumbered the white ones, and in the large straw-
berry plantations, coloured women only were picking
the fruit for the northern market. A little before sunset we took a boat and sailed out to Fort Sumter.
"Silent it lies," but on just such an April day, thirteen
years before, it had proclaimed, by a thundering roar
of cannon, that the Great American Civil War was
ended—that the slave was free.

From Charleston we went by train to the Yemesse

Junction, thence to Beaufort, where E—— met us. We crossed the Beaufort River in an open boat, rowed by negroes. The carriage was waiting, and E—— drove us ten miles to Frogmore, where Miss Towne gave us a warm welcome. "Why did you not tell me what a handsome man your uncle was?" was Miss Towne's remark to E—— M—— as soon as they found themselves alone.

We spent a delightful fortnight at Frogmore, enjoying the kindest hospitality. To travellers from the north it seemed a "bower of beauty." Ivy, roses, jessamine, mantled the long verandah and crept in at the windows; within, beautiful pictures of Miss Towne's well-known artist sister, Mrs. Darrah, of Boston, adorned the walls, while the large rooms and high ceilings promised coolness in the hottest weather. Dr. Botsford, in writing to his brother, says: "I enjoyed a fortnight at St. Helena very much. The thermometer ranged from 70° to 80°; a brisk breeze came in from the sea every day soft and pleasant. The trees were in full foliage; the orange trees added to the scene by their clusters of ripe fruit. The rose bushes, or rather rose trees, were covered with various species of roses. Phlox of every hue sprang up on the lawn like weeds; the pomegranate was in blow, and all around was one summer enjoyment. Our welcome at Frogmore, where Miss Towne and Ellen reside, was warm and hearty, and the comforts of a home added in no small degree to the pleasure of the climate."

We reached St. Helena the day before Good Friday. That day and Saturday were spent in resting, reading, talking, and walking about the garden and grounds. On Sunday E—— drove us to Beaufort to church. It was Easter Sunday, and the richest northern churches could scarcely vie with the wealth of flowers displayed by this little southern church. The chancel was banked with roses, lilies, and honeysuckle. Bishop Howe, of South Carolina, preached a magnificent sermon on the Resurrection, and it was a great pleasure to Dr. Botsford and his two nieces to meet together in a joyous Easter "celebration." It was the first and last time they did so.

The following Easter week was a school holiday, and for almost every day some pleasant drive or boating excursion was planned. One was a picnic to Hunting Island to see the light-house and the alligator swamp beyond. Dr. Botsford alludes to this in a letter: "On one of the islands we visited there was a pond, perhaps about a mile in length, and before we left a Southerner, good with the rifle, shot an alligator, which a coloured servant dragged to shore. It was between five and six feet in length. The palmetto grew in every direction, and the enchantment of southern scenery was around us. I would not like to spend a summer in these latitudes, but the spring is truly enjoyable."

These expeditions were delightful. There was so much that was new and wonderful to Dr. Botsford. The long, grey moss that, like a misty veil, draped the gigantic "live oaks;" the stately magnolia, with its fragrant white blossoms; the palmetto; the dwarf palm, with its cluster of bright green fan leaves; the Yuca gloriosa; the pink and white azaleas; the trumpet honeysuckle, and other blossoming shrubs and flowers too numerous to mention, all combined to form a picture of beauty unknown and unimagined before. But more interesting to Dr. Botsford than even these wonders of nature was the sight of the progress of the coloured people since they had received their freedom. The slave huts, in which children formerly sat on the mud floor and quarrelled like animals round the hominy pot for their food, were replaced by neat cottages, each surrounded by a small farm purchased from government by the labour of its owner. Inside there was plain, substantial furniture. Outside there were fences, hen-houses, clumps of peach trees, whose pink blossoms were just opening. The fields of cotton, corn, sweet potatoes and pea-nuts, which we passed, were clean and well hoed, and if we came across a weedy patch Miss Towne would stop the horses to inquire the cause. "Done hab fever!" or "Wife done hab fever!" was often the answer, accompanied by a request for medicine. "Come to my house at ten to-morrow morning!" Miss Towne would say. At that hour there was generally a group of invalids in the back porch at Frogmore. Young women with sick children; old women with "rheumatiz;" men with fever or wounds. Miss Towne would go round among them, distributing medicine and giving good advice, and the progress the coloured people on the island have made in cleanliness and hygiene is doubtless due, in great measure, to Miss Towne's influence.

Thus this holiday week passed quickly away. On the Monday following, at the reopening of the Penn School, Dr. Botsford would be able to see something of the educational work which had been carried on for sixteen years by the ladies whose guest he was. Before describing the school it will be of interest to

give a brief history of its formation, taken from an
annual report, printed by the scholars themselves on
their school press:

PENN NORMAL AND INDUSTRIAL SCHOOL,

Established 1862.

PRINCIPALS: MISS L. M. TOWNE, MISS E. MURRAY.

On the coast of South Carolina, near its southern border,
lie a group of islands nestling together between St. Helena
Sound on the north, and Port Royal Entrance on the south.
Beaufort, the county town, and also the old fort of Jean
Ribault, are on Port Royal Island.

St. Helena, called by the Indians, Chicola, lies between
Port Royal Island and the sea. It is about fifteen miles long,
four to seven wide, and contains a population of about thirty
whites to nearly six thousand coloured.

When, in the late civil war, these islands were taken possession of by the Union forces, among those who came down
to help and teach the freedmen were two ladies, Miss L. M.
Towne from Philadelphia, and Miss E. Murray from England.

Deciding on St. Helena for their field of work, they founded
the Penn School, so called in honour of the Pennsylvania
Freedmen's Relief Association, which had given them their
commission, and continued generously and liberally to support
the school.

When this Association disbanded, its work being done, an
Auxiliary Society, the Benezet, with the kindest interest,
cared for the school for years, and still gives occasional donations. When the Benezet support ceased, the two ladies, as
Principals of the school, with the help of their own near
relations only, undertook its support, and though necessarily
cramped for means, have for many years kept it open and in
working order.

When they first commenced they were told that the "field

hands" of these islands were too low to learn anything; that "it was a waste of time to attempt to educate or civilize them; that few of them could count their fingers correctly, their language was unintelligible jargon, and it was impossible to teach them arithmetic."

Determined to prove that

"A man's a man for a' that,"

the ladies called the school together in the Brick Church, in the centre of the island, where, in 1862, the first division of the school was made into those who could repeat the alphabet and those who could not.

Sixteen years of work lie between that time and this, and now the school has its Normal, High, Grammar, Intermediate, Primary and Infant Divisions, with its Industrial Annex.

The Industrial Departments consist of a Carpenters' Class in a shop erected by the young men of the school, and a Sewing Class.

The school has no State or County aid, and is a free school, furnishing higher instruction to the graduates of the District Schools of the island and preparing them for State examinations. Its graduates are employed as teachers in the different divisions of the Penn School, in the County schools of the island; also in other parts of the State, and as clerks in stores.

Especial attention is given to moral and religious training, and to the principles of teaching.

This brief history may well close with Gen. Saxton's comment, who, in revisiting the island after twenty years, said: "They do not seem to be the same race that we found here, their expression and bearing are so changed and improved."

The report then gives the names of the teachers, the rules of the school, and outlines the course of study for the year. At the end we find a list of benefactors, among whom Dr. Botsford appears, and also the fol-

lowing poem, written by Whittier, for the first Christmas in the Penn School:

CHRISTMAS, 1862.

O none in all the world before
 Were ever glad as we!
We're free on Carolina's shore,
 We're all at home and free.

Thou Friend and Helper of the poor,
 Who suffered for our sake,
To open every prison door,
 And every yoke to break!

Bend low Thy pitying face and mild,
 And help us sing and pray;
The hand that blessed the little child,
 Upon our foreheads lay.

We hear no more the driver's horn,
 No more the whip we fear,
This holy day that saw Thee born
 Was never half so dear.

The very oaks are greener clad,
 The waters brighter smile;
O never shone a day so glad
 On sweet St. Helen's Isle.

We praise Thee in our songs to-day,
 To Thee in prayer we call,
Make swift the feet and straight the way
 Of freedom unto all.

Come once again, O blessed Lord!
 Come walking on the sea!
And let the main-lands hear the word
 That sets the islands free.

PENN SCHOOL-HOUSE, ST. HELENA ISLAND, S. C.

L

When we reached the school-house* on Monday morning, we found the children there before us. Some of them had walked six miles from their homes, and that after having finished the "task" of cotton-hoeing required by their parents. At the sound of the school bell they formed in long lines, their erect, lithe figures and dusky faces showing to advantage in the almost tropical sunshine. They marched into school to the sound of a lively tune played by Miss E. M——, and when they were seated they recited the Lord's Prayer, and sang a hymn. Their voices are very sweet. The whole building seemed filled with sound, not a deafening noise, but full-toned music. The big boys take the bass and tenor, and many of the girls sing by ear the alto of almost any tune. The children then separated to their several departments. Dr. Botsford began in the highest room, and after Miss E. M——'s daily Bible lesson, he heard recitations in arithmetic, algebra and Latin. In the grammar department there was a geography and a history recitation; in the primary there were spelling, reading and writing, while the little ones were learning the alphabet. The next day found Dr. Botsford at the school again. This time he wished to examine the scholars himself. He was much pleased with their answers, which showed the progress they had made,

---

*The accompanying sketch of the school-house, the sketches of Westcock and St. Ann's, are from pencil drawings by Mrs. Murray, the widow of Dr. Botsford's step-brother. After her mother's death, Mrs. Murray and her daughters came out to Boston. In 1861 she accompanied her daughter to St. Helena, South Carolina. She took an active part in work among the coloured people, and died of malarial fever, August, 1867.

and the fund of knowledge they possessed. After asking a great many questions, he would suddenly put a catch question, that he might see the studious faces relax with a smile only prevented by school decorum from breaking into laughter. He had brought with him for the school, from St. John, a large engraving of the " Good Shepherd," but after getting it framed in Charleston it was forgotten in the train, so that he could not present it himself, but it reached St. Helena after he left, and now hangs in the school-house, a memento of his visit.

The time had come for saying good-bye, and on our last evening at Frogmore, a man, a former pupil of the school, who had been working for Miss Towne, sent in his account. She happened to show it to Dr. Botsford as a good specimen of handwriting. He asked at once if he might keep it, for, he said, he had never seen a white man's bill made out more correctly, or in better form. He folded it up in his pocket-book, and when on his return journey, he got into a discussion about the things he had heard and seen (and this was a frequent occurrence), if the capabilities of coloured people were called in question, he would produce this paper and flourish it triumphantly before his opponent. Even after his return to St. John, he carried it about with him, and for several months it did duty on exhibition. We took the Savannah steamer and returned via New York and Boston to St. John. We had been absent just a month. Mrs. Botsford's journal says: " May 10th. Rainy; disagreeable day; still cold, hall stove lighted. L. B. and F. returned. I am so delighted to have them home again, L. B. looking so well."

The doctor enjoyed his trip so much that he repeated it the next year, accompanied this time by his brother, the Senator. He was again invited to Frogmore, but their stay was not long, as they intended to visit Florida. The experience of travel was much the same and need not be repeated. One amusing mistake, however, occurred on their Sunday at St. Helena. E. M. took them to the Brick Church, the largest coloured church on the Island. They were ushered respectfully into a front pew. Presently an old black "elder" came bowing to the Senator: "Would the Reverend kindly give us a sermon this morning?" The idea of being mistaken for a preacher was almost too much for the Senator's dignity. He answered with a cynical smile, "That is not in my line. You had better try my brother." The request was accordingly repeated to Dr. Botsford. After a little hesitation he complied, and found himself standing beside the black preacher. It was a different audience from that which he often addressed from the Bible Society platform, and for a moment he felt puzzled, and almost shy, but remembering that God "hath made of one blood all nations of men," he told, in as simple phrase as he could, "the old, old story" of God's love and man's duty. They thanked him afterwards, and the next day he and the Senator left for St. Augustine. After a short stay they returned to New York, where Mrs. Botsford met them, and they soon found themselves in their own home again.

The next few years were not marked by any great changes. Mrs. Botsford's journal gives a faithful reflection of the usual panorama of life. Deaths occurred among friends and relatives. Governor Chandler, who

has already been mentioned in this memoir, died at
Government House, Fredericton. Two cousins, Mr.
Charles H—— and Mr. Charles D——, passed away;
and younger than any of these, Mrs. Botsford's much
loved nephew, Dr. Henry LeBaron Hartt, who had so
kindly assisted in nursing during the doctor's severe
illness, caught diphtheria from a patient and suc-
cumbed to the disease in a few days. More unexpected still was the death of the young son of Dr.
Botsford's intimate friends, Mr. and Mrs. R. P. S——.
There was a consultation, and Mrs. Botsford notes with
keen anxiety how little hope her husband could give
from the very first, and when all was over, her sympathy with the bereaved parents was great. Though
not at all well, she made an effort to attend the funeral
at St. Paul's. She speaks of " the six little pall-bearers,
the lovely flowers, the beautiful music," adding : "Farewell, little boy, till the resurrection morning. God be
with the parents and comfort them." Afterwards, both
the Dr. and Mrs. Botsford, in their occasional attendance at St. Paul's, loved to linger beside the memorial
font of " Dear little A—— S——," the doctor's artistic
eye resting with especial pleasure on the exquisite
design and almost perfect finish of the carved reredos.

Then, also, there were numerous weddings. They
are frequently mentioned in the journal, and the selection of a pretty bridal gift was one of Mrs. Botsford's
pleasures. One marriage which she notices particularly is that of Juliet D——, the beautiful daughter of
their Rockwood friends : "July 13th. This day we
attended the wedding of dear and lovely Juliet. It was
one of the best I ever saw. The church was densely
crowded; the bride's dress perfect; she herself what

she ever has been. Mr. Armstrong married them, assisted by Mr. Schofield. We drove to Rockwood to lunch, everything going on beautifully. Shortly after luncheon the bridal pair left. May she be happy. Her absence will be felt by all who knew her." How little could any one imagine, when the youthful bride bade farewell, in the fulness of life and strength, that in less than four years we should see her in St. John again, but with the smile of eternal peace on her sweet lips, her eyes closed in

> "That blessed sleep
> From which none ever wake to weep."

During these years Mrs. Botsford had several slight attacks of illness. She had to be very careful in her diet and to avoid exposure in the damp. She writes, May 19th, 1879: "Very wet and foggy. I could not go to the ceremony of laying the corner-stone of Trinity Church. L. B. and F. were present, and in the evening they went without me to a party of thirty-two at our rector's. Bishop staying there. The doctor and F. came home at half-past ten, both quite pleased;" and then, when the handsome church was consecrated, December 9th, of the following year, she again writes: "December 10th. Yesterday our new church was consecrated by the Metropolitan, and there was a lunch for the clergy and congregation in Trinity school-house. I was too ill to go. Several people were very kind in coming to see me. The doctor went to Fredericton in the morning, returned in the evening, and then went to church with F. I was quite unable to go." She was much interested in the West window, a large memorial window, with three lights, which had been given by Dr. Botsford and his niece, and Mrs. Charles Hazen. It was manufactured by Clayton & Bell, of London, but, to our great disappointment, was not finished in time for the consecration. It was not till February 21st that Mrs. Botsford writes: "Monday. Splendid day; streets dry; not cold. Went with the doctor and F—— and Mrs. Charles Hazen, to see our window for Trinity Church. Mr. Brigstocke was also there. All were perfectly satisfied, and think it most beautiful. The subject is the Transfiguration. The doctor gives the left light in memory of his father and mother; Mrs. Charles the right for her husband. F—— has the centre in memory of her father and great-grandfather, the old Loyalist, Col. Murray."

Among other notices in Mrs. Botsford's journal are those of the "Fancy Sales" she attended. She loved pretty things, and always bought a nice piece of work "to help on the cause." Dr. Botsford was generally present at the "high tea" with which these sales closed, as he desired in this, as well as in other ways, to show his appreciation of woman's work.

As a physician, he had seen the sex in its worst and in its best aspects—fretful, selfish, exacting, querulous or patient, self-forgetful, self-denying, self-sacrificing. As a physician, also, the distinction and limitation of sex had forced itself upon his attention. With Tennyson he would say, "Not like to like, but like in difference," and while he fully recognized the importance of training schools for the higher education of nurses, he did not take kindly to the idea of lady doctors.

As regards woman's political rights, Dr. Botsford held what might be called "advanced" opinions, which

VIEW OF THE WEST END OF TRINITY CHURCH, SHOWING THE WEST WINDOW (OF
WHICH DR. BOTSFORD GAVE THE LEFT LIGHT); THE BUST OF THE QUEEN,
PLACED THERE AT THE JUBILEE SERVICE, 1887; THE ROYAL COAT
OF ARMS, BROUGHT BY THE LOYALISTS FROM NEW YORK; AND
THE OLD COLOURS OF THE 2ND ST. JOHN CITY MILITIA

he did not hesitate to avow when questioned on the subject, although he never brought his ideas prominently forward. He believed in the propriety of extending the franchise to women, and when, under our new municipal law, his niece was asked for her vote, he advised her to exercise her right, and went with her to the polls.

He was sympathetic and helpful in various Ladies' Auxiliaries and Associations, and in the leisure of his latter years often assisted in the details of the work. One of these was the Ladies' Auxiliary of the S. P. C. A. (Society for Prevention of Cruelty to Animals). Dr. Botsford was a member of the Parent Society, and was particularly interested in the ladies' work connected with the Bands of Mercy. He always occupied a seat on the platform at the anniversary meetings held in Mechanics' Institute. He enjoyed seeing hundreds of bright young faces gathered from the most diverse Sunday Schools in St. John. There were Church of England, Presbyterian, and Methodist children. He watched them as they came in with their banners and badges, and he loved to hear their songs and recitations.

Another Association with which Dr. Botsford was latterly connected was the Church of England Institute. The Institute was formed in 1876 for the purpose of giving to all who belonged to the Church of England in St. John a centre for united Church work. It numbers between three and four hundred members. It has its hospital work both on Sundays and week days, its Flower Mission, its Charitable and Missionary Aid Committee, its Lecture and Religious Instruction Committee. A branch of the G. F. S. (Girls' Friendly

Society), and of the Zenana Society (for women in India), are affiliated with it.

For a time Dr. Botsford held aloof from the Institute, fearing it would maintain a "too high" platform, but when the *Record* and the *Evangelical Churchman* lay peacefully by the *Church Times* and the *Church Guardian* on the table in the reading room, he was reassured, and became a member. He spent many pleasant hours among the books and papers of the Institute, and soon got interested, and assisted in its work.

Various objects have from time to time engaged the attention of the committees. Barrels of clothing have been packed and sent to the Indian homes in Algoma; boxes of useful Christmas presents are sent to poor parishes in our own diocese; funds have been collected for an organ and invalid chairs in the Public Hospital.

In 1883 a more responsible work was undertaken. When the new cotton mill was built, a committee of the Institute collected funds, rented and furnished a large house near the mill, procured a matron, and opened a lodging-house for the operatives, who were expected to arrive shortly from England, strangers and friendless. It was at first intended for girls only, but afterwards married people were admitted. A room was reserved for meetings, and several clergymen and others kindly consented to go once a week to give simple lectures on religious and secular subjects. Dr. Botsford went several times. One lecture on the Circulation of the Blood was heard with great attention by a crowd of men and boys. After trying to explain to them a little of the wondrous arrangement by which the blood courses through our veins and arteries, he told them how to bind up wounds; when to press above and when below a cut, etc., saying that life may often be saved by a little knowledge and presence of mind.

This lodging-house was finally transferred to a respectable Englishwoman, and though the work was thus virtually given up, yet from that time a permanent improvement of the neighbourhood is acknowledged by all who live there.

This was only one of many instances in which Dr. Botsford assisted the benevolent enterprises going on around him. Owing to Mrs. Botsford's frequent attacks of illness in these last years of her life, the doctor did not often leave home except for a short time in the autumn, when he attended the annual meeting of the Canadian Medical Association in Toronto, Hamilton, Ottawa or elsewhere. In the autumn of 1882 she appeared to be a little stronger, and on the doctor's return from the medical meeting in Toronto, she was able to accompany him to Sackville, where, at the invitation of Senator Botsford, the descendants of old "Speaker Botsford" met to celebrate the hundredth anniversary of his landing in this country. The doctor looked forward to this meeting with great pleasure, as we see from the following jocose letter :

My Dear Edwin:

I received your letter yesterday, and have been as busy as a hatter ever since, and now reply to your cordial invitation. Nothing in the social line could give me more pleasure than to join the collection of the Westcock boys which you propose to have on or about the 21st of the month. As you are the head of them now, it will be but just respect to yourself and to our father, to make an effort to meet again near to, if not under, the old roof. Margaret will be there, sure, if able to travel, and F—— M—— will answer for herself very soon, for she is coming. I have only an old flute, for Bliss ran away with my very good one. He must bring that. Have you any geese? If not, you must buy a small flock, that we may make a raid upon them as in the old time. . . . I have written to George, and told him I could give him a bed and we could leave the next morning, picking up Bliss and Blair and their wives on the way.

Accordingly, George came from Fredericton on Monday, 20th, and we went to Sackville on Tuesday. The Senator gave a warm welcome to Acacia Grove, and the rest of the week was one continuous fete. Sumptuous meals were served, every delicacy in or out of season appearing on the table. Friends and young people came in the evening for music, whist or games. The "boys" chaffed each other, told stories of their childhood and youth, called each other "Whack," or "Gride," or "Pepper-pot," or "Tony," as they had done fifty years before, for the youngest was in his sixty-second year. When they returned to St. John the doctor writes: "Dec. 4th. My Dear Edwin: I believe I have settled down to a medium size and quiet disposition. We had an enjoyable time, which has dusted away any difficulties which threatened the latter days of the 'Boys.' All I think are more or less rejuvenated. Margaret has been pretty well since her return."

During the following winter Mrs. Botsford had several slight attacks of illness, and spring found her far from well. When St. John celebrated its centennial, in May, 1883, she took great interest in it. She bought a large St. George's flag, which she got Dr. Botsford to suspend from the upper windows of the house, but to her great regret she did not feel able to go with her husband and niece to Trinity, where a grand Loyalist service was held. She saw the procession from a window, and did all she could to have the house well illuminated.

At this time the journal ceases. It closes with these words: "May 24th. Queen's birthday; replied to my sister's letter. May 25th. This day is fine; I hope I may be able to go out for a very short walk, but am so weak and weary, can do so little."

As summer advanced she grew stronger, and when the doctor left in the beginning of September to attend the Medical Convention she was able to go with him as far as Milton, where she staid during his absence for about a fortnight. How much she enjoyed that last visit. The pure, sweet air seemed to reinvigorate her. She was always fond of animals. She liked to see the calves and the cows, the chickens, the big dog. All the sights and sounds of country life were a pleasure to her. Every day Mrs. R—— would take her for a drive to the beautiful cemetery of Forest Hills, to Brush Hill, to Cedar Grove. She loved children, and took particular notice of Mrs. R——'s youngest boy, a bright, curly-headed little fellow of eight years old, called LeBaron after the doctor. When she returned to St. John, however, she was again far from well, and her niece hurried home to assist in receiving guests who had been invited to attend the St. John Exhibition. Then came a long, cold winter. The doctor did all that skill, attention and love could do, but the springs of life were evidently failing. In June she had a very severe attack of illness. Then again she revived; was out almost every fine day either with the doctor or with F—— for a short walk or a drive, and when, after an absence of a few weeks at Milton, F—— returned home by boat, Mrs. Botsford drove down to Reed's Point with the doctor to meet her. That week the Eclectic Reading Club met at the house, and though Mrs. Botsford seemed a little tired, she had a bright word for each of her guests, and appeared none the worse for the exertion. In the course of the next fortnight she went out shopping and visiting several times with her niece.

On Monday, October 20th, the Governor-General, Lord Lansdowne, and Lady Lansdowne arrived in St. John. On Tuesday an address was presented by the Mayor, but Mrs. Botsford did not feel quite able to accompany her husband to the Court House. On Wednesday, however, she had a little walk in town with him, and paid some bills. That same night about three o'clock she rose to get a glass of water. A slight noise awoke the doctor. He saw her totter and sprang from the bed just in time to save her from falling. He called his niece; she reached the room quickly, but her aunt was unconscious. It was a stroke of paralysis. When Canon Brigstocke came in, his clear, deep voice in prayer seemed partially to rouse her, and his words were probably the last sounds she heard. We watched beside her Thursday, Friday, Saturday and Sunday. The only token of life was the motion of her hand as if in writing. That soon ceased, she lay very still and did not appear to suffer. Her strength gradually failed, her breathing became almost imperceptible, and very early on Monday morning, October 27th, her " worn and weary " spirit entered into rest.

Dr. Botsford himself designed the simple monument he raised to her memory—a white marble anchor and cross combined—an emblem of "Hopeful Trust," and when he wrote to Mrs. Hartt giving the details of her sister's illness he concluded thus: "It cannot be long before I shall be called to join those who have passed the bounds of our earthly pilgrimage. My hand is on the door. I feel that it may open at any time."

CHAPTER XI.

"These are Thy glorious works, Parent of good
Almighty! Thine this universal frame
Thus wondrous fair, Thyself how wondrous then."

       — Milton.

The winter that followed Mrs. Botsford's death was sad and sombre. Life's daily duties were regularly performed, but the shadow of recent sorrow rested on the household. Dr. Botsford knew what a constant correspondence was kept up between his wife and her sister in New York, and, with his usual kindly consideration for others, he occasionally took his pen to fill up, in some measure, the blank this caused in Mrs. Hartt's life. By her thoughtful care several interesting letters of the last years of Dr. Botsford's life have been preserved. One of the first letters is dated a month after Mrs. Botsford's death, November 26th, 1884:

My Dear J——:

On Sunday Ch—— (Mrs. Botsford's brother) wrote you during the afternoon. He dined with us and was very well. . . . Looking over the diary left by Margaret, there continually occurs a notice of a letter received from you, and that it was answered the same day. This agrees with what I remember, that as soon as she received a letter from you it would be answered at once — no time lost. It was a rule with her, and she always longed for your letters. . . . I am remarkably well and have seldom had such continual freedom from malaise in every respect, but cannot at my time of life (seventy-three in January) expect a long

(186)

continuance of such health. But what matters it! True, I enjoy physical life, and should not delight in pain or weakness, but, should I not have the exemption, it cannot be long before I am called to join those who have passed the boundary of our earthly existence. Miss M—— sends love to you. She is very busy in her church and school employments, and certainly will not let dust settle upon her ways.

Love to A——.   Yours affectionately,

L. B. B.

The next letter is dated March 19th, 1885:

Dear J——:

Your letter of the 19th was duly received. I will try to answer your questions. First, as regards myself, I am in good health; eat somewhat carefully; sleep as much as any man of my age; attend daily to my hospital, walking there and back, unless it is stormy, when I take a cab to save my legs. So much for No. 1. Miss M—— is very well this winter, and very busy. I do not know what I should have done without her thoughtful care since I have been left alone. Our servants also are very attentive. I have many reasons to be thankful, and try to cultivate the feeling for the few days that are now left of my life. When a man is seventy-three he may expect at any time to be called upon to put off the mortal coil then blessed if he has the hope of immortal life. [He then mentions some mutual friends, and adds]: You speak of Ingersoll and his crowded meeting. That may be for a time, but the puny efforts of man cannot prevail against the Almighty. Many silly and vicious people may wish to have it so, but the word of the Lord abideth forever, and Ingersoll will pass into oblivion as others of the same type have done before him. If men will glorify him, it will end in some way to their disgrace and punishment ever here on earth. . . . Love to Jessie.

Yours very truly,   L. B. B.

M

In the spring there was much excitement in St. John
on the subject of the "Riel rebellion" in the North-
West.   Dr. Botsford watched the progress of events
with much interest.   He was in Prince William street
when the Fredericton volunteers arrived, and saw the
troops leave the St. John station amid much enthusiastic cheering.   He prophesied a long continuance
of the contest, and was thankful when the affair was
over so much sooner than he anticipated.   During the
summer he went to Fredericton and Sackville, and
made several visits to Rothesay.   In the autumn he
attended the annual meeting of the Canadian Medical
Society, which was held that year in Montreal, spending a week at Milton on his way thither.   By the end
of September he and his niece were settled at home
for the winter.   In the following letter to Mrs. Hartt,
written December 14th, 1885, he mentions his various
engagements :

My Dear J——— :

It is a long time since I wrote to you, or have had a letter
from you.   If I mistake not, you did not reply promptly, and
that set me a bad example!   As regards myself, I am wonderfully well in most respects, eat and sleep well, but find there
are weak points beginning to show.   No wonder, when the
system has been running for near seventy-four years.   I can
hardly realize the fact that I am so old a man.   The muscles
of my legs cannot bear the brisk walking of former days.   I
feel no flagging in the mental direction, and am engaged in a
good many things.   The Bible Society must have its annual
address, and I have to attend two meetings next week, one at
Quaco and one at Upham, being one of a delegation to attend
those places.   Then comes our week of prayer, on the first of
the year, when I was called upon to preside on one day.

I have also the Natural History Society to attend to twice a month, and must be ready with the annual address, as President, on the 19th January. I attend also Mr. Armstrong's Monday night prayer meeting; also preside once a month at our Club Reading. The Marine Hospital I attend every day, and have about fourteen patients to look after. The hospital is nearly built, and a very convenient one for sailors. I think I have given a very good and egotistical account of myself. Our servants are the same, and right good girls they are, most respectable and respectful. Every Sunday Ch—— makes his appearance. . . . I have heard but very little about Fredericton. Our railroads now connect with that Celestial City, starting from our depot and crossing at the Falls over the new cantilever bridge. We are having rather tough times in the city. Business dull, but it is dull everywhere. I do not think that we have more poor than elsewhere relatively.

Yours truly,   L. B. B.

The fact mentioned in this letter that " his muscles could not bear the brisk walking of former days," was probably the first intimation he had of his last illness. In his usual morning walk to the Marine Hospital he began to have a feeling of suffocation, which ceased as soon as he stopped walking. A pause of but two or three minutes was sufficient to allow him to proceed. He supposed that this difficulty might be caused by something he was taking for breakfast. He made a little change in his diet, and the disagreeable feeling for the time completely passed away. It may have been this attack, or a talk with a friend who had recently seen his nephews in San Francisco, which induced him about midwinter to think of a trip to California. Miss M—— entered into his plans, assisted him in his preparations, and assured him that the

house-cleaning should be all done, and the house ready
for him by his return. All at once he seemed fully to
realize the length and loneliness of the journey. He
apparently gave up the project, and wrote the following letter to Mrs. Hartt:

St. John, April 7th, 1886.

My Dear J—— :

After waiting some little time, I received a reply to my
last. I was sorry to hear that you have had a sharp attack.
I trust that you have thoroughly recovered. The winter and
spring are trying seasons on this coast from Labrador to
South Carolina. Our winter has been moderate for us, and
our spring fine, though cold. The town and country are hot
enough now with elections, one for the government of the
Province on the 29th, and one day after to-morrow, to decide
the adoption of the Scott Act. The object of that act is to
prevent the ordinary sale of spirits — in other words, the
Maine law. I hope that it may be well carried, and with a
rousing majority.

Charles appeared last Sunday as usual. He certainly retains his health famously, and will outlive us all. He has
had a fit about going to Scotland, but of course it ends in
talk, like a visit to California which I planned and all but
accomplished, but it ended in smoke. I have two nephews
there, Dr. William Botsford and his brother George, the
latter a dentist. I intended to go direct to San Francisco,
then up to the terminus of the Canadian Pacific, then by that
road home. It would be a pleasant, though somewhat tire-
some journey. Our Dominion has pushed our road through
to the Pacific with greater energy and success than the people
on the other side of the line, who boast so much of their
go-a-head powers, gave them credit for. Occasionally you
are inquired for by old friends, but the people who were
young with us are fast disappearing. [Some friends are then

mentioned and the letter concludes]: You should see our hyacinths — some of the largest we have ever had. The house is perfumed by them. Half a dozen of these are placed on our breakfast table every morning, and they take the edge off the ruggedness of winter. They remind me of olden times in the country, where the hawthorn blossoms and the wild flowers deck the old ruins of Cruikston. Surrounding oneself with those old memories, how startling it is to wake to the present. *Then* there was but a far off vision of futurity. *Now* it is a reality and a few, few days before us. Love to Addie and Florrie.

Yours affectionately,   L. B. B.

Shortly after this letter had been written, the wish for the California journey revived, and as soon as his niece offered to accompany him, he decided to carry out his former plan and to leave St. John about the first of May.

Easter day was April 25th, and Easter week was such a busy week with both Dr. Botsford and his niece that but little thought was given beforehand to the expedition. Miss M—— had the arrangements for the Church Institute Fancy Sale to make and carry out. Dr. Botsford's attention was also occupied, for Bishop Kingdon (the Coadjutor Bishop of the Diocese) was his guest. Dr. Botsford enjoyed conversation, and he understood and appreciated the *jeu d'esprit* by which intellectual men often seek to conceal their depth and earnestness. So the week passed away in committee meetings and hospitable devoirs until Saturday, when the doctor purchased through tickets to San Francisco. On Sunday we were in Trinity Church and remained to the holy communion. After evening service, Canon and Mrs. Brigstocke, and the Mayor and his wife (Mr.

and Mrs. B. DeV.), called to wish us *bon voyage*. On
Monday morning, May 3rd—and a bright, beautiful
May morning it was—we started in the Boston train
on our long tour. Dr. Botsford was in a state of quiet
enjoyment. "Where are you bound now, doctor?"
said an acquaintance, as we were crossing the cantilever
bridge. "To California." "Not much," was Mr.
Robert R.'s quick answer.

Dr. Botsford, by request, gave an account of his
California trip in a lecture before the Mechanics' Institute, January 10th, 1887. This lecture is included in
the present chapter, but as there are some points not
touched, and as the return by the Panama route is but
slightly mentioned, a preliminary sketch of the journey
is given at the risk of occasional repetition.

We reached Boston and Milton on Tuesday, and,
after a pleasant day's rest, left for Chicago, where we
met some St. John friends and visited several places of
interest. On Friday night we started for Omaha by
the Union Pacific Railroad. This was an entirely new
route to us, and, instead of feeling fatigue, the farther
we travelled the brighter and more interested Dr.
Botsford became. Turning to his travelling companion
suddenly he would exclaim: "F——, do you really
feel that we are going to San Francisco?" On Saturday afternoon we passed through Council Bluffs, and,
crossing a high trestle bridge over the Missouri, we
entered Omaha and rested there on Sunday. We attended service in the Cathedral, a substantial stone
edifice. The Bishop was assisted by several clergy, the
music was good, and, from all we could learn, the Protestant Episcopal Church is making progress in the
West.

It was just a week after we left St. John when, from Omaha, we began to climb the Rocky Mountains, an ascent so gradual, so monotonous, and so utterly devoid of characteristic scenery, that when, at 10 p. m. on Monday night, we stopped at the highest station, and from the Pullman platform looked round on the low, conical hills, covered with snow, we could hardly believe that we had accomplished the great ascent, and that we were actually on the top of the Rocky Mountains — ten thousand feet above the level of the sea. The descent soon began, and in the early morning we were among the cliffs and precipices, the gorges and mountain torrents of the western side of the great mountain range. Echo Cañon, Weber Cañon are now familiar names to most people, but only those who have passed down through them can have any idea of their stupendous grandeur. Huge cliffs of fantastic shapes overhung our road; mountain torrents rushed and foamed along their rocky beds close to the railway track, or crossing beneath it leapt down the precipice on the opposite side. It was one continuous excitement of wonder and enjoyment until we reached Ogden in the afternoon. There we took the Utah train for the Salt Lake City. It may as well be confessed that feminine curiosity chiefly induced this digression, but Dr. Botsford soon found there was very much beside the scenery, beautiful as that is, to repay the traveller. It was a new experience. To stand in the " Tabernacle," a vast, low, dark and dingy building, which spreads over the ground like some monstrous fungus growth, on the ceiling of which sacred scenes from Holy Scripture, and scenes in the life of " Joe Smith" are depicted side by side, and then to go out into the brilliant sunshine, to look up at the snowy peaks of the great Wintah range, or to look down at the clear rivulets, that run pure from their mountain springs through every street of this extraordinary city. What a contrast! Vividly as anywhere on earth you feel the force of Bishop Heber's well-known antithesis:

" And every prospect pleases, and only man is vile."

Dr. Botsford, in his lecture, describes our beautiful mountain walk. As we went along we inquired our way of several women who were passing. They answered in a foreign accent. It is said that many of the new settlers in Utah, and most of the recent adherents to Mormonism, are foreigners who come out quite ignorant of the peculiar doctrines of the sect, but the Protestant Episcopal Church and other Christian organizations are holding up the standard of truth in the Mormon city, and steadily gaining adherents. There are two Episcopal chapels, and Bishop Tuttle told us that the church was making many converts, especially from among those who had come from abroad to join the Mormons without knowing much of Mormonism, and who, when they became acquainted with its tenets, drew back in disgust.

We returned to Ogden on Wednesday evening and continued our journey on the Union Pacific. All the next day we could see nothing from our Pullman but long stretches of sage grass, with its little tufts of pale green pushing through the sand; sometimes a coyote or prairie dog would come out of its burrow and look at us as we passed; sometimes in the distance a brilliantly blue lake would be seen, apparently surrounded by snow-drifts, but they were only incrustations of salt.

Thursday night we climbed the Sierra Nevada, and on Friday morning found ourselves in all the richness and fertility of the Sacramento Valley. The greenest of green grass, and the loveliest flowers, the meadows being yellow with escholzias, well named the Californian poppy. As we approached the sea-coast the soil grew more sandy and the landscape more dusty. We crossed the San Joaquin Ferry and reached Oakland about midday. There Dr. William Botsford met us and greeted his uncle with a warm Western salute. They had not seen each other for years. The nephew was a trifle taller and stouter, with a black beard and dark eyes, but the family likeness was unmistakable. Both men attracted much attention as they stood or walked side by side, fine specimens of manhood, one in the prime of life, the other in the fulness, but not the decadence, of age.

We crossed the wide ferry and were really in San Francisco, passing through the motley crowd of many nationalities which thronged its streets. Dr. William took us to the pleasant quarters he had secured in a large family hotel near his own office, that he might see as much as possible of his uncle, and he informed us with Western hospitality and generosity that we were his guests. Every day for the next fortnight was crowded with excitement and interest. Dr. William drove us to Golden Gate Park, which it is supposed will eventually rival Central Park, New York. Then we visited the Chinese quarter. We saw them worshipping idols in their temples; we took tea and tasted sweetmeats in their eating-houses; we went one evening to their theatre, and almost fancied ourselves in China. One day we drove to the Cliff House, of which

Dr. Botsford speaks in his lecture, and we watched the sun set in the Pacific Ocean. We visited Oaklands and Montpelier, one of its summer resorts. We went up California Hill in the cable cars, and saw on either side the grand residences of the Californian millionaires, among them the splendid mansion of Mrs. Hopkins, who, two years afterwards, became Mrs. Searles. We saw the Presidio (the military quarters), and last, but not least, the Palace Hotel, of which San Francisco is so proud, and where, to our surprise, we met our St. John friends, the genial Mr. and Mrs. Murray Kay. Dr. Botsford never seemed to think of fatigue; he was eager to go anywhere or see anything his nephew thought worthy of notice. The hospitals were not omitted, and while he visited them Miss M—— went to the beautiful shops in Kearny street under the guidance of a New Brunswick friend, Mrs. W. N——, the wife of a clergyman in San Francisco.*

Sunday is a most extraordinary day in San Francisco. It appeared to be a regular gala day. The large shops were closed, but bands played, processions with their banners paraded the streets, crowds moved to and fro in holiday attire. On the first Sunday we went to Trinity (Dr. Beers the rector), and on Monday we attended a church "social meeting" held in Trinity school-house. We introduced ourselves, were warmly welcomed, and spent a pleasant evening, not unlike one in St. John; pretty decorations, nice amateur music, cake and ice cream, and a profusion of flowers,

---

* The Rev. W. Neales (brother of Canon Neales, of Woodstock, N. B.). He was rector of St. Paul's Church, California street, San Francisco. He was elected Secretary of Convention for the Diocese of California, May, 1886, and died in San Francisco in 1891.

especially calla-lilies and roses. On the second Sunday we went to Grace Church, where the rector, being an old Confederate officer, preached a very martial sermon.

At length it was time to think of our intended trip to the Yosemite, for although Dr. Botsford's power of sight-seeing appeared unlimited, his time was not. Accordingly we left San Francisco by rail on Thursday, May 20th, and reached Raymond the next morning. This is as yet the last railway station, and after we had breakfasted in a large tent, with a plentiful accompaniment of flies, we took our places with eight other passengers in a stage drawn by six horses, who dragged us laboriously over rough and dusty roads. The ascent towards the Yosemite Valley, which is 4,000 feet above the sea level, was made very slowly. We saw in the morning a smoke in the woods high up among the hills, and we zigzagged all day up the mountain side before we reached it, but the magnificent scenery prevented this slow progress from seeming tedious. Then, too, the wild flowers were a constant delight. Sometimes we would walk on in advance of the lumbering stage and gather a bouquet of eighteen or twenty different specimens. The blue lupins were in such profusion that, even more than the English "sheets of hyacinths" of which Tennyson sings, they

"Seemed the heavens upbreaking thro' the earth."

When we ascended higher the curious snow-flower thrust its spike of crimson blossoms like a red finger through the dry soil. The road was too narrow for stages to pass except at certain places, where the coaches waited for those approaching in the opposite direction. There were no bridges over the mountain torrents, and the jolting was worse than that on any "corduroy road" in Canada. By dusk we had accomplished 34 miles, and we rushed down a steep hill before arriving at Warwona (Clarke's), where we staid for the night. We left early and reached the Yosemite Valley about noon the next day. The descent into the valley is long and in many places steep. The driver would gather up the reins, and drawing his horses close against the rocky wall on one side, would allow them to dash down the hill with terrific speed. At a point about half way down and 1,500 feet above the level of the valley, we halted. It was "Prospect Point." There we had a view of the mountains which, cleft apart, form the walls of the Yosemite Valley. At a little distance to our right hand was the "Bridal Veil," which bursting from the mountain side, falls 900 feet in a volume of foam. Eager to see more we hastened on till we reached Barnard's Hotel. There we found primitive accommodations. Small rooms, just large enough to hold a bedstead, a wash-stand and a chair. At table, mountain trout, and bread and butter and—New York prices. But what mattered it? We were in the Yosemite Valley. Its snow-clad peaks were around us, and on our little hard beds we were lulled to sleep by the dash of the Yosemite Falls 2,700 feet high.

The next day was Sunday. There is a little chapel in the Valley, but as this week there was no clergyman among the visitors, the chapel was not open. Dr. Botsford says of this day: "We strolled along the river, and in the shade of the trees listened to the voice of the distant waterfalls, and looked up to the beetling rocks. Then we sat down in a shady nook and read the simple service of the Prayer Book, and felt that we were in the presence of One whose works manifested His greatness. The thought stole into the heart that ' As the mountains are round about Jerusalem, so the Lord is round about His people from henceforth even for ever.' " On our return from our walk we met Judge C——, of Cleveland, Ohio. He stopped his carriage and asked us to take a drive. Dr. Botsford quietly declined. He did not wish to countenance the thoughtlessness by which visitors generally deprive this secluded valley of its day of rest.

On Monday we hired horses and guides, and with a party of ten went up " a trail," or mountain path, to Glacier Point. Some of the party went further on to the top of Sentinel Dome, wading through snow to reach the summit. From Glacier Point we had a bird's-eye view of the Yosemite Valley, six miles long but one mile wide. There, like a brilliant emerald encircled in a rough setting, it lay at our feet, with its green meadows and trees, and its little river Merced flashing in the sunlight, while around it rose perpendicular rocky walls 4,000 feet in height. All along, down these walls cascades and waterfalls threaded their way like streams of silver, and here and there a giant mountain would lift its snowy head, sentinel fashion, far above the surrounding peaks. But no words can describe the wondrous beauty of this lovely valley, nor the magnificent grandeur of the towering heights which surround it.

The ascent to Glacier Point, along a path just wide enough for the horses' feet, occupied four hours. It was fatiguing, but not nearly as trying as the descent, which was almost as slow. It was fearful to look for hours down precipices into which a slight stumble of your horse might hurl you, and although what is justly called " the grandest rock scenery in the world " was unrolled before us, it was positive relief when we reached level ground and could canter quietly to our hotel. In the evening we gathered in the " reception parlour," a large, low room built round a huge tree, from the lower branches of which lamps were suspended. It was a curious assemblage. There were travellers from almost every state in the Union; English officers from India, on their way home on leave; a large party from Melbourne, Australia, consisting of the ex-Premier of Victoria, with his daughters and friends. It was interesting to compare notes with these fellow-colonists from the Antipodes.

The next day we began our return journey. At Warwona we made a digression to visit the Mariposa Grove of " Big Trees." Dr. Botsford gives a full account of them in his lecture, so that it will not be necessary to describe them here. We reached San Francisco on the 26th, and the doctor gives his brother a *resume* of his journey in the following letter:

SAN FRANCISCO, May 27th.

My Dear Edwin: From what I see in the papers, this may have to travel by way of Ottawa to Sackville. We are so far from the Government of the Dominion that you will probably adjourn some days before we hear of the fact. I have gone over a good deal of ground since I came here. Yesterday we returned from the Yosemite Valley and the " Big Trees." We left on Thursday last by rail for Berenda, then took the stage over mountain roads to Clarke's, 40 miles, a long and rough ride; next day 25 miles to the Valley, reaching the hotel about 12 noon. The rest of Saturday, Sunday and Monday we spent among the rocks and mountains, the last day ascending and descending a mountain trail to a point of look-out 3,000 feet up. We did this on horses over pokerish roads, where a horse stumbling might throw his rider over a precipice. Fanny ascended 1,000 feet higher, but had to go through the snow. On Tuesday morning we again took the stage, reached the hotel (Clarke's) at noon, and, after lunch, visited the grove of the "Big Trees," riding to and fro and around about twenty-four miles. Next morning had breakfast at 3.30 a. m., left at 4, and arrived 11.40 at the station, where we took the cars for San Francisco, 160 miles distant. That was luxury itself compared with the tossing, bumping, shaking, and dusty mountain wagon. Strange to say I was not tired. To-day I have completed my arrangements for our return, having taken our passages by steamer to Panama and New York. It makes the journey longer, but I think it a more pleasant method of travel. We leave on Monday, 31st. To-day we go down to Monterey, which is spoken of as a lovely place. The roses are said to be in their glory in that neighbourhood, and if they surpass those we see here, they must be grand indeed.

· · · · · · · ·

We went down to Monterey by rail, Dr. William Botsford accompanying us, and remained there two days. The following account of this place is found in one of a series of short articles which Dr. Botsford wrote for the St. John *Daily Sun*, under the heading "A St. John Gentleman's Impressions on a Western Trip":

On the 27th May we took the cars for Monterey, 125 miles south of San Francisco. They claim that there are only two trains in the world that make faster time than this line. The road was built by a syndicate, few in number, but very wealthy. They purchased some thousands of acres near and around the old town, a Spanish place founded on the shore at the head of the harbour of Monterey. This harbour is virtually an open roadstead. Near this old town the company built a very large hotel for both summer and winter resort. They also have erected a large number of cottages, some with canvas walls only, others of wood of very slight construction — in fact, streets of them situated among the trees of the Pacific grove near the shore, affording accommodation for many hundreds of visitors. The old town of Monterey lies between this grove and the grounds occupied by the hotel. It is Spanish in structure and quaint in appearance. The Hotel Del Monte is built in the midst of a grove of oaks and pines, many of which, from their gnarled appearance and size, have for ten or fifteen centuries drawn their nourishment from the fields of sand and battled with the breezes off the Pacific, which have bent their branches mainly to the east. One specimen among the most exposed is near the station. Its grizzly appearance would mark it as the survivor of many centuries, probably one of the oldest trees in the grove. Its huge trunk inclines to the east, and of the many branches not one takes a westward course — all, when twigs, were forced to yield to the winds, which, in the dim distant past, blew as freely from the ocean as they now do. It might be considered a freak of nature, but others gave evidence of a general cause being in operation. The company was wise in placing their building so as to be well sheltered in making it face to the east, so that the morning sun lightened up the broad verandah, which also afforded a protection from the afternoon winds.

We approached the hotel through an avenue of large trees, surrounded with a sward of the richest green. The entrance to the hotel was flanked by beds of roses, whilst the spaces between the pillars of the verandah consisted of arches of roses, which, climbing the pilaster, had met in the centre. We entered a large square reception hall. At one side was the office for registering our names. Looking at the other side was a queer sight to be seen on the last week of May. Around a large fire-place, basking in the genial warmth of the blazing wood, were grouped some twenty or more visitors in a circle.

Before breakfast next morning we took a stroll over the grounds. A number of Chinese were employed in watering the lawn and giving the flower beds their morning bath.

In every direction water was freely used by the aid of hose upon the flowers or movable sprinklers on the grass plots. These sprinklers could be attached to the service pipes, which, running in various directions, afford an opportunity for irrigating every part of the land. No wonder the grass was so green and the plants showed vigorous growth and such a profuse bloom of roses and flowers. It is said that on any part of the sandy soil of California, with plenty of water, you can produce any result in the way of growth, and here certainly it was manifest. As there is absolutely no winter, there is nothing to check the growth of plants. A single instance will suffice to show this. On one end of the hotel was a mass of heliotrope, twenty-four feet at the base, and extending up the side eighteen feet, except where space was required for two windows to light the interior.

Sunday, May 30th, was our last day in San Francisco. We were twice at church. The convention of the California diocese had been in session, and to mark its close there was a grand missionary service in Grace Church, which we attended. The venerable Bishop Kip was in the chancel — tall, erect and portly, although upwards of eighty years of age. After a shortened "Evening Prayer," there were several stirring addresses, and the united choirs of the Episcopal churches gave three pieces of music: Mozart's 12th

N

Mass, Hayden's "The Heavens are Telling," and Handel's Hallelujah Chorus. It was an interesting close to a delightful visit.

The next morning, May 31st, Dr. William Botsford accompanied us to the "San Jose," and after many last farewell words we steamed out of the "Golden Gate" about noon. Our three weeks' voyage to Panama was not monotonous. Occasionally we were out of sight of land, but oftener we would be near enough to hear the roar of the breakers, and to see the surf as it dashed high up against the cliffs. Sometimes the mountain ranges would rise in all their greatness above the waves, and then thick mists born of tropical sunshine and ocean vapours would roll down like a curtain over the scene; only once did we see a volcano belching forth flames, stones and lava, but it was a sight never to be forgotten. Dr. Botsford always enjoyed life on the ocean, and even this long experience of it he did not find tedious. He soon struck up a friendship with Captain ——, and was never weary of pacing the deck, looking at the distant headbanks, or watching the flying fish dart past on their gauzy wings, while he listened to the captain's stories of his stormy adventures. Then at night the ocean would glitter with phosphorescence, the stars in those clear southern skies seemed larger and brighter than at home, and when we entered the tropics the glorious constellation of the Southern Cross lifted itself out of the sea and gradually rose higher and higher in the sky. The sailors, most of them foreigners, would sing in their rich deep voices Italian or Spanish songs. Altogether it was like a tale of the Arabian Nights.

The "San Jose" made several stoppages for freight,

but owing to the violence of the surf, landing was difficult. At one port passengers, who were obliged to land,
were drawn up to the wharf in an iron cage. We did,
however, spend two days on shore in Mexico, one at
Mazathan and the other at Acapulco. Mazathan was
curious with its swarthy Mexico-Indian population, but
Acapulco was unique; its beautiful land-locked harbour is considered one of the finest in the world;
even in the time of the Spanish Armada it was the
favourite resort of the galleons of Spain as they were
sailing with their treasures across the Pacific. We
entered the harbour in the early morning; the sun
shone on three mountain ranges, which, one above the
other, formed a background to the antique city and its
groves of cocoanut trees. It was Sunday. When we
landed we saw a few women wrapped in Spanish
mantillas, with books in their hands, apparently on
their way to mass. We followed them into a quaint
Templar-like Church of Adobe. Two nuns and a few
old men and women formed the congregation. After
the short service we went to the market; it was
crowded, and the shops were all open. They were
curious, long, low buildings, without a second story,
and with gratings instead of windows, on account of
the frequent earthquakes. We walked up the hill to
Fort San Diego, and on our way saw many odd things
which furnished subjects for Dr. Botsford's ready
pencil. There is a magnificent view from the fort, and
when we looked round on the tropical scenery, and in-
haled the perfume of limes and lemon trees which were
blossoming near us, we realized that we were indeed
in Mexico, the land of Cortez and Montezuma, and
the land also of Maximilian. We returned to our ship

and steamed out of this beautiful harbour in all the glory of a Southern sunset.

There were many pleasant people among the passengers, the most interesting to us being a young married couple returning with their little daughter from ranche life in the West to New York. While Dr. Botsford and Mr. R—— talked of cattle and pasturage, the ranche, and the rainfall, Mrs. R—— gave Miss M—— an insight into the experiences of a woman's life in the West. It was probably an often repeated tale of Western life. A pretty, intellectual New England girl, tempted by a high salary, goes as a teacher to the far West. The owner of a ranche, son of an ex-governor of New York, falls in love and marries her, builds a pretty house and furnishes it. Then the struggle begins. No servants, and " when I got one I had to wait on her as if she were my guest. My health gave way, for, after baby came, the work was too much for me. My husband tried to assist, and indeed he can make beds and 'wash dishes' quicker than any woman; but I could not let that go on long." So a partner was found to take charge of the ranche, and they were returning to the comforts of civilized life.

Beside our cabin passengers, the "San Jose" carried a number in the steerage. Probably they were as comfortable as are most steerage passengers, but no where do the sharp contrasts of life strike one as forcibly as on shipboard. In the steerage, crowded quarters, the plainest of plain fare; a few yards off, comfortable state-rooms, soft beds, saloons scented with tropical flowers, and a luxurious menu of five or six courses that could hardly be exceeded in the Palace Hotel.

On Friday, May 18th, we reached Panama, and were landed by boats at the railway station. We found that we had to wait two hours for the train, but when a stroll through the town was proposed we were told it would be highly imprudent. Yellow fever, intermittent fever, Chagres fever, bilious fever, Panama fever—all were floating about in the atmosphere ready to alight on the luckless stranger. So we waited on the platform and watched the motley crowd of coloured passengers in their original costumes. A bright gauze scarf round the neck, crossed on the chest, or a little cape of embroidery, with a white skirt, were generally considered sufficient attire in that warm climate. When we started every one was eager to see the progress that had been made in the construction of the Lesseps canal. A low hill, one side of which had been partially cut away, was pointed out in one place; a ditch, a few feet deep, perhaps a mile long, in another; some blasted rocks, about the middle of the isthmus, where the canal is to cross beneath the railway; but all seems little in comparison to what is yet to be done. There were many picturesque cottages built for the employes, and we saw the red roofs of the alas! too significant hospitals. The tales of sickness and death which we heard in the cars were appalling, and we found afterwards only too true. A young telegraph operator, returning north, was one of fourteen who had gone to Panama two months before—thirteen had died of one or other of these fatal fevers; this last one was hurrying away to save his life. In the afternoon a tropical shower came on, the pelting rain forming deep pools in the soft soil. At the door of a cottage we saw, as we rushed past, a mother giving her little girl a bath *al fresco* in a pool at the doorstep, quite unconcerned as to spectators in the train or elsewhere. The isthmus scenery, which was rather rocky and picturesque on the west coast, becomes more level as you approach Aspinwall. In the meadows we saw many specimens of the dove-flower. This beautiful white lily is called *Espiritu Santo* by the natives, because, when you look into it, you see, with but a little effort of imagination, that the petals are curled up into a miniature altar, behind which the stamina group themselves into the semblance of a white bird with outspread wings.

At Aspinwall the train carried us to the steamboat landing, and we went on board immediately. It is considered prudent to do so on account of the prevalence of malarial fevers. It was a large steamer full of passengers, principally Spaniards and Mexicans. Fierce hidalgo-looking men, proud women with dark eyes and flashing jewels. It was a rapid passage without any stoppages. We sighted Hayti, strained our eyes to see San Salvador, the first land that Columbus discovered, then steering out into the Atlantic and steaming due north, we saw the Long Island electric lights and reached New York on Thursday evening. Early the next morning we were duly inspected by the health officer, and after he had assured himself that we were free from yellow fever, we were allowed to land.

Dr. Botsford was full of health and life and spirits. As we crossed a square, two little bootblacks ran up with " Shine, sir ?" They looked so eager that he good-naturedly employed them both, and passers-by smiled as they saw a tall man, his shoulders propped against an iron railing, both feet elevated on stools, and a boy rubbing away on each side. He then proposed a walk across Brooklyn bridge, as he had not seen it since it was finished. On the other side we went to see Mrs. Hartt, lunched with her, and returned to New York to take the Fall River line to Boston. When on board Dr. Botsford announced his intention of retiring early, but after supper the band began to play, and he did not think of his state-room till the last note ceased somewhat late in the evening. Saturday, Sunday and Monday were spent with our friends at Milton, talking over our travelling adventures. Monday night we left for St. John, and then the first *contretemps* occurred and it was a serious one. Dr. Botsford gives an account of it to his brother in a letter dated two days after his return, July 1st, 1886:

My Dear Edwin:

I sent you a postal from Milton saying that I would be at home by the time you received it. We returned by rail on Tuesday afternoon and I was glad to be at home again, though I have enjoyed every part of my journey very much indeed. I am glad that I have had the experience by land and by sea, and what has pleased me more than anything else is the position of "the boys" in California. [He then speaks of his two nephews and continues]: Everything went well until we reached Bangor, when, after leaving the Pullman sleeper on Tuesday morning, I went back hurriedly to get my hat, which I had forgotten. The station is a dark one, and going fast along the aisle of the car, I came in contact with the steps carelessly left by the porter, and fell headlong, striking the corner of a seat. It was a severe blow. It cracked the connection of my second rib and jarred my whole body. I felt it a good deal on the train and had to avoid conversation. To-day I am decidedly better.

In the next letter written to Mrs. Hartt, July 21st, he describes the accident and says:

"After the uncomfortable symptoms abated, I undertook the hospital, and walked about a good deal settling some business. But the concussion of the nervous system, possibly of the spine, was much more than I suspected, and the muscles of the thighs and legs became disorganized in their action. I had to rest, and kept my bed for a week. I am now steadily improving, and can move about, but must take care not to repeat my indiscretion. At present I am in good quarters in Rothesay. Mrs. H—— is, and always has been, so very kind. . . . To-morrow I intend to go to Westmorland to see my brother Edwin."

Dr. Botsford seemed to recover entirely from this accident. It was the only cloud on what he often called "two months of almost perfect enjoyment."

LECTURE ON A TRIP TO CALIFORNIA.

The love of adventure is a strong element in human nature, and the desire to read of adventures, and more especially to hear of them from the living voice, is as universal as the race. Presuming upon this natural desire to hear what may be said about other lands, and other peoples, I appear before you to-night to speak of a visit lately made to the Pacific Coast.

Before entering upon the journey, it will be well to take a cursory look at the geographical relation of the country. As you are aware, the Atlantic Ocean washes the eastern coast of the continent; the Pacific forms its bounds on the west, whilst rivers, and lakes, and mountains, and broad prairies, and alkaline deserts vary the scenery as you pass over sixty degrees of longitude which divide us here in our eastern home from the eldorado of the sunset land three thousand miles away. There are three mountain ranges. They, perhaps, form the chief factors which influence the climate of the continent, especially its middle and western portions. The first range, known as the Alleghanies, commences in the south, and, taking a north-west direction, terminates on our northern border. The second is formed by the Rocky Mountains. This range constitutes the great back-bone of the continent. It runs northerly with more or less variation until it reaches the Arctic regions. The third is the Sierra Nevada range. It bounds the saline plains which stretch between it and the Rocky Mountains. Of the effect of these ranges we will have occasion to speak as we proceed.

We left St. John on May the 3rd, and arrived in Boston early next morning. On Wednesday afternoon we left Boston, and reached Chicago at nine Thursday evening, a distance of 536 miles, passing through Massachusetts, New York, Pennsylvania, Ohio, Indiana, Illinois, and skirting the southern shore of Lake Erie.

Friday we spent in Chicago. There we met an old friend, Dr. Coleman, who for some years practiced in St. John, and we passed a very pleasant evening with the doctor and his wife. The same evening we left Chicago for Omaha, 490 miles distant, passing through Illinois and Iowa. For many hours sleep and darkness ruled, but when morning came, daylight disclosed a level prairie country, well cultivated, and of much promise. Towards evening we crossed the Missouri, and rested that night and the next day (Sunday) in Omaha. It is stated that within a radius of 500 miles there is a population of 12,000,000, and 26,000 miles of railroad.

Sunday evening we left for Ogden, 1,050 miles distant, in a Pullman sleeper, and saw nothing of the Platte Valley until we reached Brady Island Station, 170 miles from Omaha. Cheyenne was reached Monday evening, 516 miles from Omaha. It has an elevation of 6,000 feet above the sea, or 5,000 feet higher than Omaha. Leaving Cheyenne we continued our gradual ascent of the Rockies; as it was dark, the only indication I had of an approach to the region of clouds was some bleeding from the nose. The air was so rarified that the vessels yielded to the force of the circulation. We crossed the crest of the Rockies during the night and descended the Western slopes the following morning, through wild scenery and mountain ranges, among them, in the distance, the Wintah. The highest peak of this range is over 13,000 feet above sea level. That evening, after passing through Echo Gorge or Cañon, as it is called here, Weber Cañon, and Ogden Cañon, with their perpendicular rocks barricading the narrow passway, we reached Ogden. There taking passage on the Central Utah road, we landed in Salt Lake City on Tuesday evening. We spent Wednesday in rambling through the streets, looking at the buildings, visiting the Tabernacle where meetings are held and worship conducted, where ten thousand people can assemble, but which has no architectural beauty to commend it. In shape it gives the idea of a large low mound, a fit emblem of their system of social life. The new temple, however, has an imposing appearance. The main building is 120 feet high, and quantities of stone are collected, hewn and ready for the towers, which are to add 120 feet more to its height — to be used, let us hope, by a people of more correct views and practice; for Mormonism is like all abnormal conditions, a local temporary disturbance in the great river of a nation's progress — a mere eddy in the stream.

Leaving the temple and the city, we commenced an ascent of the mountain slopes. On the one side was a deep ravine, worn by the mountain stream which flashed from the depths below; on the other the wild flowers tempted us to loiter on our way; cattle were browsing lazily around. Again, the mountain side above us was alive with thousands of sheep, passing like a white cloud along its broken surface. At length we reached a point at which a panorama opened before us; Salt Lake city, with its temple and buildings, was but a spot beneath us; the plain extended to the right and left, and before us, until it touched the lake, which stretched far away to the west and north; whilst the mountains with their peaks and sides covered with snow (this was May 12th), encircled a valley, fruitful now, but made so by man's energy, and by the melting snows which yield abundant waters for the irrigation of the land.

The Mormons immigrated to that valley in 1847. The following year the whole country was ceded to the United States. In the first years of its settlement money was hardly known, there not being more than $1,000 among them. But now all is changed. Money is abundant, and a number of fine stores offer good opportunities to spend it. Among these was one large one with its sign stretching over three or four entrances, "Zion's Co-operative Store." There were many divisions and entrances, and each division confined to a special class of goods. In this store, as in Utah generally, copper cents were not used, and nothing less than a five cent piece would be taken. In all the streets water was running freely. During the heat of summer this must prove refreshing to the eye and ear. The lake is 80 miles long by 50 in width. It is intensely salt, more so than sea water by six per cent.

That evening we returned to Ogden, took our places for San Francisco, and faced the great desert which intervened. Of its desolation we were not conscious for some hours. The night closed in, and dreams of the desert may have flitted through the brain, but they did not trouble us. Next morning we awoke to the realities of that weary way. Stretches of alkaline plains, with stunted sedge grass struggling for its existence; mountain ranges far, far away, as if to mock the speed and endurance of the iron horse; rocky cliffs of every shape and size closing in as if to stop our progress; the white salt that formed the boundaries of the desert lakes, the track along which, in past times, emigrants to the west threaded their toilsome way; and now and then the one solitary wagon, with young heads looking curiously from beneath its canvas cover at the passing train, and one stout heart that for wife and family was bravely facing some hundreds of miles of sandy waste which lay before him.

This dreary valley lies between the Rocky Mountains and the Sierra Nevada, and, though a valley, is in no place less than 3,900 feet above the level of the ocean. It is surrounded with mountain ranges, which chill and rob the moist winds of their treasure, blow from what quarter they may.

About three in the afternoon we stopped at Humboldt, 450 miles from Ogden. At this station our eyes were greeted with a real oasis in this great desert; there trees, the first seen since we left Ogden, were flourishing. The grass formed a rich green sward. A fountain sent forth sounds like sweet music. Here fruitful trees were repaying the labour of man, and the yield of the universal potato was abundant. All this is the result of irrigation. Here in this great desert, with moun-tains on the one side, and a huge alkaline flat, with its barrenness and desolation, on the other, nestling under the towering cliffs as though it would claim shelter and protec-tion, is the oasis of the desert. This successful experiment proves that the desert can be reclaimed and made to be fruit-ful, and the snows which gather in winter upon the mountain will descend in rivers of blessing.

Another hundred miles, and the shadows of another night were settling down upon us. We were approaching the Sierra Nevada, and the conversation naturally turned upon the scenery before us. These mountains were the last barrier that, in former times, met the emigrants who had crossed the sandy plains. Should their journey be in winter, the snows, which are then heaped on those mountain tops from 10 to 100 feet in depth, would offer more danger to their progress than did the hundreds of miles of dreary desert which lay behind them. Many a poor wanderer, in his efforts to cross those summits, had perished, having the snow for his winding sheet. Near the summit is Starvation Camp, fitly named. Here, in the winter of 1846 and 1847, a company of 82 persons, many of them children, were overtaken by snow. They lost their cattle, and were reduced to such straits that many of the survivors fed upon the remains of their starved companions. Thirty-six perished. Of a party of thirteen who went for help, only three survived. Early in March relief was sent, but it was impossible to save them all.

How different is the lot of the traveller now. In the Pullman car we were passing over the scenes of many a hopeless struggle, and when morning lightened our road, we found ourselves rolling down the mountain slopes to the plains of California. We missed the imposing grandeur of the snowy heights. But here trees were around us in luxuriant verdure; the mountain slopes were clothed with grasses in all their freshness; vineyards dotted the hillsides and valleys; wild flowers decked the embankments; canals and ditches afforded evidence of former mining operations and of present irrigation.

The transition from the dreary wildness of the salt plains, and the beetling cliffs, with their deathlike stillness, to scenes of such living beauty, must be made before one can realize the fulness of its pleasure. Passing through Sacramento and a great extent of low, wet lands, covered with reeds, we reached the level farming country. Here a change was noticed; the winter rains had given place to the cloudless sky of spring and summer. The green of the mountain sides was replaced by the tawny hues of juiceless grass. Fields of harvested hay or ripening grain suggested autumn rather than our month of May. The surface was becoming parched and dusty; vegetation wilted, except where water for irrigation could be obtained. In fact, the earth was entering upon its period of rest, to sleep until the heats of summer were past.

Thirty miles from San Francisco we crossed the river formed

by the junction of the Sacramento and San Joaquin. Our train was run on a boat about 500 feet in length, and sufficiently broad for four railroad tracks. At this point ships and sea-going steamers were at anchor, discharging and receiving ocean freights, thus affording evidence of the great facilities for shipping in the bay and harbour of San Francisco.

Skirting the eastern shore of the bay, we approach Oakland, which is separated from San Francisco by a ferry six miles wide. Oakland is to the city what Brooklyn is to New York. It had a population of 50,000 in 1880.

Noon, the 15th of May, we embarked on board the splendid ferry-boat, which soon landed us at the foot of Market street. When we went on board we were warned to put on our overcoat to be guarded against the wind, which was fresh and cold. I expected to meet with cold when crossing the mountains, and was prepared for it, and little dreamt that the necessity for extra clothing was to be first experienced when about to enter the Queen City of the West. We took outside seats on the cable car and rode up the principal street of the city. Many people were moving on its sidewalks, among them ladies dressed in furs and seal-skin sacques, and then I felt the benefit of the caution about my overcoat, and, buttoning it more closely, enjoyed its protection against the cold, chilly wind we had to face as our car moved rapidly along. The Palace Hotel, the largest in the Union, is on this street. Other hotels and places of business line either side of the broad roadway. Cable cars, horse cars and 'busses, and men and women and children, and almond-eyed and felt-footed Chinese, were going to and fro in all the bustle of a large city.

One of the first places visited was the market. Beef, veal, mutton and lamb abounded. But, though the display was good, yet compared with similar articles in our market, I did not see anything that would be ranked among our first-class meats.

On the afternoon of the 16th, we drove in an open

barouche through the Golden Gate Park to the Cliff House. The park lies between the city and the coast. The grounds consisted of sand hills, but have been reclaimed. The grass is fresh and green, the trees are thrifty and abound. Trees which grow in southern latitudes, suggest thoughts of unchecked vegetation, and hold out the promise of increasing enjoyment for the citizens. The Cliff House is a place of much resort, and hundreds daily visit it. It is situated on a bluff which overlooks the Pacific Ocean, and above it, on a hill, there is the residence of Mr. Sutter, one of the rich men of California.

This house had beautiful surroundings, upon which its wealthy owner has lavished large sums. Leaving our carriage we ascended, by many steps formed in the solid rock, until, from its parapets, we had a view of the Pacific Ocean stretching to the west, whilst to the north and south a line of breakers rolled ceaselessly against the shore. Immediately in the foreground were the islands, which are the resort of the sea lions. These animals are specially protected by a State law. Some were basking in the sun; some were floundering with an ungainly gait; others were fighting, which they do furiously; whilst above the noise of the surf was to be heard the mournful hollow bark of the contending animals.

When preparing for this visit to the Cliff House I was again advised to take an overcoat. Again we met the chilling wind, but with a winter coat and warm knee blanket, we were well guarded. This strong sea breeze, or rather, trade wind, prevails during the summer on this coast, and makes extra clothing necessary.

Looking at the geography of this western country will enable us to understand the peculiarities of its climate. Running parallel with the coast and 150 miles from it is the lofty range of the Sierra Nevada Mountains. Along the coast are hill ranges. As summer advances this whole country, 150 miles wide and extending through several degrees of latitude, becomes heated by the sun's unclouded rays. The warmed and rarified air ascends from the heated earth. The lofty Sierras shut off all wind from the east, the supply of the displaced air must come from the Pacific Ocean. The temperature of the waters of this ocean does not vary more than two degrees during the year. The air which rests upon or moves over its surface has a corresponding temperature, and becomes saturated with its vapour. This western breeze is therefore comparatively cold when it strikes the land, and only loses this sensation when it reaches a few miles inland. San Francisco is seven degrees further south than St. John, yet its mean temperature in the month of July is 57 degrees. The months of June, July and August, when the trade winds are strong, are called their foggy season. I have stated that the ocean breeze in the first instance is loaded with moisture, but an increase of temperature doubles the rate of evaporation for every 20 degrees ; the capacity of the air to contain vapour also doubles at an equal rate. Air at 70 degrees contains twice the quantity of water that it does at 50 degrees. But not only is the chill removed by the warmer air of the land, but the greater capacity for moisture prevents the formation of any clouds, and therefore from spring to autumn, there is one blaze of sunshine over this land from the coast to the summit of the Sierra Nevada.

During the winter months the sun returns to the south ; his slanting rays no longer overheat the earth ; gentle western airs from the Pacific meet a cool reception, and unload their moisture over the land. The same winds which, in summer, felt cool on the coast, produce an opposite feeling during the winter. They are warmer than the air on the land, and make the country agreeable to all who dislike and shiver at the cold. There is no check to vegetation. Roses of every kind flourish. Shortly after my arrival I was greeted with a bouquet from an old friend, which was a foot in diameter. It contained fifty roses, among them the moss, the cabbage, the yellow, and others of various hues. The lawns of dwellings in Oakland abounded with them. The trellis work of cottages was interwoven with vines of red and white roses.

The city does not differ much from other cities on the continent, except in not being so regularly built, and in having more wooden structures. San Francisco must progress. Her harbour is a bay of vast facilities. She must continue to be the centre of business of that coast for hundreds of miles. The country around is rich in agricultural products—wheat and cattle; vegetables and vineyards; fruits of various kinds —the orange, the apricot, and the pear; with abundance of snow stored up every winter to yield its waters for summer irrigation. All these must make a city so situated continue to prosper.

Two features peculiar to the city are the cable cars and the Chinese population. The car is double. The chief one is similar to the ordinary horse car. The front of it is a cab, with open seats on its sides for passengers; with a central space for the engineer; also for the gearing which connects the car to the cable, which is beneath the roadway. In Market street, one of these cables has a length of 18,000 feet, or more than three miles. Several streets to the north of Market run parallel with it, some of them up grades steeper and longer than our King street. The ordinary speed is eight miles an hour. At this rate we went up the steep grades of California street, having a good view of the houses of the wealthiest citizens. Some of these palaces cost over a million of dollars.

The Chinese number about forty thousand. They occupy a section by themselves, and this in the very heart of the city. A visit to their quarters throws you among a people and customs as distinct as would be met in China itself. There were stores for goods; shops containing every Eastern curiosity; stalls for meats in queer forms and sizes, or for vegetables various and strange in appearance; barber shops with

o

a razor gliding deftly over tawny bare skulls; eating-houses
where you were served with tea made in Chinese fashion,
handed to you in Chinese cups by Chinese waiters on Chinese
trays; also conserves of strange substances.   There was the
Joss House, or Idol Temple, where hideous gilded images
appeal to the fears of superstitious worshippers.   There the
theatre, with the actors dressed in gorgeous robes, long feathers
floating from their head-dress, and all the tinsel paraphernalia
of Eastern life, whilst the speakers in shrill voices kept time
to a music of harsh sounds from clanking drums.   Add to
this an audience of stolid faces, as if cut out of motionless
stone.   Such scenes leave the impression that by a rub of
Alladin's lamp a genii had transported you to the flowery
land itself.

[Dr. Botsford then enters at some length on the subject
of emigration to California.   His opinion may be briefly
summed up in his own words]: From a limited personal experience, confirmed, however, by what I have heard, it appears
to me that capital is as necessary for success in California as
elsewhere.

[He then proceeds to make some remarks upon the rainfall, and says]: The winter rains stimulate vegetation of all
kinds.   Nothing could impress this more forcibly than the
"Big Trees" of the Mariposa Grove.   We visited them on
our return from the Yosemite Valley, where we had seen
nature in some of her grandest aspects.   This valley is
hemmed in by mountain walls, which average 4,000 feet in
height.   In some places they are perpendicular, in some over-
hanging, and everywhere so steep as to shut out the possibility
almost of scaling the barriers.   On our left, as we entered,
was El Capitana, with its broad front 4,000 feet.   Near it the
Falls of the Yosemite, which, at its first bound, does not
touch the mountain side for 1,500 feet, then dashing through
a rocky channel for 600 feet, again makes a sheer leap of 400
feet to the talus at the foot, or 2,700 feet in all.   On our right

"This Tree was Growing when the Sun Shone on the
Pageantries of Mummied Pharaohs."

the Bridal Veil was pouring its waters in a mass of white spray and mist as it fell 900 feet. A little beyond this was Glacier Point, about 4,000 feet high, from which, before we left, we had a panoramic view of the valley and its mountain guards, and also of two falls on the Merced River, the Nevada and Vernal, one 750, the other 350 feet high. On the north towered up the Half Dome, 6,000 feet, as if it were the pillar upon which the blue heavens rested. The whole scene was oppressive, and a deep awe fell upon us as we gazed upwards and around at the results of primeval forces. Huge masses of rocks, thrust far above the earth's surface, have remained unmoved through untold ages. Silent greatness was the impression made by the Yosemite, but life and its wondrous results is the thought suggested by the Mariposa Grove. Entering it, a number of trees from three to six feet or more in diameter commanded our admiration. Their stems, like shafts, rose to a great height before the foliage of their branches formed a canopy over our heads; but standing apart, in all the majesty of a monarch, was the oldest living tree in that Grove, the Grizzly Giant. The diameter of this tree at the ground is 33 feet. At 30 feet from the surface the trunk has a diameter of 18 feet. This it retains for about 100 feet, when it gives off its first branch, which is six feet through. Soon after, another giant stood directly in our way. Our horses stopped for about a minute, and then horses and carriage entered an archway cut through the tree. Here we stopped to realize our position. There was wood on our right and on our left and overhead, for the tree was 300 feet high. The coach (carrying six passengers), as well as the horses, were all contained in the archway. Here we are in contact with a principle of life—a principle by which this tree through many, many ages had gathered from the earth beneath, and the air above, the material which formed its growth and strength. How long? Who can tell? It is surmised 5,000 years. The shattered branches of the old

Grizzly Giant show that old age has overtaken it, that time is placing its mark upon it, as it does upon all things having life ; but the tree was old before the pioneers of the American nation landed on Plymouth Rock ; old before Columbus ventured across the western ocean ; old when the Druids worshipped amidst the oak forests of Britain ; old when the twin founders of ancient Rome drew their life from the dugs of their fierce foster mother ; old when Moses stood on Pisgah and looked upon the land where his people were to dwell.

It was a living tree when Egyptian serfs toiled to raise the Pyramids, and when I touched this living tree, I felt that my hand was on the living link connecting the present with the old, old dead past, for this tree was *growing* when the sun shone on the pageantries of mummied Pharaohs.

To return to the climate. The mildness of the winter commends itself to those who shiver at the idea of cold. The thought of grapes and oranges appeals to the imagination, and men picture to themselves a veritable Eden, where such fruits are found. But luscious fruits are not the whole of life. To bask in the warmth of a cloudless sky is not the only source of health. Other ingredients must enter into our enjoyments to produce a vigorous existence.

Wide experience shows that in the most favoured lands there will be conditions wanting for the full development of man. That a law of compensation reigns and causes an equality among the countries of the earth. That while each may excel in some special points, there are other points in which it is deficient. That the superiority of no country can be inferred from a few favoured localities, nor from a few exceptional conditions. Regard must be had to every circumstance before a balance can be struck. Let this be done, and I am inclined to look upon the claims of our own country as being equal to, if not beyond, that of the western coast.

In connection with this subject, let me state a circumstance which came under my notice some few years ago. When I

was a younger man, young enough to go upon a fishing expedition with a brother doctor, we went on wheels thirty
miles on good roads, and then some distance over a by-road,
threading our way through mud, over cradle hills and young
granite boulders until we reached a farmhouse situated on the
border of the lake, where we anticipated a good day's sport
among the fish. I need hardly tell you that though we fished
and paddled, and paddled and fished all the next day, we did
not catch a single fin. Perhaps the fish recognized our professional prowess. Well, it was late when we reached the place,
and, being tired, we intended to take to the hay mow for the
night. A hay mow, I always thought, as a boy, was a grand
place to sleep in. But no, the owner of the farm insisted
upon showing us hospitality, and persisted until we yielded.
The dwelling was a log house, but the barn was of good size
and a well enclosed framed building. The fields were well
cultivated, though in many parts the stumps still held possession. There was a look of comfort around and a look of
content in our host. During the evening the farmer let us
into the secret of his success and his contentment. Some
years before he had thought his native land a poor place, too
poor for a man who had muscle and sufficient self-assurance
to make his way in some more favoured land. He sought
the Western States, then spoken of as a land of great expectations. He sought and obtained labour in the Mississippi
Valley—worked for an employer who exacted a full return
for the wages given. He saw and felt that there was more
work for his muscles than in swinging the scythe or handling
the hoe. In fact, that fever and ague was master also, and
that the chances of being a landowner were not great. He
left and tried Upper Canada, with no better prospect. It
ended in his return to New Brunswick, his settling upon a
wilderness farm, and his being in a condition to look with
great satisfaction upon the result of his labour, and upon the
health he enjoyed. This man's experience is not a solitary
one ; it is, I believe, one among many.

Of our own country, what can we truly say? We have a climate that is healthy. We have a land well watered in every part. Springs, and brooks, and rivers abound. We have a soil that gives liberal returns. Our yield of hay is equal to that of the most favoured State in the Union, and greater than in most. Our oats, and barley, and wheat give generous crops. Our vegetables are good and prolific. Our meats — beef, veal, mutton, lamb and pork — are fit for any market. Our poultry of all kinds cannot be excelled. Apples and plums grow well. The smaller fruits are abundant. Shellfish are plentiful on our coasts, and some of the finest fish in the world are to be found in our lakes, and rivers, and seas. We may be surpassed in some particulars by other countries, yet, looking at all the conditions of existence, there is no place which can show a better average, nor hold out greater inducements to an industrious man.

In conclusion, instead of swelling the cry of discontent, and fostering a feeling of dissatisfaction with our country, every person, whilst admitting the just claims of California, should maintain the true position of our own Province:

> " Lives there a man with soul so dead,
> Who never to himself hath said,
> This is my own, my native land."

CHAPTER XII.

Sunrise and *morning* star,
    And one clear call for me,
And may there be no moaning of the bar
    When I put out to sea.

Twilight and evening bell,
    And after that the dark,
And may there be no sadness of farewell
    When I embark.

For though from out the bourne of time and space
    The flood may bear me far,
I hope to see my Pilot face to face
    When I have crossed the bar.

                    —Tennyson.

The secrets of the future are shrouded from our view, and when Dr. Botsford and his niece welcomed the year 1887 to their home, none could foresee that it was to be the last year of his busy, energetic life.

In the previous autumn a pleasant visit had been made to us by Mrs. Greaves, an English lady who came from the Church of England Zenana Society to interest Canadian women in their untaught sisters in India. When in Halifax she received an invitation from Dr. Botsford to stay at his house while she remained in St. John. We went to Rothesay to meet her, and she could scarcely believe that the brisk, ruddy faced man who asked for her in the cars was the Dr. Botsford who in Halifax had been described to her as "an old gentleman past seventy."

The winter was spent in his usual employments. The three following letters, written at this time, show the drift of his thoughts, and contain allusions to several incidents that occurred:

DECEMBER 12th, 1886.

Dear J——:

It is Sunday, and C—— is sitting opposite me looking at the *Graphic.* . . . I was at Fredericton not long since. I went to see Helen, my brother George's daughter, who died after an illness of three weeks. She spent some time with me last summer when Miss M—— was with her sister. She was a very general favourite with both old and young, so bright and cheerful. Her death cast a gloom over society, and is a terrible loss to her family. My brother George is 79 this month, a pretty good age; my brother Edwin 82; Charles 80. I am 75 next month, Bliss 73, and Blair, the youngest, 65, all healthy and apparently with a promise of some further time. I think, however, the next break will be here in St. John. If I attain 75, I do not anticipate any further addition. But man cannot tell. It is all in wise hands, and He will do as will be best. . . . On the 10th of January I visit California before an Institute audience. Writing out my lecture was like going over the country again.

JANUARY 22, 1887.

Dear J——:

I got your letter in due time; that is to say, after waiting a due time. . . . You seem to have had a sharp winter for New York. We have been highly favoured the whole of the summer, autumn, and winter thus far. During the present month there is snow sufficient for good sleighing. I occasionally take a cab to pay my visit to the hospital, but not often, as I regard it better to walk there for exercise. I know that if I did not have some inducement, I would not take sufficient exercise for health, would grow lazy and musty, and bluemoulded. I think people often suffer in old age and shorten existence by yielding to a fireside life. You will recollect that in four days I will have completed my 75th year. "Three-quarters of a century, Miss Jessie." Well, I cannot say much for the opportunities being improved. In fact, looking back, as I was doing this evening, does not give any comfort to the soul, and it is only by looking to "the refuge" that the past can be blotted out. I have a little book given me by Catherine Bogle, in Glasgow, more than fifty years ago, with a prayer and a promise for every day in the year. The text for to-day is, "Have mercy upon me according to thy loving kindness, O Lord, according to Thy tender mercies blot out my transgressions." The promise is, "I, even I, am He who blotteth out thy transgressions and remembereth not thy sins." Much do I require such a promise when I look upon the past. Poor Catherine had a short experience of life, and I believe had a firm hope when called to surrender her spirit to God. How much has taken place since then. . . . Whilst writing I have just had a beautiful bouquet sent in — roses of different varieties, Roman hyacinths, English violets, and smilax. New York can match but not beat them. Miss M—— is enjoying the flowers and arranging them. She is very busy these times; just now especially engaged in a meeting of the Bands of Mercy. . . . I have escaped colds and influenza so far this winter.

JANUARY 31ST.

My Dear J——:

We have had a long thaw and a great deal of rain, which has almost bared our streets. All in all, our winter has been a fine one, though not Californian in character. I am wonderfully well for a seventy-five year old animal; no complaint to make save that I cannot run as fast nor jump as high as I did forty years ago. We are in the midst of an election for the Dominion Parliament. I hope, and I believe, that the Government will be sustained. . . . I am expecting my brother Blair this evening. He has started for Florida, where his son, the doctor, now resides and practices.

A few weeks after writing this last letter, Dr. Botsford found himself unexpectedly in New York. His brother Blair, after staying some time in Florida, had left in apparently good health. He wrote from Jacksonville that he had never felt better in his life, but on the return voyage he was attacked with malarial fever, and when he landed in New York he was so ill that his own medical man, Dr. M——, of Dorchester, and Dr. Botsford were summoned by telegraph. For three weeks there were many fluctuations of hope and fear. Dr. Botsford watched over his brother with untiring devotion. He called in the assistance of the ablest advice, but nothing could arrest the progress of the fatal fever, and on April 7th the youngest of the Botsford brothers entered into his rest. Dr. Botsford returned with the remains to Dorchester, where, on Easter Day, all that was mortal of the popular "Warden" was committed to the grave in the "sure and certain hope of a joyful resurrection." Dr. Botsford speaks of this sad event in a letter to Mrs. Hartt, dated May 2nd, 1887:

My Dear J——:

It is time that I answered your last kind letter. I was sorry that I could not again visit you before I left New York. I was very much occupied; in fact, I did not leave my brother the last four days of his illness neither night nor day. I felt that he was in the most critical state, and I did not want to lose the smallest chance for a recovery. The case was rather singular — the result contrary to what the medical men anticipated. With a naturally strong constitution, I hoped that he would be able to throw off the disease, but the malarial poison kept too tenacious a grip of his system. His sufferings were not severe. Mrs. Botsford, at the time of his death, was too ill to travel, and did not reach home for some days after the funeral. He has left four married and one unmarried daughters, and two sons, one in Florida, the other, until now, in the Maritime Bank. The failure of this institution will throw him out of employment for the present. . . . The failure of the Maritime Bank has been a miserable failure. There will be more than a million of debts unpaid when it is wound up. I shall lose my stock, and have to pay as much more on account of being a shareholder — what they call double liability. Happiness does not depend on the amount a man possesses, and it is well that it is so. Fredericton people will suffer a good deal by the failure. There was a branch there, hence their trouble. With love to J——.

Yours affectionately,   L. B. B.

Apart from the fact of being a shareholder, and of having a nephew employed in the institution, Dr. Botsford was especially interested in this ill-fated bank. When it was reorganized in 1881 he was asked to become one of its directors, although he could bring to the position neither wealth nor business experience, but only his credit for integrity and uprightness. He rather reluctantly accepted the office, and endeavoured to fulfil its duties to the best of his ability. Any salary he received was handed over to an especial object of destitution in whom he was interested. He alludes on September 30th, 1881, "to the new position in life," which he has assumed, that of "Director of a Bank and Vice-President," and in April 17th, 1882, he writes:

"Thus far our Maritime Bank is doing well, as you will see by our monthly return when published. I was engaged to-day in. counting up the cash. We commenced with a few dollars to spare. To-day we have about $13,000 in gold, and $70,000 Dominion legal tenders. The books and cash on hand tallied to a cent. Our president is making up a regular inspector's report for the board and for the stockholders' annual meeting the first week in June."

Writing again in April, he says:

"Our Maritime Bank seems to be doing a very good business, and the directory expect to show a very good state of affairs at the annual meeting. . . . Between ourselves, I shall retire from the directory when a new board is called, for I do not feel myself sufficiently versed in mercantile matters, and in the knowledge of the mercantile community, to feel that I am in the right place."

The annual meeting was held in June. Dr. Botsford did not resign — for he was not re-elected. But until the crash came on March 8th, 1887, he never lost confidence in the bank nor in its president. Guileless himself, he was unsuspicious of others. On April 27th, 1887, a meeting of the creditors of the bank was called, and Dr. Botsford was asked to act as chairman. It might have been a wild and stormy scene, for the disappointed creditors were angry and excited. Muttered words could be heard in the crowd, accusations of "imbecility," "political partiality," "superficial piety." The weak tears of the president tended to increase rather than to diminish the general indignation. But the respect in which the chairman was universally held, the calm dignity of his manner, and the business-like way in which he conducted proceedings, enabled him to preserve order through a protracted meeting, which lasted, with but a short intermission, from 11 a. m. to 8 p. m. Business was resumed and finished the next day. The following day Dr. Botsford went to Fredericton. He laid his papers before the Chief Justice, Sir John Allen, remained one hour, and returned at once to St. John.

His own brief account of this meeting is given in a letter to his brother, April 30th. "There was material on hand for any amount of confusion and fight. But from the start I took charge. I showed no disposition to dictate, but let them know that I was firm and I kept them to work on system. I had the moral support of the sensible and order-loving members of the community. I have several times been congratulated on the meeting. . . . But what an exposé! I cannot understand it."

A few weeks after this unfortunate affair had monopolized public attention, St. John became absorbed and interested in another and more pleasing object, the Queen's Jubilee. Like almost all the houses in St. John during this memorable week, Dr. Botsford's house was filled with guests—some of his New Brunswick relatives and some of his Milton friends. He went about with them, and entered with great interest into the various ways by which St. John citizens endeavoured to demonstrate their loyalty. The Sunday services, the procession, the regatta, the fireworks, the trooping of the colours, the illumination. And at the close, on Saturday, he was on the platform

of the Mechanics' Institute, and his voice joined the
Bands of Mercy when for the last time in that happy
week the children sang " God Save the Queen." He
delighted to honour the Imperial Lady, not only as the
embodied representative of the greatness of the British
Empire, but as the highest type of the nineteenth century woman; a home-loving woman, fulfilling her
duties as wife and mother, and making her court a
model of morality and purity; an accomplished woman
with literary tastes and art culture; a wise woman,
taking intelligent interest and exercising judicious
influence in the political questions of the day, which
so deeply affect the well-being of the nation. Above
all, a good woman, setting an example of attention to
private and public religious duty.

Shortly after the Jubilee week, Dr. Botsford met, for
the first and last time, our great Canadian statesman,
the late Sir John Macdonald. There were various
entertainments given during Sir John's short stay in
our city, but the weather was not very favourable, and
Dr. Botsford only attended a splendid afternoon reception given at Duncraggan, by Mr. and Mrs. Murray
Kay. There, however, he had an opportunity of con-
versing with the able man, whose sagacity he held in
great estimation, and whose policy he so thoroughly
endorsed.

During the remainder of the summer there were
several pleasant outings in which Dr. Botsford took an
active part. As president he attended a field-day of
the Natural History Society, and had a long, scrambling
walk to the top of a hill near Lawlor's Lake, where
Professor Bailey gave an interesting address on the
rocks that rose round us.

As president, also, Dr. Botsford went up to Clifton with a large, " social " picnic of the Eclectic Reading Club. The officers of H. M. S. Bellerophon were invited, and the doctor, as active as many a younger man, was much amused by the merry games played by the " Middies " and young people of St. John, and on returning in the boat three cheers were given for the " President of the Club." Thus " swift as a tale that is told," the bright hours of the summer passed away.

In September he made his autumn visit to Milton. This year he staid longer, and seemed to enjoy it, if possible, more than usual. He was much thinner, but still he was apparently in perfect health. He would be up in the morning roaming through the fields an hour before breakfast. He was interested in watching the building of a stone bridge across a stream which ran through the farm. Sometimes he would walk beside the tall southern corn and calculate its height, or look at the busy machine at work chopping the corn and filling the Silo with the ensilage fodder, for he always entered with interest in the life that was going on around him. One day he went to Nahant to visit his niece, a daughter of his brother Blair, and he much enjoyed the breezy trip down the harbour. On Sunday, as Phillips Brooks had not yet returned, we did not go to Boston, but walked a mile through the woods to the Memorial Church at Mattapan. It was a beautiful autumn morning, bright and balmy, and as we walked under the shade of the trees, amid the ferns and wild flowers, listening to the song of the birds, Dr. Botsford enjoyed every step of the way. The service was simple and unpretentious, the rector not unlike Dr. Botsford's old friend, the Rev. G. M.

Armstrong, and this last Sunday at Milton was probably for the doctor an ideal Sunday.

When his niece returned to St. John, he met her at the station. It was only a fortnight since they had parted at Milton, but she observed that even in that time he had grow thinner and paler, and when in repose there were deeper lines on his open countenance. On inquiry, she found that within a few days he had had a return of the suffocating feeling in walking which had attacked him two years before. He said very little on the subject, appeared bright and cheerful as usual, but made arrangements for driving daily to the Marine Hospital instead of walking there. As the autumn advanced the difficulty of breathing increased. It, however, only interfered with his walking; he read, wrote, and talked as usual, and friends, though anxious, were not much alarmed. When his medical adviser, Dr. H——, was questioned, he was, of course, as reticent as Dr. Botsford himself.

Winter brought its busy occupations; there were one or two pleasant gatherings at the doctor's house, and he seldom refused the invitations of friends. He did not, however, feel quite able to be present at the annual supper given on Christmas Eve to the sailors of the Marine Hospital by the ladies of the Church of England Institute. On Christmas Day we attended the 11 o'clock service in Trinity Church, remaining to the Holy Communion. The next day, Monday, we went to the pleasant Christmas gathering at Mrs. R. P. St——'s. On Tuesday Dr. Botsford left for Sackville to spend a few quiet days with the Senator, returning at the close of the week.

The year 1887 was ended. When his niece looks

back on this time she can remember that a change was gradually taking place. There was a peace, a calm, pervading the atmosphere round him which made itself felt but cannot be described. It is, perhaps, partially expressed in the following lines from a volume of poems by Bertha, the daughter of the Scotch geologist, Hugh Miller. The book was owned and valued by Dr. Botsford :

> In secret love the Master
> To each one whispers low,
> "I am at hand ; work faster,
> Behold the sunset glow,"
> And each one smileth sweet,
> Who hears the Master's feet.
>
> Have we not caught that smiling
> On some beloved face,
> As if a heavenly sound were whiling
> The soul from our earthly place,
> The distant sound, and sweet,
> Of the Master's coming feet.

On New Year's day, 1888 (Sunday), Dr. Botsford and his niece were as usual in Trinity at the 11 o'clock service, and they again remained to the Holy Communion. The month that followed was to be the last, and perhaps the busiest of Dr. Botsford's life. On Thursday, January 5th, he presided at the annual meeting of the Bible Society. His earnest address on that occasion has already been given. He also that week presided over one of the noonday meetings for prayer, held in connection with the Evangelical Alliance on the first week in January.

In the second week in January he presided over the annual meeting of the Eclectic Reading Club. Notwithstanding the bitterly cold weather there was a

P

large attendance.   Dr. Botsford was one of the readers, and his selection was a bright, humorous piece, describing an Irishman's first experience in America.   He read it with keen appreciation of the wit, and sat down amid laughter and hearty applause.

At the beginning of the third week in January, Miss M——'s Sunday school class were invited to the house to take tea.   The doctor looked in upon them and spoke a few pleasant words.   One poor girl had been suffering for some time.   Her friends had urged her in vain to submit to a medical examination. Something in Dr. Botsford's manner, however, inspired her with confidence.   She consented to make an appointment for the next day.   Her case was thoroughly looked into, and she was assured that her illness would give way to proper remedies.   She followed the advice, and after a few months regained her health.*   This kindness to poor S—— T—— was probably Dr. Botsford's last medical act, apart from his hospital work.

The next day, Tuesday, January 17th, the Natural History Society of New Brunswick celebrated its twenty-fifth anniversary.   Dr. Botsford presided.   He opened his annual address with these pregnant words :

"'The thing which hath been it is that which shall be.' There is no new thing under the sun.   In the infinity of differences, there is, after all, an infinity of similarities."

---

*Since writing the above, one of Dr. Botsford's patients, the mother of a large family, tells me that the doctor had wonderful tact, in making his medical examinations, especially with children.   She says that instead of frightening them, he could examine a child's eyes, ears, lungs, heart or limbs, and the child would not be aware that anything was being done except that the doctor was playing with it.

The greater part of this address was given in Chapter VII., in connection with the history of the Natural History Society and Dr. Botsford's work in it. The closing paragraphs were as follows:

"During the past century science has wonderfully advanced, and as the years roll on it will lay an ever-widening basis upon which to build substantial palaces of knowledge and truth, at the same time (let us hope) with such good results materially, as well as intellectually, as will enable the race to enter upon the greatest possible amount of enjoyment. . . . But science, however definite and universal it may become; literature, however brilliant; and wealth, however enormous it may be, cannot, singly or combined, secure a permanent civilization. This can only be enduring when based upon the high principles which flow from the throne of God, for it is righteousness which truly exalteth a nation!

"In conclusion, I beg to thank you for the honour conferred upon me for many years. The society has existed for quarter of a century. During the most of that period I have occupied the chair. I am perfectly aware of my short-comings in that position. Your work has made the society what it is. The time has come when I must yield up my position into more efficient hands. 'The thing which hath been it is that which shall be.' The old must disappear from the scene, and the young must take their place. It is so ordered. It is not necessity, but duty, which demands the change. Not only do I wish that great success may attend the future of the society, but I feel assured that such will be the case. You have material that would secure a prominent position to any society, and I have no doubt that a first rank will be maintained by the Natural History Society of New Brunswick among those of the Dominion."

Dr. Botsford's idea, that " duty required a change" in the presidency, was not endorsed by other members

of the society. He tried for a time to resist his renomi-
nation, but finally yielded to the earnest solicitations
of all present, and was re-elected president.

Following his footsteps closely in this last fortnight
of his life, we find him on Thursday, January 19th, at
a large "reception" at Mrs. G. F. S——'s. There he
was uncommonly bright and cheerful. He found himself surrounded by many old friends; he chatted with
the ladies, and escorted several to the luncheon room;
he exchanged jokes and talked politics with the men.
He looked thin, but the excitement of the occasion
ligted up his face, and none could foresee that it would
be the last time that his bright smile would be seen
and his cheerful voice heard in a St. John social gathering. He speaks of this reception in a letter written
the next day to Mrs. Hartt, the last letter she received
from him. It is dated January 20th, 1888:

My Dear J—— :

Your letter of the 9th duly received. C—— came to dinner
on Sunday, and was glad to get the reading of it. . . .
To-day we have a high wind, which is drifting the snow that
fell yesterday. The temperature for the month has been well
down to zero, for a few days from two to nine below, sometimes above. Pleasant weather compared with the blizzards
of the western country. The accounts are dreadful — the loss
of life enough to make a man shiver at the bare idea of winter. I have not heard of a death from frost in either of our
Maritime Provinces. . . . I saw Mr. Armstrong at a
reception of one of the members of his congregation, Mrs.
G. F. Smith — an "At Home" from 4 to 7. Miss Murray
and I were there — a goodly turn out of the city (over two
hundred), and not less than eight doctors among the crowd.
Mr. Armstrong is very much broken, but is as cheerful as if

he had power of speech and muscle. Our city, you see, is not dead yet. It is now conceded, even by pessimists, that business is better, and affairs moving more satisfactorily. You would be surprised to see the railway station, and the bustle, and moving to and fro of the cars, and goods, and passengers.

Our street railway is well patronized, and has not been interrupted by snow as yet. It is very convenient now, and when extended round the back of the town will be more so.

The people of Fredericton have celebrated the Queen's Jubilee. Lady Tilley had a grand bazaar during the summer to build a hospital, and last month a series of tableaux, also to raise funds. They were said to be remarkably effective. Mrs. F—— and Miss N—— are living in Fredericton—Miss N—— deaf, Mrs. F—— deafer. It only wants one more to make the superlative. I certainly have started on that road, and already find it troublesome to hear conversation unless near and directed to me personally. Can't expect much else. Next Thursday, if living, I shall be threescore and sixteen years old—six years more than the allotted average. I can't expect the dial to go back, and as certainly cannot look for its continuance much longer. I saw Prudie the other day; quite proud of her baby. N—— I saw on Tuesday at the meeting of the Natural History Society. She is looking well. Her husband, Mr. G. U. Hay, promises to rank high as a member of the society in many respects, but especially in botany. I made an effort to resign the office of president, but they insisted that I should continue in it. I "guess" another year they will be glad to have another president, perhaps be *compelled* to do so. I have been president from its beginning—a quarter of a "century, Miss Jessie."

With love to Addie, in which Miss M—— joins, I must bring this scrawl to an end.

Yours affectionately,

L. B. Botsford.

On Thursday of the following week, the last week
in January, a few friends had been invited to spend
Dr. Botsford's 76th birthday with him, but on Wednesday night he had a severe attack of pain during
the night; he did not explain to his niece the nature
of the attack, but he said if it had lasted much longer
he could not have lived through it.   He seemed weak
and weary through the day, which was damp and
rainy.   The little gathering was postponed.   The next
morning, Friday, the doctor rose early and appeared
as bright as ever; he wrapped himself in his cloak
and muffler, and to his niece's astonishment told her
he had some business to transact with Dr. Steeves,
which would probably detain him all day.   He returned from Carleton in the evening, none the worse
for his exertion.   On Saturday he went to the Marine
Hospital and spent the rest of the day as usual.   On
Sunday, January 29th, we were in Trinity, and in the
evening, after some hymns had been played and sung,
the doctor called for recitations, he himself repeating
that picturesque poem on the death of Moses beginning "By Nebo's lonely mountain."   He said it was
the only poem he did or could' remember.   On Monday he went to the hospital, and in the evening while
Miss A——* played some lively marches, the doctor
walked up and down the drawing-room marking the
time vigorously with his footsteps.   He retired early,
and when his niece went to his room to inquire if he
wanted anything, he asked her to read his daily bible
verses to him from the little book to which allusion has

---

*A young friend from the country who was staying with us for a few
days.

been made in one of his letters. She did so, and the last good-night was said without any anticipation of sorrow.

The next morning, Tuesday, January 31st, his bright, cheery voice was heard on the stairs: "Fanny, it wants but ten minutes of eight." "Please ring for prayers. I am all ready," was the answer. The bell was rung. Miss M—— came down stairs and entered the breakfast-room. The light of a bright winter's morning was streaming in, a large fire blazed in the grate, the bible was lying open on the breakfast table, but the beloved uncle, who had been always ready to meet his niece with a cheerful morning greeting, was not standing in his accustomed place on the hearth rug. He was lying unconscious on the sofa, breathing heavily. To ring the bell and send for a medical man was the work of an instant. Before any one came a few simple restoratives were tried in vain. The laboured breathing ceased, the kind blue eyes opened once more, but the mystery of death had already veiled them, and with that last effort the spirit departed. When the medical man came a hasty examination was made. The heart had ceased to beat, and those saddest of all sad words were heard, "He is gone."

During the next two days the house was filled with many coming and going. All wished to take a last look at the noble features so calm in the repose of death. Thursday was a bright winter's day. Trinity Church was crowded. The sunshine poured in through the West window, and rested on the "Resurrection flowers" with which loving friends had almost hidden the dark coffin. There was no gloom. You seemed to realize the scene in Bunyan's great allegory where friends accompany the "Pilgrims" with music and singing, as they move towards the Dark River upon which the glory of the Celestial City shines. The first words of the first hymn gave the key-note to the service, "Forever with the Lord," and the whole congregation appeared to take up the triumphant refrain:

> "Forever with the Lord!"
> Amen, so let it be;
> Life from the dead is in that word,
> 'Tis Immortality.

"The funeral was attended by a very large number of citizens representing every walk of life. The pall-bearers were Messrs. John Sears, S. S. Hall, T. W. Daniel, Boies DeVeber, W. Girvan and R. W. Crookshank. The chief mourners were Hon. Senator Botsford, George Botsford, Clerk of the Legislative Council, and Judge Botsford of the Westmorland County Court, brothers of the deceased, and following them in the long funeral procession were judges, including the Chief Justice, clergymen, senators, barristers and indeed eminent representatives of every profession and calling. The New Brunswick Medical Society came directly after the mourners, almost all of the local members attending, and then came delegates from the Natural History Society, the Historical Society, the Bible Society, the Evangelical Alliance, the S. P. C. A. and other bodies, with all of whom the deceased had been connected. The impressive burial service of the Church of England was conducted by the Rev. Canon DeVeber, and the Rev. A. J. Gollmer (Canon Brigstocke being absent from the city). As the funeral procession left the church, the Dead March in Saul was played on the organ."—*St. John Daily Sun, Feb. 3rd,* 1888.

The place where Dr. Botsford's remains rest in the Rural Cemetery is marked by a simple marble monument, on the top of which rests a beautifully sculptured open Bible. Across the leaves are the words,

"He was not, for God took him."

Below the name and date is the sentence,

"A Christian Philanthropist and man of Science,"

and one side of the monument bears the inscription,

"For twenty years President of the New Brunswick Auxiliary of the British and Foreign Bible Society."

On the Sunday following Dr. Botsford's death, an earnest sermon was preached in Trinity Church, which was thus reported:

"The Rev. Canon Brigstocke preached yesterday morning, in Trinity Church, on the character of a godly man, from Psalm i, 1, 2: 'Blessed is the man that walketh not in the counsel of the ungodly, nor standeth in the way of sinners, nor sitteth in the seat of the scornful. But his delight is in the law of the Lord, and in his law doth he meditate day and night.' And after dwelling on the different features of that character as set forth in that passage, and holding it up as an object of high ambition, that God may bless us and make us a blessing, he referred to the late Dr. Botsford as follows: Such, we believe, was the ambition, and such the scriptural attainment of him who, in God's mysterious providence, was called so suddenly and so peacefully to his rest during the past week. Possessed of strong individuality of character, which was guided and moulded by a simple and firm faith in his God and Saviour, he was ever ready to devote his talents and opportunities for the promotion of the intellectual, the moral, and the religious interests of this community. The number, and the nature of the positions he occupied, testify to the respect in which he was held, and his

readiness for every good work. Of these there was none in
which he took greater delight or interest than in the New
Brunswick Auxiliary of the British and Foreign Bible
Society, over which he presided for so many years. Lover of
the Bible himself, and knowing it to be a revelation of God
to man, he took delight in promoting its circulation throughout the world. And was it not significant of this feature of
his character, that his last act was to open the sacred volume
for his accustomed family reading when his summons came to
call him away from his earthly labours, and to enter into rest.
It was a peaceful and merciful end of a godly life. As an upright citizen, a Christian friend, a godly layman; as a moral
and spiritual power he will be greatly and widely missed; but
he has left behind him the record of an unblemished life, and
the name of LeBaron Botsford will ever be held in blessed
remembrance. And why may we thus speak and think of
him? Because, like all believers, he walked with God, and so
was blessed himself and a blessing to others. His sudden
and unexpected call did not find him unprepared, because a
steady and unconscious preparation was going on in days of
quiet routine and in times of tranquility and health. How
would it have been had the summons come to ourselves?
Are we prepared to give up our account and to stand in some
immediate manner in the awful presence of God? Now is
the time given for gaining a true and firm trust in God. It
is now when nothing disturbs; now when no pain afflicts,
when faculties are not clouded, that we can learn to believe
and love and obey God. Let the suddenness with which God
was pleased to visit his servant lead us to consider our latter
end, so that we may be ready whenever our summons shall
come, and be able to respond to the voice that calls, ' Even so,
come Lord Jesus.' "—*St. John Daily Telegraph, February
6th,* 1888.

On the anniversary of Dr. Botsford's death the following poem, written by his niece, Ellen Murray, was

sent as a memorial to relatives and friends, and with
these verses this memoir closes :

I.

Oh! not with tears
They greet the hero when his work is done,
And with the glories of the setting sun
    His home he nears.

The bells ring out,
The road is deep with shining leaves of bay,
His friends and kindred crowd the homeward way
    With song and shout.

Arch after arch
Spans with its banners sunlit path and gate ;
The highest in the city, robed in state,
    Attend his march.

The joyful ranks,
With sound of viol, enter through the gates
To where enthroned his smiling Sovereign waits
    With gracious thanks.

II.

Oh! not with tears
They greet in heaven Christ's soldier brave and true,
The faithful proved all life's long journey through,
    From youth's bright years.

The silver bells
Ring in the Holy City, open wide
Stand the great portals, all the river tide
    To music swells.

Kindred and friend,
Souls he had helped, sad ones he comforted
Throng out, in glad procession. "His," they said,
    "Joy without end."

And up the golden street
They lead him smiling.   High uplifted there
The Central Glory shines.   He kneels to hear
The welcome sweet.

III.

So not with tears
We to the nearer shore accompanied him ;
Our earth was darker and our homes more dim,
Yet without fears.

We said " Farewell,"
While hymn and organ chanted " With the Lord ;"
And from the window with the Form adored
The glories fell.

Among the flowers
We took the last long look and let him go,
Content that never loss nor grief nor snow
Should blight his hours.

Content towards
Fair Paradise to look, and, trusting, say,
" He is not dead, but, happily, to-day
Is with the Lord."

— Ellen Murray.

APPENDIX.

MEMORIAL LETTERS.

Many kind letters of sympathy were received after Dr. Botsford's death. Extracts from a few are given, as they seem to throw a side-light on the memoir:

[From Sir **Leonard Tilley**.]

GOVERNMENT HOUSE, February 28, 1889.

I thank you very much for the "In Memoriam" (the poem) kindly sent through Lady Tilley. To be reminded of the life and lovely Christian character of so good a man as was your uncle must be of service to all who had the pleasure of his acquaintance, and the reminder thus given by the "In Memoriam" is therefore of great value.

Those who knew him best esteemed him most. It may truly be said of him, "Being dead he yet speaketh."

Again thanking you, I remain,

Yours very sincerely,

S. L. TILLEY.

[From Rev. Edmund F. Slafter, D. D., Registrar of the Diocese of Massachusetts.]

BOSTON, 249 Berkeley Street,
February 4th, 1888.

I need not tell you how much surprised and grieved I am to hear of the death of the good and noble Dr. Botsford. I most sincerely sympathize with you in this inexpressible loss. Your whole community will feel the blow. A pillar has been removed from your social edifice, and a strength and vitality has gone out of it that can never be restored. It is difficult fully to estimate the power in a community of a strong, good

(251)

man, who is always on the side of right, never swayed by any
selfish motives, and never driven from the path pointed out
by a clear, healthy and sensitive conscience. Of such men
the world has not too many. Their presence is more than a
benediction : it is a gift of unseen spiritual power that elevates,
enriches and sanctifies all about them. Such was Dr. Botsford's whole life, and its withdrawal from the society of St.
John will be seen and felt by all who knew him well. . . .

EDMUND F. STAFTER.

[From the Rev. Frederick S. Sill, Rector of St. John's Church, Cohoes, N. Y.,
former Curate of St. Paul's Church, St. John.]

THE RECTORY, February 17th, 1888.

I want to add my token of sympathy for you, and to express my own sense of a friend lost for a while. Every day
you must miss your uncle more and more. . . . I have
read with much interest the notices of Dr. Botsford's death
in the St. John press, and was glad to see how a man of his
many-sided traits was so well appreciated by his contem-
poraries. One could not be brought into contact with him
without being impressed with the great reserve force of
gentleness and manliness he had. Whether as physician,
philanthropist, scientist, or public-spirited citizen, one might
meet him ; one would like him best for being the true, sincere, upright, Christian man he was.

Certainly the circumstances attending his death, the preparation for the morning prayer, the last thoughts evidently
on things of God and eternity, made it seem more like a
translation than a dying.

It must have been a great comfort to you, in Canon Brigstocke's absence (which no doubt he regretted very much),
to have Canon DeVeber perform the rites of burial. We
were all so much associated together at Trinity and St.
Paul's, and especially close were Dr. Botsford's relations
with the rector's family for so many years, that it must have
seemed a most fitting thing for him to give burial to his old
friend's body. . . .   FREDERICK S. SILL.

[From H. W. Frith, Esq.]

JANUARY 31st.

I have just heard of the **very** sudden death of Dr. Botsford. I suppose that the gathering of a ripe and godly Christian into the garner of **the Lord** should not **be a matter for** mourning; but to **you,** who **have** been so **long his companion** and sympathizing **friend, the** loss, however much **in the** course of nature, **must be very** great, and all the more so from the very **fitness of your uncle** for the change. Few men could **be more missed either in** private or public life. His activity, his genial **hilarity,** his participation in so **many good** works, and **the grand** example of his sterling **character, combined** to make **him a** citizen, rare in these days, **and whose** place will not soon be filled. . . . **H. W. F**RITH.

[From James R. Ruel, Esq.]

FEBRUARY 7th.

I received this **morning the** enclosed pamphlet **for your** deeply regretted relative, **Dr.** Botsford, from an **old friend,** Mr. Swabey. He will **learn the** sad news **from me in a few days,** and like all **of us in** this city, will **mourn over our loss.** It is right **to weep on such an** occasion — we **have sacred authority for it; yet as** true Christians **we should rejoice —** rejoice at the happy reunion with those we have in another and a brighter world. Surely it may be said my friend was translated — a moment here, the next in glory, seeing the King in all His beauty. God grant that my last end may be like his — the sudden summons, the glad awakening. . . **J**AMES **R. R**UEL.

The following quaint, kind letter was written by the late Mr. T. M. Deblois when he was upwards of ninety years of age:

134 F**EDERAL S**TREET, Salem, Mass., Feb. 2, 1888.

Dear Miss Murray, — On reading a late St. John *Globe* last evening, I was sadly grieved to notice that it had pleased the

Q

Almighty Disposer of events suddenly to remove from the midst of his many friends your kind-hearted and, in every sense of the word, good uncle, Dr. Botsford. I deeply sympathize with you, his relatives, and the community, on this melancholy occasion. I shall feel his loss greatly. Our acquaintance extended over half a century, during which he had been a warm-hearted, kind friend. When absent from St. John we were frequent correspondents; to me his letters were always very acceptable and interesting. It was only the other day I received a kind letter from him. Little did I expect our correspondence was so suddenly to terminate. I intended to have written him this morning relating to the Rev. Dr. Courtney, of Boston, a gentleman highly esteemed in his profession. Thus it is, "*L'homme propose, et Dieu dispose.*" I shall write our mutual friend, Mr. Swabey, advising him of the sad loss so many have sustained. He will feel it sadly, as we all do.

I remain, my dear Miss Murray, yours truly,

T. M. DEBLOIS.

APPENDIX II.

"MEMORIAL RESOLUTIONS"

PASSED BY SEVERAL SOCIETIES AFTER DR. BOTSFORD'S DEATH.

I. COLONIAL AND CONTINENTAL CHURCH SOCIETY.

Memorial Minute to the Memory of the late LeBaron Botsford, M. D.

The Corresponding Committee of the "Colonial and Continental Church Society," at their first meeting of committee after the removal by death of the late Dr. Botsford, place upon record of their minutes that they lament very much the decease of their highly valued friend and fellow-labourer, Dr. LeBaron Botsford, who was so suddenly, but so peacefully, removed from them on the 31st January, just after he had entered on his seventy-seventh year, they would record the sense they retain of the many important services rendered by him in various ways to the society they represent.

It was in the year 1851, when the association was first formed, that Dr. Botsford joined its ranks, and has ever since continued a steadfast supporter of the organization, and they can fully testify that they have ever found in him an earnest and intelligent colleague, comprehensive in his views, sound in judgment, and intensely desirous of upholding the principles of the society and those great evangelical doctrines which have been the strength of the church at home and abroad, contributing to its efficiency and usefulness.

The number of societies with which he was connected were represented at his funeral by sympathizing mourners. This of itself testified the deep and wide-spread esteem which his high character and honourable career had gained for him.

"The memory of the just is blessed."

(255)

II. BIBLE SOCIETY.

At a meeting of the Committee of the New Brunswick Auxiliary Bible Society, held 7th February, 1888, the following resolution was moved by the Hon. John Boyd, seconded by Rev. A. J. McFarland, and unanimously adopted:

"Since our annual meeting it has pleased Almighty God to call home our dear brother, Dr. LeBaron Botsford, whose bright, cheerful, joyous spirit calmly and peacefully left its earthly tenement, when he gently fell asleep on Tuesday last.

"At this, our first meeting after, we desire to express our thankfulness to God for the long, useful and eminently benevolent life He permitted to our friend, for the quiet influence of that life in many a sick chamber, and the wider sympathy of its spirit in public, largely permeated by that Word which he took as his daily counsellor, and which led him to co-operate with all who were joined together in the circulation of that Word, through the organization of this society. For nearly half a century was he a member of this committee, for very many years vice-president, and twenty years president of this Auxiliary of the British and Foreign Bible Society, for which office he was specially fitted by his catholicity of spirit, and we desire to place on record our estimate of the unwearied diligence, unswerving fidelity, and continued devotion to its interests which so eminently distinguished his course, more especially during the latter period of his life, after his marvellous restoration to health some fourteen years ago. His tireless activity in every good work of a national, social, educational, scientific and religious character, gave hope of even a longer life than the seventy and six years permitted to him, now so peacefully ended by his entrance into that ' Rest which remaineth for the people of God.'

"This Committee desire also to express their sympathy with his niece, the home friend and companion of his later years, and other relatives in whom his departure awakens sad and tender recollections."

III. YOUNG MEN'S CHRISTIAN ASSOCIATION.

At a meeting of the committee of the Y. M. C. A., the following preamble and resolution was passed:

Whereas, It has been the pleasure of Almighty God to remove from our midst and take to Himself Dr. LeBaron Botsford, who, at the age of seventy-six years, peacefully fell asleep in Jesus on the thirty-first day of January last, while in the act of religious duty; and

Whereas, For many years our beloved brother was actively identified with our Association, holding official relations as President, Trustee and member of our Managing Committee, and manifesting his interest, not only by personal endeavour but by a most generous financial support in advancing its welfare, we remember him as being amiable in disposition, generous in sympathy, sincere in friendship, faithful in good work, and faithful in the discharge of duty, doing justly, loving mercy and walking humbly and in integrity before his God, we feel that it may be said of him that the law of his God was in his heart, and that, having fought a good fight, having finished his course, having kept his faith, henceforth there is laid up for him a crown of righteousness which the Lord, the righteous Judge, shall give him at that day;

Resolved, That we cannot allow the occasion to pass without recording our profound respect to his memory, for his public and private worth, and to extend to the relatives and friends of the departed brother our sincere sympathy, and to commend them to the care of Almighty God, and the comfort and consolation of his Holy Word.

IV. EVANGELICAL ALLIANCE.

Resolution adopted at the Annual Meeting of the Evangelical Alliance of St. John, N. B., held March 19th, 1888, with reference to the late LeB. Botsford, Esq., M. D., &c.

Resolved, That, by the decease of Dr. LeB. Botsford, the Evangelical Alliance have been deprived of the society of a member whose services, alike on the score of his ability and of the spirit displayed by him on all occasions, were simply of inestimable value.

Sound in judgment, and single-minded in his every aim, governed by the loftiest sense of duty so far as his own conduct was concerned, and yet singularly conciliatory and generous in his bearing to others; at once firm in his attachment to his own views of truth, and catholic-minded in the construction placed by him upon the views of those differing from him, Dr. Botsford presented in his demeanour the happy blending of well nigh every quality of disposition requisite to the character of an ideal Christian gentleman.

Profoundly philanthropic and overflowing with interest in every matter bearing upon the public welfare, his estimates of all questions arising in these connections were invariably based upon the dictates of that Book which was to him in very deed "A light unto his feet and a lamp unto his path;" that Book, the study of which, under the guidance of a scholarship various and accurate, was his daily pleasure, and labouring for the wide-spread diffusion of which was the source of his deepest joy.

In his decease the Evangelical Alliance lament the withdrawal from their ranks of one of their oldest and most loyal members, of an attached and sympathetic friend, of a counsellor than whom no one was listened to with more profound respect, of a man to whose example they could ever refer as that of the kindliest and most uniformly consistent of Christians.

In common with the whole community, the members of the Alliance mourn the departure of one to whom all looked as to a father, because of his dignified wisdom, and to a trusted friend because of his genial courtesy. They rejoice, at the same time, in their remembrance of the many proofs evincing that "his path was as the shining light," and in the conviction which they can confidently cherish that their loss is his gain, being persuaded that their brother, having "fallen on sleep," has "entered into the joy of his Lord."

In name, and by appointment of the Evangelical Alliance of St. John, N. B.

D. MACRAE,
Corresponding Secretary.

V. PROTESTANT ORPHAN ASYLUM.

Resolutions adopted relative to the death of the late Dr. LeBaron Botsford.

The Directors of the St. John Protestant Orphan Asylum, at the first meeting after the death of the late Dr. Botsford, adopted the following resolution :

Whereas, It has pleased Almighty God to remove from among us, our late lamented colleague and fellow-labourer, Dr. LeBaron Botsford, who has been a Director ever since the organization of the Institution ;

Therefore Resolved, That the said Directors desire to give expression to the sense of personal loss they have sustained by his death. They would record their high estimation of his character, and of the valuable services ever rendered by him since the formation of the Orphan Asylum. Immediately after the sad visitation of Asiatic cholera in our city in 1854, our late brother was appointed one of a provisional committee of seven laymen, of whom only two now survive, to solicit funds for the erection and endowment of an Orphan Asylum, and at a subsequent public meeting held in the Mechanics' Institute, he was the first ably to advocate the necessity for such an institution, and towards which he gave two lots of land on Summer street, Portland, N. B., which are still the property of the Board. He had ever contributed largely towards the maintenance of the Orphanage, and in various ways manifested a deep interest in the work, which he regarded as a special charge committed by God to himself, and his fellow-workers, thus to care for the spiritual and temporal welfare of destitute orphans in the community.

VI. HOME FOR AGED FEMALES.

At a meeting of the President and Directors of the Home for Aged Females in the City of St. John, held on Thursday, the 23rd day of February instant, the following resolution was moved by the Rev. G. M. Armstrong, seconded by Mr. Crookshank, and unanimously adopted :

The Directors, in recording with deep regret the loss which this institution, in common with many others of St. John, and even with the city itself, has so recently suffered by the sudden, though happy, removal of Dr. LeBaron Botsford, would humbly praise God for the many graces given to his servant, their friend and brother, who so peacefully entered his rest on the 31st day of January last. As a physician, his ability and benevolence were highly prized by many inmates of the institution, while his happy and lively disposition endeared him to all. By his Christian self-devotion and nobleness of character he was a living witness unto the truth, and, while he had the courage of his own convictions, he respected those of others, causing his presence at the Board, which he constantly attended, to be sorely missed, and the Directors tender their heartfelt sympathy to the niece and other bereaved relations of their loved and valued colleague.

[Extract from Minutes].

H. LAWRANCE STURDEE,

Secretary.

VII. NATURAL HISTORY SOCIETY OF NEW BRUNSWICK.

Copy of a Resolution passed by the Natural History Society of New Brunswick, February 6th, 1888.

Resolved, That the New Brunswick Natural History Society place on record an expression of the loss it has sustained in the death of its late President, Dr. LeB. Botsford, who, since its organization, has been so closely identified with its interests ; who had entered so heartily into all its aims and objects, and had given it that support and encouragement which his generous and self-sacrificing spirit prompted.

W. J. WILSON,   G. F. MATTHEW,
    Recording Secretary.   *President.*

VIII. ST. JOHN ANTI-TOBACCO ASSOCIATION.

At the regular meeting of the St. John Anti-Tobacco Association, held last evening, Capt. Pritchard presiding, the following resolutions were adopted:

Whereas, It has pleased Almighty God to remove from the scenes of his earthly labours, Dr. LeB. Botsford, Vice-President of this Association; and

Whereas, This Association, by the death of Dr. Botsford, loses one of its most faithful co-workers in the cause for the suppression of the use of tobacco, and all the evils pertaining thereto;

Therefore Resolved, That this Association, while humbly bowing to the will of our Divine Creator, deeply regret the demise of our late Vice-President, whose genial disposition and untiring zeal in all good works for the religious and moral advance of his fellow-beings, made him an honoured member of the community and a true friend to the needy; and

Further Resolved, That a copy of these resolutions be sent to the different city papers for publication.

APPENDIX III.

NOTICES OF THE PRESS.

DEATH OF DR. LEB. BOTSFORD.

Dr. Botsford, whose sudden death yesterday morning caused such a profound sensation throughout the city, was a son of the late Hon. Wm. Botsford, one of the Judges of the Supreme Court, and formerly Speaker of the House of Assembly, and grandson of Amos Botsford, Esq., a Loyalist, formerly of Newton, Conn., who was Speaker of the first assembly elected after New Brunswick was constituted a separate province. Dr. Botsford pursued his medical studies at the University of Glasgow, where he graduated in 1835. On his return to this province he entered into the practice of his profession in Woodstock, and some time later, in 1840, he established himself in St. John, where he had enjoyed a successful practice for near half a century. For about twenty-five years he had been attending physician at the Marine Hospital, and was the incumbent at the time of his death. He was appointed one of the physicians and surgeons of the Provincial Hospital when it was opened June 13th, 1865, and in March, 1868, he resigned his connection with that institution. Dr. Botsford was married to Miss Main, of Glasgow, who died in October, three years since, leaving no issue. He was an active member of Trinity Church, for several years President of the Bible Society, was for about twenty-five years President of the Natural History Society, and was deeply interested in the Historical Society, the Evangelical Alliance and the Y. M. C. A., and everything tending to the welfare of the community. His cheery bearing and pleasant manner made him a universal favourite.

For some time Dr. Botsford had felt apprehensive of sudden death from an organic disease of the heart. The attack

(262)

yesterday morning was unlooked for by his family, and terminated fatally before Drs. Harding and Johnston, who were instantly summoned, could reach his residence.

Dr. Botsford was a gentleman of good natural ability, enriched by a life of extensive reading and study. Readers of the *Sun* will recall with pleasure his interesting and instructive letters in this paper, while on a visit to the Pacific coast, and which afterwards furnished the material for one of the most interesting lectures in the Mechanics' Institute course of last season.—*St. John Daily Sun, February 1st*, 1888.

THE LATE DR. BOTSFORD.

Seldom has the sudden death of a citizen given a stronger shock to the community than was made by the announcement of the death of Dr. LeBaron Botsford yesterday morning. He had been long a prominent and active figure in our midst, and though he had considerably passed the allotted three score years and ten, he was yet full of energy and usefulness. As a physician of good skill and judgment he had long since won success in his profession, but it was in other lines of intellectual, moral, and religious activity that he has been chiefly known to the public of late years. With the work of the British and Foreign Bible Society, the Evangelical Alliance, the Young Men's Christian Association, the New Brunswick Historical Society, and the Natural History Society he was actively and prominently identified for many years down to the day of his death, and in several of these he had filled the highest positions.

He was a man of strong individuality, extensive knowledge, and humane and generous impulses. In Dr. Botsford the poor had a sympathetic friend, while among all classes he was ever ready to every good word and work. Those who knew him best know how well he deserved the titles of a true friend, a good citizen, and a devout Christian.

The manner of his death was, we think, eminently happy and desirable. He had lived a good and useful life, and one of untiring activity in the service of his fellow-man. He had filled up the measure of man's allotted days, retaining till the last the full possession of his physical and intellectual powers. Then he was permitted in the quiet of the home he loved to close his eyes peacefully and painlessly for the last sleep. To him death came suddenly, but with no harsh summons—rather as an expected and not unwelcome messenger, inviting him to rest and reward. In the calm of the bright morning hour he passed out into the fuller light, liberty and repose which lie beyond the confines of earthly life.

Dr. Botsford's demise creates a sad blank not only in the home circle, but in almost every line of moral and religious activity in our midst, and in the larger circle of citizenship as well.—*St. John Daily Telegraph, February 1st,* 1888.

A GOOD CITIZEN.

Probably no citizen of St. John was better known at home or abroad than Dr. Botsford. His genial, cheery, hearty manner, his friendliness, his activities in many directions, brought him in contact with people of all classes and creeds. Notwithstanding his natural kindness he was a man of strong views and decided convictions, and sometimes he did not hesitate to sharply express himself. Thirty-five to forty years ago he was an active figure in our political affairs, although, we believe, he never sought representative honours. In the work of the New Brunswick Association in 1849–50 there was no more active man, and he declined to accept the presidency because it was not as decided as he thought it should be. He strongly resented the interference of Earl Gray and the Colonial Office in our affairs. As we write we have before us a letter of his, in which he ably sets forth his views on the Colonial future. In church matters he was an active Low Churchman, and did not hesitate so to declare himself. . . On almost every subject inviting the attention of an intellectual mind Dr. Botsford had opinions. His appointment to a public position—a matter which at the time excited a very hot discussion in St. John, and caused a sharp feud in the Liberal ranks—withdrew him to some extent from active participation in public questions, but he was a man whose intellect never dulled, and whose interest in the works of humanity never slackened. His works of benevolence and charity were unending, and in all conditions of life there are many persons who, by his death, will lose a sincere friend.—*St. John Evening Globe, January 31st, 1888*

INGENIOUS CONTRIVANCE.

Dr. Botsford, of St. John, New Brunswick, forwards to us an ingenious contrivance adapted to the lifting of patients. It consists of a framework the size of the bed or mattress, the sides of which are made of wooden bars, and end pieces of plate-iron an inch and a half wide and three-sixteenths of an inch in thickness, pivoting in the centre. These are so contrived that when the lift is placed on the bed, the framework falls on each side, the canvas is slackened, and the patient rests on the mattress or bed provided for him, but when the framework is lifted, a catch prevents the pivot acting beyond a straight line. Transversely across this framework canvas is securely stretched, excepting for about the middle fourth ; here one or more wide strips are fastened by hooks, and are readily removable. Strong cords are fastened to the framework of the lift by means of hooks and rings, four in number, and are attached to a ring through which the hook at the end of a lever, six or seven feet long, is passed. This lever has a second hook, which is attached to the end of a chain suspended from the ceiling, and at its extreme end is a chain which can be fixed to a staple or some secure hold while the patient is being attended to after having been lifted from the bed. This lift, which can be easily and cheaply made, has been tried by Dr. Botsford in the Marine Hospital of St. John, and would be very useful in cases where the medical man was shorthanded, and the patient required much nursing.—*Extract from the Lancet, January 2, 1886.*

ADDRESS BEFORE THE NATURAL HISTORY SOCIETY ON "THE THUMB."

AN EXPLANATION OF ITS WONDERFUL CONSTRUCTION, IMPLYING DESIGN AND A DESIGNER, AND AIDING THE INTELLECTUAL AND MATERIAL PROGRESS OF MEN.

The subject which I submit to-night for your consideration can hardly be termed scientific, and yet it certainly is one which bears, though indirectly, upon our position as a Natural History Society, for it treats of a condition which appears to be necessary to progress among men. It will suggest thoughts to a reflecting mind, and perhaps lead to metaphysical questions, as to the why and wherefore of our existence, and more especially whether design reigns in the world of which we form a part. Man is an intellectual being. He soars upward in his contemplation of the material universe, penetrates the vast profound filled with dazzling suns, measures their distances, and analyzes the very elements of which they are composed. On the other hand, by the aid of instruments, he investigates the secrets of nature hidden from the unaided vision of mortals, and seems to measure not only the minutest organisms of living existences, but to scrutinize the infinitesimal molecules in their action and relationship.

It is evident that without the aid of instruments it would be impossible to arrive at the knowledge we now possess. How could man, with even his great mental faculties — and we must acknowledge them to be very great — how could he tell us what the materials are which enter into the composition of the heavenly bodies? Yet we know of what those materials consist, as definitely as we do of those of the matter which we touch and handle and measure. Without the spectroscope

(266)

this would be impossible. We might make a good guess, but it would be nothing but a guess.

Thus, however powerful the mind of man may become by training and culture, it is an indisputable fact (and I want to impress *this* fact upon your attention) that even to develop the power of the mind there must be large aid from the accidents or circumstances attending its working. And it is not possible to conceive how mind, unaided by external and complex instruments, ever would, nay, ever could, rise above its lowest and dormant condition. To show how much it is dependent upon instruments will be my object to-night, and for this purpose I will direct your attention to the Human Thumb. It may be thought a singular subject for the annual address of the president of your society. I trust, however, it will prove interesting and instructive. We will point out the bones of which the thumb is composed, the position it occupies, the muscles which are engaged in its movements, its functions or office. Looking at the hand, we find eight small bones which form the carpus, or wrist; these are attached by articulations to the bones of the forearm on one side and to five long bones on the other side, called metacarpal bones. To these latter are articulated the phalanges of the fingers and those of the thumb. The metacarpal bones of the fingers run a parallel course, are bound together, and form the basis for the palm of the hand. The metacarpal of the thumb differs from those of the fingers, being more movable, with a bevelled articulation, and when bent takes a diagonal position across the hand, thus bringing the end of its second phalanx into contact and opposition to the ends of the phalanges of the fingers, which latter, when bent, form a point of resistance to the thumb. Each finger is composed of three pieces of bone, which makes them longer than the thumb. When the hand is closed the points of the fingers form a straight even line, and the last bone of the thumb lies bent at right angles and supports the fist when doubled. Such is the bony structure of the thumb and its relation to other members of the hand.

We will now consider the muscles connected with these parts. A muscle is a band of flesh which can contract, and being fastened by its two ends to different bones, will bend one or both of them in the line of shortening. Thus we have muscles which arise from the back of the arm, pass on and are attached by cords and sinews to the wrist and to the back part of the fingers, and are called extensors. Others again which are called flexors start from the forearm, pass to the wrist and under the ligament to the fingers, and by contraction draw the fingers together, or in other words close the hand. The flexors are more powerful than the extensors, as the work they have to do requires more force. The thumb is also supplied with flexors and extensors. But besides these, which correspond to those of the fingers, the thumb has other muscles which are powerful in their action and exert a strong antagonism to one or to all the fingers combined. You can form an idea of them by examining the mass of muscles which form the ball of the thumb and which connects the first bone of the hand (flexors and adderators). Again, if we examine the position of the thumb and fingers when acting in antagonism, we see that the pressure in the case of the thumb is in a line with the axis of the bones, and it is thus enabled to afford greater resistance. Externally the thumb has the usual covering of skin and cellular tissue, whilst, at its extremity, as at the end of the fingers, there is a broad cushion of material, supported by a nail, which enables the thumb to oppose with force a sensitive surface to any resisting medium with wonderful accuracy. The nerves, which are bountifully supplied to this part of the thumb, afford the sensation so necessary for its efficiency. In a member so constructed, there is an innate power to perform the most varied movements. On account of the antagonism which the thumb presents to the fingers, implements can be securely held and efficiently directed for the production of other instruments which the mind may devise, by which the power of working may be indefinitely increased.

We can now somewhat appreciate the great importance of this factor in helping man in his advance towards civilization and the attainment of knowledge. Without such an agent (evidently designed for the purpose), even the progress of the race must have been arrested, and the higher faculties of the mind paralyzed for want of use. We have already alluded to the discoveries made by the use of the spectroscope. The manufacture of this instrument requires minute manipulations; its construction requires much skill, its adjustments call for great exactness in its details. It has to be manufactured (and the word defines itself, "made by hand,") and without its aid it would be impossible to arrive at the knowledge now attained by its use. If the hand had not been so wondrously adapted for strength and precision, the instruments which now surround man could never have been made; his daily wants would not have been supplied by machinery, complicated in its character; there would be no loom to weave his clothing; no foundries to cast and mould his engines; no factories to shape his tools; nay it is doubtful whether the stone axe or the flint arrow head would have been made. In such a case man would have to be content with the simplest and rudest forms of aid, and the mind remain dwarfed though endowed with almost divine potency. Let us suppose that instead of a thumb the hand had been formed with five fingers — all similar in character; their movements when they closed would be the same, their grasp might be firm, but in minute things there would be a want of precision, and man would have to content himself with the rudest implements. He might live in those parts of the earth where he required no clothing to protect him from the changing seasons, or if he extended his home to the north or the south he might cover himself with the skins of animals; but this resource might fail him, as he would not be able to compete with the wild beasts who would physically be his superior, and render his very existence a doubtful problem.

R

I repeat the fact again. The mind of man would to-day be ignorant of the composition of distant worlds unless it had been aided by instruments, and it is no disparagement to its wondrous powers that such is a fact. Our whole advance has depended upon the rise of agents or instruments by and through which it acts, and it cannot detract from the power of mind to say that its development has been intimately associated with the hand, but more especially with one member of it, and that is the thumb; for without its peculiar construction we may fairly conclude there could be none of those many complex instruments which now minister to our sustenance, to our comforts, to our knowledge, to our civilization (I had almost said to our existence). I do not wish to be understood as suggesting that the hand is the origin of the mind, for then we would naturally expect that the quadrumana, *our Darwinian ancestors*, would precede us in the scale of being.

It is true there are many factors, all of which are necessary for the manifestation and development of mental activity. But of all these factors the thumb I regard as the most potent in the great problem of life. The ethereal mind is dependent upon the material body. The body and its various members minister in various ways to the mind. Adaptation of many members to a common end, each member perfect in itself, yet dependent on the others, and all conspiring to a glorious end, force the conclusion upon us that the principle of design must be acknowledged. And if design then of necessity, the existence of One who planned all things. The unseen of whose existence, power and wisdom we ought to know something from His manifold works which surround us. "He that planted the ear shall he not hear? He that formed the eye shall he not see? He that teacheth men knowledge shall not he know?"

LECTURE ON HYGIENE.

The importance of the study of Hygiene can scarcely be overrated, if we accept as its definition "The knowledge of all the elements which conduce to the health and amelioration of society." This will include every department of physical nature, also the evolution of the intellectual and moral powers of man. The air we breathe, the water we drink, the food we eat, the social habits we form, the government which presides over us, all exercise their influence and shape our physical state, now degrading us to a lower level, now lifting us by the silent operation of centuries to a higher state of being. The effect of external circumstances upon the character are apparent wherever man is found. Whence, we would ask, come the steadfastness of purpose and mental vigour of the North, so different from the impulsive character of the South? Whence the intellectual and social characteristics which mark the governments in different climates? Characteristics so strongly impressed upon the northern and southern people that, as has been truly said, " We might as reasonably expect to educate the Italian greyhound into a Newfoundland dog, as to teach the Hindoo how to enjoy and maintain a free government." Ten centuries would be uselessly spent in the attempt to annul the climatic effects of fifty or sixty centuries.

General views of this nature should impress upon legislators the assistance they might derive from a knowledge of hygienic influences if they wish to act upon broad and far-seeing principles. But perhaps it is too much to expect that men will so act until the demand for legislation is too urgent to be overlooked. To the medical man hygienic principles are important, as they will lead him to a more correct estimate of circumstances which may be of service to the well-being of those who commit their health to his charge. A knowledge of the effects of climates in forming certain temperaments and conditions will enable him to meet the requirements of special cases even by artificial means. But whilst general causes act over large areas, there are a multitude of minor agents which are probably more important in their influence upon communities and more or less affect vitality in every locality. Among these, diseases, general or local, take a prominent stand, and more prominent than disease itself are those conditions which, acting upon the animal economy, weaken its powers of resistance and render fatal what would otherwise be a passing disturbance. Our profession stands first, and pre-eminently first, in its qualification for investigating this broad field of causes. The legislator may apply his regulating powers when he has sufficient knowledge to act. The divine and philanthropist may urge the consciences of individuals or communities to obey the requirements which reason and law would enforce; yet, though the law-making power and the moral teacher may both help in demonstrating the many evils to be avoided, the medical man, by his acquaintance with disease, by his study of the circumstances which enter into its production or prevalence, must occupy the vantage ground in hygienic investigations. He knows best what value to place upon collected data, and is ever seeking for causes to account for them. Many, if not all, reports upon sanitary matters have been furnished by him, or he has supplied the data upon which they are based; and in the future this must continue to be the case. Medicine is a noble profession, and we cannot too highly esteem the men who adorn it in their endeavours to remedy the ills and assuage the pains of their fellow-men. And surgery, which grapples with the destroyer and snatches so many victims from his grasp, stands in the foreground of praise. Yet both must be regarded as *specialties* in themselves. Advanced as they are, and wonderful as they are, they but contend with the *visible* results of noxious principles. A much higher and a more advanced position will be occupied by hygiene, which combats with the numerous and ever-working sources of disease and suffering—an ignorance of which may render futile the most masterly performances of the surgeon's hand. Medicine may do battle, even successful battle, with the armed men who sprung up from the sown dragon's teeth. Hygiene destroys the seed ere they touch the mother earth. Surgery, like Hercules, may strike off the heads of the hydra; hygiene sears the roots from which they continue to reissue.

It must be evident to all, that in order to establish a true hygienic system, the foundation must be laid by a thorough registration of the deaths which occur. These must be registered not by practitioners as such, nor in limited areas, but must be exacted by a government system general in its operation, and embracing a whole people. A mere record of deaths can be accurately accomplished by any civil machinery, but will be of little use unless the cause of death is also ascertained. At this point comes in the importance of the medical profession, an importance increasingly acknowledged when the effort is made to ascertain the remote and subtle influences which intensify the death rate.

As the death rate is not uniform, but varies in different localities, and at different periods, the next step will be to ascertain the conditions which precede or attend the mortality, and this opens up all the causes which diminish the vital powers of man. Among these may be ranged mental depression, social habits, local influences, meteorological influences, food, drink, overcrowding, bad sewerage, and whatever in fact tends to undermine the functions of life, and subjects the animal to premature death.

Diseases which are communicable have long occupied the attention of governments as well as of the profession. They are palpable, and force their consideration upon all. Terrified by the destructive power of some, governments have been

compelled to take measures to avert evils which sweep over
kingdoms, and are not stopped in their course by the widest
oceans. A wild terror has too often suggested ill-judged
means of prevention, and quarantine, right in itself, has
frequently violated all common sense. To be properly carried
out, quarantine requires a great deal of accurate observation
and a great deal of philosophical thought; for, however much
has been done, there exists still a great ignorance of the conditions of several of these diseases, and, until a more exact
knowledge is attained, errors in quarantine must arise. Medical men even differ upon the essential characters of diseases
—some maintaining those to be epidemic which others as
firmly maintain to be contagious, and both may be ignorant
of the region to which their propagation may be limited.
The disease germs of many are not known. The characteristics of one, however, are too palpable, and small-pox, one
of the most virulent, has to be met by the most stringent
isolation.

The office of hygiene will be to ascertain the exact nature
of these scourges—the virus which propagates itself in the
animal economy; their epidemic character; whether it de-
pends upon the increased subjective poison, or upon the
objective conditions, or upon both; their habitat, whether
general or local. When these facts are known, then may we
look for wise legislation in the direction of a thoroughly
sound quarantine.

Diseases personally induced form a large class, and arise
from causes which, being generally known, can be avoided.

Inherited diseases embrace a numerous and deeply interesting class. They are the result of a train of external
circumstances which, during a shorter or longer period, impress a character upon the animal economy. All these
diseases may, under ordinary circumstances, have a tolerably
uniform death rate, each of its own; but they are subject to
influences which may greatly increase or modify their inten-

sity. And it is to these influencing data that our further attention must be directed. Taking inherited diseases as an illustration. They are the result of *tendencies* already brought into existence by exposure to external causes, aided by the habits of life of former generations. A concentration of these causes will develop a further increase of diseased action until the death rate from its prevalence shall be greatly in excess of the average, and when depressing agencies lower the vital resistance the disease will assume the character of an epidemic. Scrofula is undoubtedly an inheritance, and yet may not scientific hygiene determine the conditions which are favourable to its production, and may not the tendencies to such diseased action be steadily beaten back by a removal of the disturbing elements which call it into being and activity?

Death, which, as a rule, is the result of diseased action, may, and often does, become more frequent owing to disturbing causes which act injuriously upon the vitality of communities. And hygiene can only become acquainted with these noxious elements by an extended observation of the physical conditions which operate upon the animal economy. Among these meteorology holds a prominent place. Climate, which embraces changes in the relative degree of moisture and temperature, and also differences in the barometrical state of the atmosphere, exercises a modifying power over the human system. The physique of man in different countries demonstrates this, and in many cases we may expect a deterioration of a race by a change of climate until an adaptation to the new conditions is developed.

It is questionable whether the constitutional characteristics of the people of this continent will not require a long time before they settle down upon a permanent basis. Some causes are so palpable that their results are recognized at once, and yet, simple as they appear, are so mixed up with other disturbing elements springing from a common source that they will require careful elimination before their true value can be realized.

Cold affects the mortality of the aged, and we might naturally expect this, when we consider that as age advances the power of generating animal heat grows less. On the other hand, heat produces the greatest death rate among the very young, the class in which the generation of heat is greatest.

The effect of water is well illustrated by the experience of the Millbank Prison in 1854. The water from artesian wells was introduced, and the result has been the virtual extinction of typhoid and other diseases of the same class which frequently prevailed in the institution.

The effects of continual moisture, or of an electrical state of the atmosphere, can only be determined by observations over large areas, liable, however, to errors, as various conditions may give rise to many and subtle influences.

The food we eat, and the liquids we use, constitute important items among the causes which tend, and largely tend, to affect the stamina and vital powers of man, especially the quantity and quality of the former at various periods and under varying circumstances.

The conditions under which water, coffee, tea, and other liquids are most beneficial, require experimental observation. Theory cannot solve these questions unless theory is based on facts.

Locality must be well considered, and this will require extensive observations to elicit results which arise from similarity either in geological, meteorological or topographical conditions.

The phenomena which are grouped, rightly or otherwise, under the head of social influence, largely affect the organism of man, and it is questionable whether, under this head, we do not have to deal with elements as destructive to human life as from all the causes we have previously noticed, inasmuch as all these are intensified by the social condition of the race. Governments which vary in their tendency to elicit human thought and to develop self-government, will vary in their power of grappling with social evils. Despotism which dwarfs and represses thought can only be surpassed in evil results by the licentiousness which characterises the other extreme when every man does that which is right in his own eyes. Customs which prevail in communities produce in individuals those habits which are injurious or beneficial, and both are apt to escape strict investigation as they commence with our existence and are strengthened with our growth. We look upon the fashion or custom of the Chinese woman in repressing the growth of her feet, and the still more injurious fashion of the European or American woman in contracting her breathing space, as a violation of natural laws, and yet there are evils connected with our every day life more injurious from their frequency, and if the attempt be made to obviate them, the general body of society will resent the effort as an unnecessary interference.

Custom prevails in our buildings, in our ventilating systems, in our eating, clothing and drinking; and social habits, familiar from childhood, too often pass unquestioned, and yet there is no one part of our every day life but might be based upon a truly scientific foundation. It is only of late that attention has been directed towards these objects.

There is one custom of society which as yet has had but a partial investigation — a custom too strongly rooted to permit an honest consideration. The mortality directly arising from the effects of alcoholic drinks form quite a percentage in the annual death rate, but who can tell the number it adds to the general percentage by diminishing in the system the powers of resistance to diseases which might not otherwise terminate in death.

Overcrowding, whether of dwellings or localities, tends to increase the number of deaths, and it is only by the most perfect hygienic arrangements that injurious results can be obviated when the population in a given area becomes numerous.

It is through the agency of the intellect that we must look for a regulation of the conditions which will result in the greatest possible physical good, and these regulations can only be wisely made when observation has laid the foundation by recording all the possible facts connected with disease and death; and just in proportion as this is done will legislators be enabled to enact their laws upon a scientific basis.

Laws necessarily override individual and commercial rights when the exercise of these rights might be injurious to the people generally. Compulsory sewerage, restrictions as to buildings and the number of occupants, width of streets, and numerous other things require the exercise of restrictive legislation. In Great Britain sanitary regulations, though numerous before 1837, were in that year included in a general Act, and a system inaugurated by which every part of England could avail itself of law to carry out the necessary reforms.

A few remarks upon the sentiments will close my paper. They must necessarily occupy a place among the influences which operate upon the human economy; they form the substratum of our duties, and, exercised in their due relationship are conducive to a healthy state, whilst, on the contrary, they may injuriously affect not only the individual but the masses at large. Hopeful expectation has been the cause of the success of many a quack, and is a good working ingredient in producing a reputation for the regular practitioner. On the other hand, the absence of hope demoralizes the man prostrates his energies, renders him the easy victim of disease and, to escape its misery, drives him to stimulants. History is full of examples of defeated armies wasting more from disease than the sword, and as rapidly recovering their morale and physique when the tide of warfare has been rolled back And when pestilence has commenced its ravages, how many rushing into vicious indulgence, have become the food of the plague.

The magnitude of this question has compelled me to curtai

my observations to the smallest compass upon the various subjects, any one of which would require more than one paper to eliminate it. My object has been to give a bird's-eye view of what the study of hygiene really involves. When we look back we find that general education has hitherto embraced almost everything except those relationships which man holds to the physical world. He was taught to lift his eyes to the stars to scan their movements and to measure their distances, and yet was left in ignorance of the effects of his cramped up rooms and of the mephitic air which entered every moment one of the citadels of life. Knowledge of every department of nature has been accumulating until creation has been spoiled of its teeming infinite facts, and it is only now that the necessity is felt that man, who is the creature of the influences around him, should devote his study to the circumstances which mould his destiny.

To secure a hygienic education we must look to three sources: Governments, universities, and individual exertion. Governments only can obtain returns of vital statistics from a whole country by compelling a registration of deaths and the causes of death. They also can secure meteorological observations from every quarter, and, by a central department, have all the data collected and tabulated. From individuals as such, or associates, and chiefly from those of our profession will come the condition of localities, the elements of disturbance, and all the facts which, requiring a quickened intelligence to eliminate, bear upon this question. But chiefly upon the centres of education will devolve the duty of imparting to their alumni the knowledge obtained from all sources. And if in every medical school there was a Professor of Hygiene, who does not see that with leisure and ability to investigate the numerous facts now being collected, such professors would be able to generalize and elicit the relationships which exist among all hygienic phenomena, and to place intelligibly in a few months before the students, that which could not be attained in a lifetime of individual exertion amid the cares of a professional career. And not only so, but in every university there should be established similar chairs, so that the relationship between man and his physical surroundings should form a part of the education of those who, in the nature of things, must be the future legislators of the land, who, if instructed in these relationships, would be ready to legislate wisely and intelligently instead of leaping in the dark. And who can tell the grand results, when the material condition of the race shall be advanced by enlightened sanitary knowledge and regulations; when the causes of disease are attacked in their stronghold; when national enjoyment shall supersede the discordant sounds of the revel; when the wants of the system shall be supplied with proper foods; when the physical state of man shall be elevated, and reacting upon his intellectual and moral powers, shall raise the race to the highest attainments possible.

THE SUPERNATURAL,

BASED UPON SCIENTIFIC INDUCTION; OR, INTERRUP-
TION THE MOST UNIVERSAL LAW.

Law evidently reigns everywhere; but to understand what any law is requires persevering efforts, first to ascertain and determine the facts, and then to decide what is the law engaged in their production. To assert that law reigns in all places and among all things, and that we can only satisfy the demands of science by strictly adhering to the principle of induction, may lead some to think that we bind ourselves down to a hard and fast positivism, and that in doing this we shut out the possibility of any higher relationship of life, especially the intercourse of man with a personal God. This is, in a measure, both true and false. True, as regards the unchanging potency of each law; not true, inasmuch as there is no law but which, at times, ceases to produce its results because it may be and often is interfered with by some other. And this interference or interruption of law by law is a principle forced upon our convictions by the strictest induction from facts. Let us illustrate this more fully. The principle of inertia, or that matter without applied force, will remain in the same place, is a pure induction of the reason, based upon a number of facts; and that, without a disturbing cause, it must remain in the condition it is found. Again: that gravity, or attraction, or cohesion will keep it in position; and moreover, we cannot conceive it possible but that these qualities or powers shall exist and exercise their influence.

But another set of facts compels us to infer the existence of another law which overrides the inertia of matter and the

(281)

force of gravity. Observation shows that matter is interfered with, and changed both in form and position by the principle engaged in the formation of crystals, in all their varying forms. Again: animate and inanimate organisms interrupt the above determining causes, for not only is matter moved from its position in spite of the law of gravity or cohesion, but the crystal becomes decomposed to yield obedience to a stronger force.

We cannot stop here, but are compelled by the same inductive system to look for the solution of new changes proceeding from higher forces, and consequently a further interruption of laws which, left undisturbed, would hold their sway for ever. Yes; above the lower forms of inanimate and animate existences there are organisms which interrupt and override all that is below.

Matter is carried by birds in their flight from one part of the earth to another, and its inertia and gravity are in complete abeyance to animal functions. Animate and inanimate forms are reshaped and forced into other and different channels, and all that would otherwise be permanent is interrupted.

Again: by the logic of facts, we are compelled to admit other disturbing elements. The mental phenomena of life appear upon the scene, and the silent strength of the eternal law is broken, and matter becomes the servant of mind. In spite of its inertia or its manifold combinations, the human mind acts upon and changes every aspect of nature. It makes seas give place to land; it turns the lonely desert into the happy homes of thousands; it raises mounds and pyramids until they touch the clouds.

We have briefly touched upon the interruptions which are everywhere manifest in physical, organic, and in the mental regions; but all these are again subject to an expressed wish or command of one human being, as when in modern times hundreds of thousands swept over desolated countries,—they themselves to perish beneath the northern snows, or to fall before the retributive anger of outraged peoples. Or, as in olden times, millions followed their Eastern leaders over the plains of Asia.

But to come down to the acts of every day life. What are they but asking questions and receiving answers? Answers which, in their completion, continually override the laws of nature. Yet these laws are not done away with ; their potency exists ; they exert their force on matter, but have to yield to the demands of the higher forces which control their powers and hold them in abeyance. Philosophy demands of us, and we admit the demand, that right inferences, based upon facts, form the chief, if not the only method, of gaining scientific ends ; and this same method compels us, by its inexorable logic, to acknowledge that interruption of law by law is the most general of all facts. That whilst we admit that each and every law, under similar circumstances, will be recognized by its effects, and be permanently endued with power to produce such effects, yet it is universally true that each and every law is being continually interfered with, and overridden by others. When by observation a law is once determined, the idea of permanency is associated with it. To such a degree is this the case, that it is constantly affirmed that a natural law cannot be broken. Now, if we understand law to be a force ever tending to operate, it will be true. But it is equally true that the power of a natural law may be superseded, and its results interfered with by other causes. Mind itself is subject to laws which rule its operations; yet, interference and interruption are recognized facts in its working. An important question here arises. Wherein does this principle of interference or interruption differ in matters of philosophy, and in the region of religion? Or, indeed, can it be said to differ? Both have to admit an interruption of natural laws. Both demand it as the result of observed facts. Throughout nature the lower series of laws are, perhaps, more universal in their operation, and as we ascend the disturbing forces are not so extensive and the most powerful ; those arising from mental sources may not be so palpable nor so frequent. It is therefore philosophical to assert that the law of interference is limited to what we see or feel, and that whilst human beings act and react upon each other, and respond to the demands or requests of their fellow-men, even to an interruption of physical laws, there is no force beyond man to change and mould the facts of nature in compliance with man's petitions. As well might the diatom on the floor of the ocean limit the power of change to its locality and deny the possibility of higher forces in operation, when at the same time the mighty steamer plows her way over the surface of the same ocean, the results of the mind of man — going as he directs, coming as he commands.

Let us conclude with a practical illustration. A man is seated by his evening fire resting his weary limbs after the labours of the day. All is bright and quiet within, but without the rain is falling, and darkness adds to the chill of the night. Hark? There is a quick, short bark, and then the gentle whine of his dog seeking his well-known shelter. The cry is heard, and affection for a faithful and dumb animal stirs up the half slumbering brain. The will assumes command of the body, and rising from his seat of comfort, he turns the key and swings open the heavy street door to receive his dependent. Now, what is the sequence of facts called into existence by the appeal of a loved favourite? The waves of material sound were put into motion; through the ear they pass to the brain, and reach the sentiment of love. This again disturbs and wakes the will; this rouses into action the functions of the muscles; a heavy weight is lifted; inert matter is put into motion, and its condition is changed. In other words, the mute appeal occasions physical and chemical changes, inertia is overcome, and iron itself yields its cohesion to the force of friction. Shall the principle stop short here? Shall it be unphilosophical for man to lift his voice to a source higher than himself? Must we stand in the dark, and not look for light? Shall doubts and fear chill our souls, and there be no hope either here or beyond? Are we bound down by chains of adamant, with no chance of ever being delivered? Shall the cry of the dumb brute cause the fixed laws of nature to yield to the stronger forces in nature? And shall the cry from human hearts find no response from the strength of the Infinite?

Manifold interruptions in the physical, the intellectual, and moral worlds surround us. This is the undeniable result of the phenomena of existence. This is truth, based upon induction, and more than this is not demanded by natural or revealed religion. This is a general, an essential truth, or the inductive principle ceases to be a source of the true and the philosophic.

But, no! Science is based upon the rocks of time. Religion is founded upon the Rock of ages. Twin sisters, they walk hand in hand. Daughters of one common Father, they bow their heads in adoration. One pours forth the song of praise, "Bless the Lord all his works in all places of his dominion." The other responds, "Bless the Lord, O my soul."

www.ingramcontent.com/pod-product-compliance
Lightning Source LLC
Chambersburg PA
CBHW020901020726
47497CB00005B/1508